Identity

Robert Abbamonte

PublishAmerica

Baltimore

First printing

ISBN: 1-59129-974-8
PUBLISHED BY PUBLISHAMERICA BOOK PUBLISHERS
www.publishamerica.com
Baltimore

Printed in the United States of America

*This book is dedicated to
that special someone who entered my life
and gave me the motivation to write.
She will always be in my thoughts and my heart.*

*I also dedicate this book to
my mother who gave me life so I could become a writer.*

I would like to thank my brother Phil and his wife Alice,
who took the time to read my early attempts
and give me good solid criticism so that I could make this book a success.

I want to also thank my good friend Stefan Brand,
his wife Robin and his mother-in-law
for their valued interest in my endeavors.

And I thank Wendy Spindelman
for her time and patience in taking such a good picture of me.

If it weren't for the good counseling of Andrew Belton and his patience
and confidence in me, I would never have pursued my dream.

Chapter 1

The airport was its usual state of chaos for a Sunday evening after dusk. Delayed flights, people running for flights about to depart, and the delayed arrivals all looking for those that were supposed to meet them but had somehow gotten lost in the mayhem. Amongst those late arrivals, a well-dressed and distinguished-looking gentleman strode confidently out of the terminal and across the sidewalk to a remote corner and a waiting car with its driver inside. In the lighting of the roadway and sidewalk, the figure in the car appeared to be no more than a silhouette, hardly distinguishable.

Confidently he gave a brief wave at the driver, opened the passenger door of the car and got in. The car made a slow entrance into the flow of traffic and, once in the stream, made its way around the airport road to the exit. Entering the main streets, it picked up speed and silently left the glow of the airport behind. It was a routine seen many times over, and drew no unusual attention from the surrounding populous.

Apologizing for his late arrival, the man settled back in the seat and watched as the endless path of red tail lights made a pathway for his vehicle, as if beckoning them to proceed along the same route in total confidence. He said nothing further as they sped along towards the suburbs and, he hoped, some peace and quiet. He leaned his head back against the headrest and closed his eyes. After a few moments he began to feel himself drifting comfortably into a state of semi-consciousness as the fatigue of the busy day he had left behind took hold of him. He was looking forward to a night of rest.

As suddenly as the sleepiness had come, so did a sensation of pressure around his neck. It was so strong and forceful that he could feel the opening in his throat become pinched shut by the effect. He quickly opened his eyes and tried to speak to the driver to ask what was happening, but could only sputter a quick gurgling sound. Reaching his hands to his throat, his fingers caught the feel of a large cloth-like object wrapped around in such a manner that he was unable to get a grasp around it to pull it away. He tried to wiggle loose from the vise-like grip of the object around his throat, which only pressed him closer against the back of the seat. Reaching over, he pulled on the driver's arm. Then, when that produced no response, he began to pound his fist on the driver's arm.

The pounding continued until the man lost consciousness. As quickly as the car had entered traffic, it left and traveled down dimly lit streets until it reached the side of a creek. The driver got out and walked over to a shadowy figure standing at the side of the road. After exchanging conversation, they both walked back to the car and opened the passenger door. Looking inside, they agreed that the man in the passenger seat no longer needed plans for the evening. The man was dead.

Detective Lieutenant James Hargrove arrived at his office earlier than usual that Monday. Jim was a tall man with broad shoulders. For an Afro-American in his early fifties, he still had a full head of hair, though it was almost completely gray. His face showed that he had come to this point in life through hard work and many years of stress. The past few weeks had been rough and he wanted to wrap up the case he'd been on as quickly as possible so he could take some vacation time, which had already been postponed twice.

As he entered his office, a slender woman with high cheekbones and jet black hair greeted him with a smile. When she did it accentuated her dimples. Debra Simms was also of Afro-American heritage and had shared many investigations with Jim even though she was an automobile insurance investigator. As usual, Debra made no secret about starting early each day. He had gotten quite used to her being where he least expected her to be. Forgetting the formalities that Jim liked to extend, he immediately started in on the task at hand for the day.

"Well, Debra; I see you've gotten the upper hand on this morning, and as usual I'm sure you've got everything under control."

"Why do you always start the day by persecuting me for my ability to be earlier than you? And besides, I was actually about to compliment you for showing up early for a change."

"You don't know how to compliment anyone. The word isn't in your vocabulary."

"Now Jim, and after the wonderful evening we spent yesterday, with dinner and all! My, how quick we are to forget. Remember how you said you loved me?"

"Did I say that? It must have been the wine."

Then out of guilt, and the need to make things right or hell would prevail throughout the day Jim leaned forward and kissed Debra. She smiled and returned the kiss.

"That's more like it! If we're ever going to wrap this thing up, we had both better be on the same side. And besides, the kiss was nice, very nice."

"The feeling is mutual on both counts."

Jim smiled back at Debra. He could see in her a woman of perseverance, yet warmth. They had so much in common. Both had seen tough times as youngsters; and both had made their mark in the world and achieved success. He still could remember when they had decided to make a truce to their constant taunting. It had been right after the accident involving a woman client of Debra's, when the entire incident had gone from one of frustration at trying to prove guilt to one of complacence on the part of the courts. If it hadn't been for Debra, Jim would never have succeeded at proving anything. He had discovered the softer side to Debra at the same time. Since then, they were inseparable.

As Jim put the final touches to the paperwork, the telephone rang. He picked it up and asked who was calling. The frown that came over Jim's face indicated whoever it was, the call was not a good one. As he listened the initial look of disappointment became a look of anger. Jim finally hung up and muttered out loud.

"Damn it, there goes the vacation plans. Some fool put his car into Tonawanda Creek."

Debra gave Jim a look of sympathy. After a brief description of what had been found, the two agreed that though it appeared clean and simple, until he saw the accident scene, anything was possible.

Jim resigned himself to the fact he would have to investigate a car that had mysteriously ended up in Tonawanda Creek. The driver was missing, so there were suspicious circumstances involved. Debra asked if she could tag along for support.

"Sure, why not? I needed a little something more to complicate matters, like no driver. I see this as doomsday. Why me, Lord, why me?"

Debra and Jim had planned to take this time off in the hopes that a vacation

9

together would lead to a permanent arrangement between them. She tried to console Jim as best she could.

"Stop being a pessimist! Think positive!"

Jim just nodded in dismay and gestured toward the door.

"After you, my dear."

The two headed for the elevators and to the street where the car was parked. Jim had conceded to having Debra ride in his police vehicle. The department frowned on it, but since it was only on investigative work, and not arrests, they turned a blind eye. But not his peers and subordinates, who constantly referred to Debra as his "partner" and knew them as the Erie County Dynamic Duo of Investigation. Debra thought it was cute, but Jim thought it was degrading.

Jim had become recognized in the department for his hard work and efforts in tracking down the facts in an investigation. It had led him to his recent promotion to Lieutenant. But all the promotion had done was give him a bigger office and some extra pay. The work doubled, as did the responsibilities. Jim could give the task of checking out the scene of the accident to a subordinate, but that would not alleviate the need for him to review the findings and recommend the action to be taken. So why not do it yourself and circumvent the middleman. It might shorten the time of the investigation.

Jim pulled out of the parking spot and immediately threw a bubble onto the roof of the car and began using his siren. Debra just looked over at him and smiled, giving him her cute but sarcastic type of expression.

"Where's the fire, Jim? It's not like you to use that thing unless it's a real emergency."

Jim wanted to get to the scene as quickly as possible. He wasn't about to fool around with the morning rush hour traffic. But not wanting to admit a selfish motive to his action, he played as though he couldn't hear her.

"What's that? I can't hear you and the siren at the same time. Did you say something?"

Debra was no fool, and immediately picked up on his not wanting to justify the use of the siren. She was getting to know him better than he realized. But she respected his desire and didn't pursue the question. Within twenty minutes they were at the scene of the accident. Jim wasn't kidding when he said he wanted to complete the investigation as quickly as possible. The speedy ride was proof.

As Jim emerged from his car, a policeman from Tonawanda who had responded to the call came over to him. Jim could spot a rookie a mile away, and this one not only looked it but gave it away as the officer addressed him.

"I've got everything under control. It looks to me like someone pushed the car into the creek and took off. No one is inside and there isn't any sign of foul play."

Jim was in a hurry to expedite things, but he still knew that he had to help channel some teaching towards the officer. To instruct the man in proper communications, he first corrected the officer's approach.

"Excuse me, but do you have any idea who I am? Have I got a badge showing, or some form of identification showing that I am a policeman? You're first step should be to find out who I am before you start telling me what you've found."

The officer just gave Jim a look of authority and spoke back defiantly.

"You pulled up in a car using a siren and with a bubble on it. You do not have the right to address me in that manner. I am the authority here, not you."

"Is that right? Well I am Lieutenant Hargrove with the Sheriff's Department's Investigation Unit. And until I determine the causes here, I am in charge. Understood?"

As Jim spoke he pulled out his badge and ID and held it in front of the officer. The officer turned his head away and uttered a profanity under his breath. Then he spoke to Jim.

"Sorry sir, I didn't mean to offend you. I just thought—" Jim cut him off.

"Well, stop thinking so much and show me this water-bound car."

By this time Debra had gotten out of the car and as Jim and the young officer started towards the water, she hurried until she was next to them. Within a minute they were at the edge of the creek looking at the roof and windows of a car sitting almost in the middle of the creek. Everything else was under water. Jim turned to the officer and asked him a few questions.

"So you think it was pushed in, is that right?"

"Yes sir."

"How did you come to that conclusion?"

"Because no one is inside the car. How else could it get into the water?"

"Well, that's why I'm here, son; to properly direct this investigation with a little use of what is known as common sense. First of all, that car couldn't have gotten all the way out to the middle of the creek just by being pushed. Between the weight of the car and the density and movement of water, it would only have made it a few feet in, with the back end almost completely exposed. There's an appreciable amount of mud and sludge on the bottom which would also make the entry difficult."

There was a definite look of embarrassment on the young officer's face. Jim was taking his time in the process of instruction.

"The other thing you mentioned was no sign of foul play. How did you reach that decision? Have you examined the vehicle physically?"

"No sir, but it looks OK from here, and there are no footprints along the path the car took from the road to where the car is that indicates anything out of the ordinary."

"Why should there be, if it was pushed as you thought? Now, what we have to do is call for a tow truck and someone dressed for wading out to the car. When they pull the car out we can have a good look at it. And before the truck gets here, let's walk the theoretical path together. This time we will look for what should be there but isn't. You make the call while I jot down some notes."

"Yes sir."

As the officer left to call his dispatcher for a tow truck, Jim took out his notebook from his inside jacket pocket and a pencil. All this time Debra had said nothing. Now she had a chance to speak to Jim without the young officer around to hear her.

"Don't you think you were a little tough on him? He's just getting his feet wet, and you let into him mercilessly."

Jim began scribbling something in his notebook. As he did so he responded.

"No. The man has got to start out doing things right the first time. I wish I had a mentor to help me when I was a rookie. I could have avoided a lot of stupid mistakes and many embarrassing moments. He'll learn, and thank me some day."

The officer came over to Jim and reported that the truck and driver with wading pants would be there in about forty-five minutes. Jim suggested that while they waited, they should walk the path of the vehicle. Jim looked at the rookie's nametag, which read Benson.

The two walked the path the car took, with Jim explaining that if the car had been pushed, it would have taken a few people to move it. It would have had to be as fast and as close to the edge of the creek as possible before it entered. Seeing no large number of footmarks in the grass meant very little. Footmarks would be lost due to grass usually coming back to its normal position within a short time. Therefore, that was insufficient in proving one way or the other if the car was manually pushed. Besides, such a large group of people would have never gone unobserved by someone passing by.

"Have you found any witnesses?"

"No sir."

"Did you ask the people standing around, or didn't you?"

"No sir, I never thought to ask."

"Always talk to people standing around. Sometimes it takes a little coaxing to get someone to speak up. Sometimes you can even find someone guilty of some participation by talking to him or her. Like a pyromaniac; they almost always show up on site at a fire they started to admire their endeavors. Understand what I mean?"

Then Jim looked at the possibility that the car was pushed, not by people, but by another vehicle. Tire tracks through grass do stay for a while due to the weight plus the traction made by the wheels. However, only one set of tracks was visible. Assuming they belonged to the car in the water, and since they were the only ones, it must be assumed that the car drove into the creek under its own power. To do that would take a driver.

"Then there has to be a driver, and he's missing."

Jim smiled.

"You'd think so, wouldn't you? Let's see what we find when we look inside the car. Gas pedals have been known to stick, sometimes deliberately."

That statement alerted Debra. If that were the case, this was no accident. That would be very significant to her company, if she were involved.

"Sorry I didn't pick up on those things, sir. I need to do a lot more looking in the future."

Jim patted the officer on the shoulder.

"You'll learn. By the way, in case you didn't pick up on this when you checked my ID, the name is Jim."

The rookie looked relieved for the moment, and smiled.

"That much I did, and thanks for the help, Jim."

"Anytime."

The officer excused himself and walked off towards the group of people that were accumulating at the edge of the creek to provide a little crowd control. Debra grabbed at Jim's arm and tugged it.

"That was nice of you. He really was thankful. You do have a heart after all; it just takes a while for it to emerge."

"I'm just thinking ahead. Someday I may want to retire; there has to be someone to replace me, or I'm destined to work this damned job forever."

Debra smiled and held his arm tightly. She knew better than that; Jim did have some modesty in him.

As soon as the tow truck arrived, and the driver had gone out to the car to hook up his tow chains, Jim went down to the edge of the water. When the driver returned, Jim decided to ask him some questions. He identified himself and began with a simple question first.

"How much undercurrent is the creek producing? Is it making your walk difficult?"

The driver shook his head negatively.

"Very little. Actually the creek here is rather low compared to some places further downstream. The bottom is slippery and you can feel it giving under you as you walk."

"Do you think if someone were in the car when it went in could walk back to the ground?"

"I'd doubt it; unless the person removed their shoes first, walking back would be almost impossible."

Removed their shoes. Jim pondered over that analogy. If someone wanted to drive into the creek deliberately, they would either remove their shoes in advance or not wear any at all to begin with. That is if they knew what they were planning. Very interesting. Jim thanked the driver, who had already started to operate the winch.

The car moved almost effortlessly until it rested at the foot of the creek. There was mud up to the top of the rims, indicating the mud had let the car settle into it to a depth of about seven or eight inches. A person would not sink that far, but sink they would. Jim felt that walking the bed would be difficult. If anyone had done so, he was sure they would have slipped a number of times. That would mean they would have emerged soaking wet.

Jim asked the tow truck driver to open a door on both sides to let the accumulated water out. As the door to the driver's side was opened, a moderate flow of water spilled out onto the grass. Jim watched closely as this happened. Debra was watching Jim the whole time. She was fascinated by what he was doing, but couldn't figure out why.

"Jim, what are you looking at? It's just water that got inside the car."

"Oh, it's more than that. I'm looking at the volume of water that is coming out. You see, if someone had driven into the creek and then got out of the car the level of water inside the car would match the level of water in the creek. As you can see, the level in the car was much lower. No one was inside that car when it went in."

"But Jim, you just told that officer the car must have been driven into the water."

"No, Debra. I suggested it might have, or the accelerator was accidentally or deliberately stuck. That would be my current theory since I've seen the water."

Jim and Debra walked over to the car that had stopped expelling water and looked inside. Since the body of the car formed a shell inside, there was about an inch or so of water still in it. Debra saw nothing unusual. Jim looked down at the gas pedal, leaned into the car and started to run his hand along the base of the pedal.

"Ah ha! What have we here?"

Jim retreated his hand from the car and opened it. In his hand was a nail about one and a half inches long but without any head on it.

"There's the driver of the car. This little baby was put just under the pedal shaft where it enters at the firewall. Notice it has no head. That's because in order to put the car into gear, the nail cannot be pressing against the gas pedal. But once in gear, the perpetrator of this deed has to hit the pedal with, Oh say a long stick since they aren't in the car to step on it, which snaps the head of the nail off and away goes the car. Neat little trick, wouldn't you say?"

Debra stared at Jim in awe.

"My, you sure know a lot about cars and gimmicks. Where did you learn all that?"

"Well, let's say it's reminiscent of those days when I was young and foolish. Remember I grew up on the streets of Buffalo. We did a lot of crazy things back then. Some of the things I wish I could forget, and some come in handy, like today."

Debra shook her head and muttered something about the youth of yesterday. Jim just ignored her and continued to look around the inside of the car. He asked her to look inside the glove compartment for a car registration to identify the owner of the vehicle. As she opened the compartment and sifted through it, she looked at the insurance card that is usually in there as well. Her eyebrows rose as she read it.

"Jim, I've got the registration. I've also got the insurance card and guess what. The insurance company is mine. It looks like we'll be together all the way through on this one."

"How fortunate." Jim said as he closed his eyes in a momentary act of prayer. *Why me, oh Lord, why me?*

"I can read your mind, Mr. Hargrove. Don't get smart with me; we're a perfect team, and you know it."

Jim smiled, took the cards from Debra and read the name of the registrant

15

out loud.

"Mr. Robert Thomas, 32 Binder Street, Evans, New York. Now why would someone from Evans come all the way to Tonawanda to sink their car? And why in a part of the creek that isn't deep enough to submerge it? Unless they wanted it to be discovered, and fairly quickly. But for what purpose?"

"Maybe it's a stolen car." Debra suggested.

"Maybe. I'll check on that right now."

Jim walked back to his car, radioed in with the license plate number and asked for a stolen vehicle check. He was back at the car with Debra still searching the glove compartment within ten minutes.

"It's not hot. I guess the next step is to locate this Robert Thomas and find out why his car is not reported missing. That is, of course, unless he knows where it is. Then I think he will have a lot of explaining to do."

Debra had just pulled a large sheet of paper from the glove compartment as Jim had finished speaking. On it was a poem, a name and a date. Debra handed the paper over to Jim and shrugged.

"What do you make of that?"

Jim looked at it and rubbed his chin. The poem had just four lines. It was hand printed and irregular; an apparent attempt at disguising the author's handwriting.

**THERE ONCE WAS A MAN THAT THOUGHT HE KNEW
EVERY ANSWER; BUT ALAS, HE KNEW TOO FEW.
SO NOW HE RESIDES WHERE ONLY ANGELS ROAM
AND ALL THE ANSWERS ARE NOW AT HOME.**

Under the poem appeared the name of Richard Barksdale and yesterday's date. Jim had a look of discomfort on his face that Debra had seen many times before. It was the look he made when his thoughts focused on a scenario that was unpleasant.

"I have a feeling the owner, or driver, of this car left this in the glove compartment deliberately."

Jim called the tow truck driver over, asking him to bring a crowbar with him. As soon as the driver appeared with the crowbar, Jim asked him to pry the trunk lid open. The driver hesitated for a second, then decided not to argue with Jim, and did as he was asked. As the trunk popped open, what the three of them saw was what Jim had feared. In it was the body of a man.

Debra turned away. She was a strong willed individual, but one thing she did not like was to see a corpse. Her stomach did a somersault and she had to breath heavy for a minute to calm the nausea down. Jim could tell from the color of the skin and the fact that there was no odor of decay that the man had been dead for just a few hours. The date under the poem appeared to corroborated his theory of the time of death.

"Well, it looks like vacation for me is out for a while. All I need to find out is who the corpse is, who the killer is and the motive. A piece of cake."

Jim had readily accepted his promotion, even though he knew that the added responsibilities might jeopardize his vacation plans. Before he had been responsible only for investigations that were accident oriented. But now his jurisdiction took him into all fields of investigation, including homicide. He did feel the need for assistance on this one, as he was a bit green himself regarding homicides. There was a Sergeant Mansfield that was well respected, and familiar with the territory. Jim was going to need a strong leader on this one.

Jim walked over to Debra and placed his arm around her shoulder.

"Are you going to be all right? I regret exposing you to that; I wasn't thinking when I suspected a body was in the trunk. I just automatically assume the people at a scene like this are hardened to such things. Again, I apologize."

Debra thanked him for his concern, said she would be fine, and asked Jim what he was going to do next.

"Well, first thing is report what I've got here and call for the coroner. The second thing is to get you away from here. This is no place for a civilian to be when the news media show, as I'm sure they will once the call for the coroner is made."

"What about my investigation? Should I get involved? It is still my insurance companies' responsibility to ascertain all the facts and make a report."

Jim pondered that for a moment and then gave Debra a green light to continue her side of the investigation.

"In fact, you can help me by letting me know if and when this Robert Thomas calls regarding his car. It is bothering me that he should have a car that is involved in a murder and yet he doesn't acknowledge the whereabouts of his vehicle. It's just something very odd about the relationship. If I weren't involved, I'd sure like to know where my car is, wouldn't you?"

"Absolutely! And again, thanks for the concern. I think sometimes I don't appreciate you as much as I should."

Jim smiled, led Debra back to his car, and asked her to wait there while he informed Officer Benson of what was happening. He recommended that the officer call his department for some help at the scene, as the media would be showing up to announce the addition of another murder in the Queen City. Buffalo and the surrounding areas had built quite a number of homicides so far that year. Another one was bound to stir the pot up, with Jim in the middle of it.

Once that was done, Jim radioed for the coroner, took the bubble off the roof of his car, and headed for headquarters. *No need to hurry now,* he thought. This was going to be a very long day.

Chapter 2

After dropping Debra off at her office, Jim returned to headquarters and searched the telephone directory for a Robert Thomas. He was amazed at the number of people with the name of Thomas that were in the phone book. There had to be well over six hundred. Thankfully, there were only nine with Robert before it, and only one of those had the Evans address. He dialed and waited. An answering machine picked up the call, so Jim hung up without leaving any message. He wasn't sure of what involvement, if any, that Robert Thomas had regarding the dead body. It was best not to leave to chance a sign that the police were looking for him. He decided to check on Sergeant Mansfield and find out the status of his workload.

Jim found the sergeant in the break room having coffee. Harold Mansfield was a man in his middle thirties, tall and well built. He had a full head of wavy brown hair that was long enough to reach his broad shoulders. A man that looked every bit like he should have been in show business, he also sported a full mustache and goatee. He would have made a perfect Robin Hood or Sir Lancelot. Harry was not originally from Buffalo, and as soon as he spoke to you, his English accent gave his true origin away. Originally from Gloucester, he had come to the United States at the age of nineteen to seek his fame and fortune only to find himself in need of a good paying job. If you asked him now if he had found it, his answer would be the same as his greeting when he saw Jim entering the room.

"No!"

It had already reached the ears of headquarters that the Sheriff's Department had discovered the sixty-first murder of the year in the greater Buffalo area early that morning. Details were sketchy, to say the least, and the media was having a field day ostracizing law enforcement about their lack of being able to control crime in the region.

Jim had already had to confront his superior Captain Frank Hopkins regarding the events and give a comforting assurance that he would personally handle the case and resolve it quickly. A tall order for what appeared as a total lack of any concrete leads as to how, who or why this had all happened. A lot of weight was being brought to bear on the department from the media, the local politicians, and the people as well.

No one wanted the reputation of the area tainted so as to diminish the tourist trade, which was already hurting since legalized gambling had been approved. The new casinos had brought financial prosperity, but along with it an economy that was a boon not only for merchants, but the criminal as well. Jim knew he had his hands full, and the only reprieve came from knowing Harry Mansfield was his ticket out of disgrace for the department, his fellow officers, the County, and himself.

Jim smiled at Harry and sat down next to him.

"No, what? I haven't said anything or asked you anything yet."

"But you will! And the answer is still no, my good fellow. I have seen that look before, and it usually means I'm in for a big and tough assignment. I have enough to keep me very busy already."

Jim touched Harry on the shoulder and spoke in a soft voice.

"But I need you on this case. It's a homicide, and I am not sure where to begin or in what direction to go. You have such a terrific handle on things of this nature, it would be a pity not to let you help me on this one."

Harry just huffed at Jim as he finished his tea.

"Flattery, my good man, will not sway my feelings. I knew you would be looking me up. I heard about the body in that car you found in Tonawanda Creek. Maybe you should ask your partner to help you. I understand she has quite a handle on many things, particularly on you as of late."

Harry smiled. He had to get his comment in quickly, or the atmosphere would turn strictly businesslike. When Harry smiled, his face took on a devilish appearance. Jim would have said something in retort, but looking at Harry smiling could do nothing short of causing amusement.

"She's not my partner, and don't underestimate her abilities. She's a sharp lady."

"She has to be to control the likes of you."

The two laughed and as soon as Harry had placed the empty cup in the sink, he followed Jim to his office. The atmosphere turned serious once the two sat facing each other.

"Harry, the car was where it could be seen and easily towed out. A poem in the glove compartment tells me that whoever did this wanted the body found fairly quickly and easily. The name of the victim has been handed to us. It almost looks as if the murderer were challenging us to figure out who he or she is. It's weird, Harry; very weird."

"Where's the owner of the vehicle? Has he reported it as missing?"

"No. That's another weird thing about this case. If I were the owner of the car, I certainly wouldn't be the killer. If I were, I wouldn't have left the correct plates on the car and my registration and insurance information in the glove compartment. And yet the owner seems to be unaware of his car's whereabouts. I tried to reach him by phone, but all I got was his answering machine. He probably went to work. What do you think of all this."

Harry scratched his chin and looked off towards the window. For a few moments both men were silent. Then Harry asked if Jim had checked on the victim's residence, or what he did for a living.

"No; that's where I need your help. I really have no clue as to where this Richard Barksdale lives or even if he lives locally or is from out-of-town. How do I start finding out about the victim without any identification. The murder happened so recently that even a missing person's report is too premature. I feel lost on this one. But we have to start soon, or the trail may get cold."

"I doubt that will happen, Jim. If what you think about the murderer challenging us is true, and I may agree with you on that, I am sure he or she will make sure you get enough information. Otherwise, as you say, the trail will get cold and the challenge as well. I think the first thing to do is locate the owner of the vehicle. He may be able to shed some light on what we are to look for; he may even know the victim."

"Then it's settled? You will work on this case for me, right?"

"Only because you would probably flounder. Certainly not because you pulled rank on me, mind you! You're rank doesn't affect my decision in any way. I just don't wish to see a good man go down in defeat on his first homicide."

"Why, how thoughtful of you. I appreciate the help, Harry."

"You shall appreciate the help by being at my side through this. You're not going to just walk away and leave everything to me."

"You do realize, Harry, that if I am at your side, so will my 'partner' be at your side as well."

Harry frowned at the thought of a threesome. Jim just shook his head to gesture that it was inevitable.

"I suppose if it must be, then by George it must be. I just hope that the two of you will behave in a civilized manner throughout this investigation. No romancing while on duty, or some such thing as that, ay what?"

"Would I ever do that? Harry, please, you insult me."

With the ground work and understanding established, the two sat and made a list of steps that were needed. First, a complete set of fingerprints should be obtained from the victim and sent to Washington to be identified. Even if the owner of the car knew the victim, it would be important to know if the victim had a criminal record, or if he were involved in some way with drugs; anything out of the ordinary. Somewhere in this there had to be a motive for the killing. Neither Jim nor Harry believed it was just a wanton murder for thrills or for the challenge alone, though even that premise could be true.

Next, a complete background check had to be made on Robert Thomas. Though not likely, it might turn up some information about his lifestyle that would set him apart from the norm, such as being a gigolo, or a man of strong religious ties. Was he deeply in debt, or did he have an unusually large amount of money in the bank?

Third was to check the history of the vehicle involved. Did Thomas purchase it new or did it have a previous owner? Was it ever involved in an automobile accident; was it ever stolen? The list became a total of eight items, four of which only a man with experience and know how could accomplish; Harry took those. Three were simpler, and Jim took those, with the knowledge that he would be tagging along on some of Harry's to broaden his experience in homicide investigations.

As for the one involving the vehicle Jim promised Harry that when it came to investigating cars there was only one expert. Harry agreed; so Debra would do that one with gracious generosity and as a favor to Jim.

As they finalized their plans, the phone rang. Jim put it on the speaker mode. It was the captain, his voice anxious to know what was planned. Jim explained what they had and how they understood the pressure that was bearing down on the department. Captain Hopkins had made a commitment to have answers within the next couple of days for the media and the public. He expected Jim and Harry to come through for him, or all hell would break loose.

By the time Jim hung up the phone, Harry had already left with his list of tasks. Jim assigned the subordinates in the homicide division to the fingerprints and the check on Robert Thomas. Jim prepared Debra for her part by taking her to lunch.

"You what? Jim, that's taking our close relationship a little too far. I can see giving you the history of the car from the insurance angle, but checking as to who owned it when and for how long, that's unfair. It's also out of my jurisdiction as an insurance investigator. What if someone found out I was obtaining that kind of information as a favor? I could put my job in jeopardy."

"No one's going to find out. Besides, it would only look like you were really trying to give a super extra effort in your research. How could that jeopardize your job? If anything, you might get a raise."

"A raise! Huh, that's not likely. Getting a raise in my company is tantamount to discovering you just became a billionaire. It just will never happen."

"Please accept my apology Debra. I didn't think you would mind. I presume too much of you. I just thought of you when it came to being the best at what you do."

Debra looked at Jim and could see the sincerity in his eyes. She loved Jim, and her being his only thought when it came to efficiency made her feel good. She sighed and gave in.

"Just this one time, Mister Hargrove. Don't let this happen again, or you and me are going to have quite a battle of terms and conditions regarding our relationship."

Jim thanked her, told her all the required information that he would need, kissed her, paid for lunch and went back to his office. As he walked towards his desk he heard the voice of Harry at his back.

"Everything work out smoothly with your partner?"

"Smooth as silk. And she's not my partner, she's my close friend and confidant."

"You're in love. I can tell it in your voice. By Jove you're hooked man. She has you in her grips."

"Maybe, then maybe not."

Jim smiled at Harry, and Harry just made an expression on his face that looked like a cross between an angel and the devil all rolled into one. Then he smiled and walked away. Jim decided to try calling Robert Thomas again, but only got his answering machine. He tried several times later in the day, but got the same results.

Jim occupied much of his time that afternoon with other cases that had come across his desk for review, then decided to head home, taking the phone number of Robert Thomas with him. He would probably have a better chance later on in the evening. The day had been a long one, a very long one.

The next morning started out routinely, with very little change in the status of the background regarding the body in the car and the whereabouts of Robert Thomas. Jim had tried to call several times during the evening, but no one answered the phone. By eleven o'clock he had given up and gone to bed. He called Debra and asked if she had any information back on the car. The answer was no. Jim asked if she might also have the opportunity to look at the files of her client to see if a job and job phone number was in the files. There was an audible sound of dismay at the other end.

"Jim, there you go again. You know that information is private and if I disclose it without my client's permission, I am in big trouble. You will have to get that information on your own. Sorry Jim, but I have to draw the line somewhere."

"I understand. It's just that it's becoming irritating that this Thomas person is nowhere to be found. I am almost willing to ask for a warrant for the apprehension of this guy on the premise that he was driving that car and has fled the scene of an accident."

"But Jim, remember the nail?"

"So? Besides you, who knows about that? No one. Maybe I should throw it away and play dumb."

"That's tampering with evidence, Jim. I don't like what I'm hearing. It's not like you at all."

Jim gave a long sigh and let a few moments pass before continuing.

"You're right; I won't do that, and you know it. I'm just frustrated with this homicide shit. I should have stayed right where I was. I was comfortable with the work and didn't have to hunt down every Tom, Dick and Harry to find out if they killed someone or not. This is much more stressful and involves too much dependency on getting information from nothing. It's easier to get blood from a stone."

"Now Jim, you love challenge. So now you have lots of it. You should be happy."

Jim told Debra to let him know as soon as she hears about the car, told her he loved her, and thanked her for her patience and understanding. She promised she would, said she loved him too, and told him to relax and things would happen. The conversation over, Jim hung up the phone just as Harry came into his office.

"Good morning, old chap! So, how'd the little conversation with Mister

Thomas go yesterday?"

"It didn't. This guy is somewhere, but so far there isn't a clue as to where. Maybe I should assume he is the killer and put out an all points bulletin for his arrest."

"That's risky, Jim. If this Thomas is away on some legitimate work, or on vacation, or whatever, and he isn't the guilty party your ass is in a sling."

The two sat looking at each other for what seemed like an eternity. Suddenly Jim had an idea.

"What if I went around to the major banks and asked if they had an account under the name and a matching address. Would it be feasible to request the business address and business phone number? It's not like asking for anything personal about the man, like his financial status."

"I don't know for certain where the law places the limits regarding a person's privacy. It might be worth a try. I think it would be best if you did so personally. Your badge and rank might allow a bank employee to be more free with that information rather than giving it to a uniformed policeman."

"You mean more intimidating?"

"Now that's your word for it, not mine."

Jim decided it was worth expending the time in the hopes of extracting the much needed information. He set out immediately, and hit pay dirt on his fourth stop. He returned to his desk by late morning with the information. Also on his desk was an autopsy report from the coroner's office on Richard Barksdale. Jim picked it up, scanned the report, and raised his eyebrows when he got to the line for probable cause of death. Then he placed it down, took out his notepad and dialed the number he had been given for Robert Thomas's place of employment. The phone rang twice, and a pleasant soft voice came on the line.

"You have reached the offices of Unisearch Corporation. All of our service representatives are busy. Your call is very important to us, so please hold for the next available representative. If you need immediate assistance, or would like to speak to the operator, please dial zero now."

"Damn, who runs this world, us or the computers?"

Jim dialed zero and waited. The phone began to ring again. This time he was given a menu and a list of options to choose from. He heard something that sounded as if his call would fit with that option and hit the corresponding number. He got another phone ringing, and the same recording he had heard before came back on. Muttering a profanity, he dialed zero again and went through the same procedure. By the fifth try, he was finally directed to dial zero followed by the pound key for the operator.

"Damn it, why didn't you say that the first time!"

Of course Jim got no response. He was still dealing with the computer. Finally he heard a voice on the line.

"Can I help you?"

"Finally! Are you real?"

"Yes sir. How may I help you?"

"I'm looking for Mister Robert Thomas. I was told he works with your firm. I need to speak with him on a matter of great importance."

"I'm sorry sir, but Mister Thomas is out of the office on an assignment. Do you wish to speak to his voice mail?"

"No thanks. When do you expect him to return?"

"In about three days. Are you sure you don't want his voice mail? All our representatives check their mail daily. I'm sure he will return your call as soon as possible."

"Three days? What kind of assignments do you people have to keep a person away that long?"

"We research people to retrieve lost or unknown wealth. Sometimes that takes our people out of the country, which could involve weeks. Three days is actually a very short time."

Jim was hesitant to leave any message, but with days involved he was left with very little choice.

"Fine, give me his voice mail."

Jim left a message that was brief but didn't hint that there was anything unusual. He gave his name, his office number, and left word that Robert Thomas's car had been involved in an accident. It would sound innocent enough. He also made it sound urgent enough so that Jim's message would produce a quick response. As soon as he had hung up, his phone rang. It was Debra.

"How's it going Oh Great Sleuth of Erie County?"

"Lousy. I just got off the phone after spending damn near fifteen minutes battling with some stupid computer. All I wanted was to speak to a human being. Is that such a crime?"

"It is in this day and age. I know the feeling."

"Well, I finally got what I needed to know. Robert Thomas is an investigator for a search company that retrieves monies for people that don't know the money exists. He's out of town and not expected back for three days. So I guess you won't be hearing from him until he returns the call I left on his voice mail. At least that gives him an alibi for the night of the murder, and the reason why he doesn't know about where his car is."

"That's odd, because I called to let you know that Robert Thomas just notified his insurance agent that his car was involved in an accident at Tonawanda Creek."

Jim sat quietly as Debra's words sank in. He was at a loss as to why or how Thomas knew anything about the accident since he was away on an assignment. Unless he **was** involved and didn't actually leave town until after the accident. If that were the case, the timing would have to be extremely precise. He would have to tread very carefully when Thomas returned his call. Things were not looking good for Debra's client.

"Thanks for the news. I'll get back to you as soon as I hear from Thomas. Oh, and incidentally, you'll never guess how Richard Barksdale died."

"How?"

"He suffocated."

"Suffocated? Like in lack of air?"

"That's right. There could be a possibility he wasn't actually dead until after he was put in the trunk."

"How gruesome! What a horrible way to die."

"Which now casts some doubts as to this being a deliberate act of murder. Except for that piece of paper from the glove compartment and the poem, there is no actual link between Barksdale's death and the accident. Maybe whoever placed him in the trunk didn't actually plan on killing him. Maybe the poem was supposed to be more of a threat rather than an admission of a crime. I'll have to read the poem a few times and see what I can make of it."

"Just be careful, Jim. I don't like this cloak and dagger business you're getting involved in. I almost wish you hadn't taken that promotion. I love you, even if you are stubborn, and I don't think I could bear to loose you. Please promise you'll be careful."

Jim promised, said he'd call her at home later, and hung up the phone. He opened the file folder on the case and picked up the paper with the poem on it. Then it struck him; maybe it wasn't too late to check it for fingerprints. Damn, in such a hurry to get Debra away from the body and the scene, he hadn't even thought about the paper as a potential fingerprint source. It just proved Jim's point. He had a lot to learn about thinking homicide instead of accidents.

Jim copied the four line verse onto another piece of paper, then placed the original paper neatly between two blank sheets and took it over to the lab for testing. When he got back to his desk, Harry was sitting there waiting for him. He had picked up the poem and was studying it intently. Without looking up, Harry addressed Jim.

"Just turned in the original for testing, I'll bet. They won't find anything I'm willing to wager."

"Why not?"

"Because, dear fellow, the paper was handled too much, and most of those prints on it are blurred and are probably only yours, your partner's and mine."

"You think the killer wore gloves to write it?"

"Probably. If this person is out to challenge us, he or she is certainly not going to give us anything as definite as a fingerprint. At this stage of the game, the upper hand is theirs. No, slip-ups are the product of panic or stupidity. This person has their course well plotted, and so far we haven't done anything that would pose a threat."

"I guess you're right. And stop referring to Debra as my partner. You know how annoying that is to me."

"Pity."

As the two pondered the meaning of the poem, the phone rang. He asked who it was, then waved at Harry to listen to the conversation as he switched the mode to speaker. The caller was Robert Thomas.

"Lieutenant, I received your voice mail and wanted to call you as soon as possible. I'm rather confused at this point. I already know of the accident, and have reported it to my insurance company. Is there anything that you know that I should know?"

"How did you find out about the accident, Mister Thomas? I was told that you were out of town on an assignment when it happened."

"A fellow worker called me around ten that evening and told me he had the accident. I had lent him my car while I was away because his car was in the auto shop undergoing repairs."

"Could you give me the name of that individual?"

"Sure. His name is Richard Barksdale."

Jim and Harry looked at each other. Jim couldn't believe what he had heard.

"Would you repeat that name again, please?"

"His name is Richard Barksdale."

Jim sat silent for a moment. He wasn't sure if he should mention the present state of Richard Barksdale or not. He looked at Harry and silently mouthed the words 'should I tell him?' Harry nodded his head.

"Mister Thomas, I haven't completed my investigation of the accident, but I feel there is something you should know. Mister Barksdale was found in the trunk of your car."

There was silence at the other end. Then laughter.

"That Rich, he's quite a character. Did he tell you why he was in there?"

"I'm afraid you don't understand. Mister Barksdale was dead when we found him."

There was another long period of silence, then an exclamation.

"Shit! I don't believe it. He seemed fine when he called me that night. A little shaky, but I would be too after driving my car into a creek."

Jim decided to pursue the conversation a little farther.

"Did he sound drunk?"

"No. He wasn't a drinker to begin with. No, he spoke as if he was cognizant of what he was saying and what had happened."

"And you said it was what time when he called you?"

"Around ten o'clock. I'm positive of that because the local newscast came on shortly after his call."

"When are you scheduled back in town?"

"Day after tomorrow. I'll contact you as soon as I arrive and let you know when I can meet you. I'll call the office and let them know. This has upset me, Lieutenant, more than you know. Rich was like a brother to me. I can't believe it."

Jim hung up the phone and stared at Harry. Harry shook his head as if he was trying to ease a stiff neck. Then Harry made a profound observation.

"I think we are beginning to see where the challenger is taking us, and that's in many different directions all of which appear to be false trails."

"Harry, that's not fair. I still have a body that is identified, and a cause of death. Just because it happens that the body and the person using the car are one and the same really doesn't matter. We are still clueless as to motive and who did it. Let me look at that poem again."

Harry handed the poem to Jim, who placed it down in front of him and read each line aloud.

"'There once was a man that thought he knew every answer.' What do you think that statement refers to; is the man in the poem the victim? I think it has to be."

"How's that, good fellow? At this point, we do not even know what the questions were."

"But in a way we do, Harry. Barksdale was a sort of investigator; an investigator looking for someone's money. That was his job. As such he was searching for answers so that he could retrieve that money for a client. What if he had found what he thought to be the answers he was searching for and was about to reveal his findings? But in doing so he discovers his investigation wasn't thorough enough. See how that fits in with the next line? 'But alas, he knew too few.' What do you think?"

"Too perfect. When you've been investigating homicides as long as I have, you'll realize that anything that even closely resembles a perfect solution, question it. In most cases, it's a false trail."

Jim shrugged the comment off and continued to read.

"'So now he resides where only angels roam'. See, again it's referring to the deceased."

"Really? Then suggest a correlation for the last line. 'And all the answers are now at home.' What answers? Home where? Did he find them all and leave them at home? God, man, how far do you wish to stretch this?"

Just as Jim was about to protest the sarcasm and defend his theory, the phone rang again. It was Robert Thomas.

"Lieutenant, I just got off the phone with my office. I don't know how you identified the body in the trunk, but it can't be Richard Barksdale. He's in the office at the moment and quite alive."

Jim's mouth dropped to his chest. Stunned, it took a minute before he could answer.

"Thank you for letting me know. Please give me his extension. I need to ask him a few questions."

After jotting down a number Jim hung up and stared at Harry, who had caught Jim's expression and was curious to find out what caused it.

"You know, Harry, I'm really developing a great deal of respect for your approach to things. You certainly were right about questioning everything that seems to fit."

"How so, my friend?"

"That was Robert Thomas. He just informed me that Richard Barksdale is alive and working in his office."

"There you are, chap! All that poppycock over the poem was foolhardy now, wasn't it?"

"It sure looks like it. I'll let you make the call to Barksdale. I'm not sure what to ask or say at this point. You'd be better at handling this one."

Harry changed chairs with Jim and placed the call. As soon as Richard

Barksdale answered, Harry introduced himself and led the conversation to what he hoped would be a logical conclusion.

"Lieutenant Hargrove and I are concerned over your accident of two days ago. Could you tell me what happened?"

Jim watched as Harry began taking notes as he listened. As Harry posed question after question, he wrote more notes. Finally, it was time to conclude the interview.

"Well, that certainly sheds some light on the matter. I wonder; would you object to coming to the morgue and make an attempt at identifying the body? I know that's not pleasant, but under the circumstances. You would? Great!"

Harry gave directions, set a time and hung up. Jim sat waiting to hear what the story was. Harry stood up and stretched. He seemed to be savoring the moment, and Jim was becoming impatient.

"Well? What's happened?"

"It turns out that Mister Barksdale received the poem at the office that afternoon. The secretary said an anonymous benefactor had left it on her desk. She placed his name and the date on it. She thought he might think it cute. He merely placed it in the glove compartment intending to read it later that evening. Of course, with the accident and all, he completely forgot about it. However, I detected some surprise at the first mention of it. Almost as if he didn't know of its existence."

Jim felt lost. His whole idea of the implications and the meaning of the poem was now a dead issue. And his identification of the body was premature and without foundation. Jim looked stupid, and he felt that way at the moment.

"As for the body in the trunk, he claims to have no knowledge of it or who it could possibly be. He is willing to take a look see and maybe he can recognize the man."

Jim frowned. He wished that the fingerprints they had taken of the deceased would be processed and identified quickly. He had an uneasy feeling that the person they found had some link to a deeper and more ominous involvement than just a simple killing for revenge, money or the like.

"How did he explain the car ending up in the creek without him being in it?"

"Simple. He wanted to shine the lights down onto the creek to show the lady friend he had spent the evening with how it looked. She was not from Buffalo. They got out, and as they looked at the creek lit up by the headlights, the car started to move. He had left it in gear and running. He was too slow to react, and by the time he realized it, the car was moving too fast to stop it."

Sounded good, except for the nail that Jim had found jammed into the accelerator pedal. Even Harry was not aware of the nail, and it was that one thing that made Jim disbelieve the story.

"And the body? What about the body, Harry?"

"He's baffled. He claims he went into the trunk earlier in the evening for something and the body wasn't there at that time. Maybe it was placed there after the car was in the creek."

Jim knew that couldn't be, since it took a crowbar to open it at the scene. Unless, of course, the murderer had keys to the car. Who had keys to the car? Only the owner and the driver. And besides, the condition of the footing in the creek's bed would have made carrying a body out to the car and holding it until the trunk was opened to deposit it was inconceivable. Plus, the body had not been wet when discovered. And Jim still couldn't see the car picking up enough speed to enter the creek and ending up midway.

"That whole story has its flaws. I don't buy it, Harry."

"So, did I say that I believe it? I just repeated what I was told. That's why when we meet this Barksdale chap, we are going to watch his reaction when looking at the cadaver rather closely for some sign of indifference; maybe discomfort. Who knows? Signs of guilt."

Jim hoped something would surface. He had never experienced such frustration over an investigation before. He also dreaded having to inform the captain that they had been totally wrong in their identification of the victim.

As the hour for their meeting at the morgue approached, the two headed downstairs, both anxious to meet the now infamous Mister Barksdale.

Chapter 3

Jim and Harry entered the hall of the city morgue where the security checkpoint was set up. They identified themselves, were told to pass their weapons through to the guard on the other side of the scanner, and then walked through. Once they had their weapons back, they took the elevator to the lower level where the vaults that held the corpses were located. As they approached the glass doors at the end of a long corridor, they saw a slender man sitting in one of the chairs that lined the corridor just before the doors. He looked at them and stood up. There was a look of discomfort on his tanned face, and he seemed a bit nervous as he extended his hand to Jim.

"Lieutenant Hargrove, my name is Richard Barksdale. And you must be Sergeant Mansfield."

As Harry shook Barksdale's hand he could almost sense a slight tremor to it. This tall man in his early forties with long blonde hair tied back in a ponytail was nothing even close to what the cadaver looked like. He was glad no one else had seen this comparison. It would have made the department look very foolish. Jim spoke to Barksdale for the first time.

"Mister Barksdale, we're glad you could do this for us. I hope you are not squeamish about looking at a dead person. Especially since this one hasn't been made to look as if they were sleeping, as does a funeral parlor."

"I hope not either, Lieutenant. I've never done this before."

Harry placed his hand on Barksdale's shoulder.

"Just relax dear fellow and it will be over with quickly. It's about the same as in the movies, only this time you get to see it up close and in person. If you wish to back out, we'll understand."

"No sir. I said I'd look at the body, and I still wish to help out, if I can."

"Excellent! Now, what we are looking for is simple. Either you know

33

who it is or you don't."

"I understand. Can we get this over with now?"

Both Harry and Jim could see the effort Barksdale was making to hurry through the ordeal. Jim thought it to be a normal reaction. Harry thought it to be phony.

They entered through the glass doors and approached the desk that was occupied by a rather sultry looking individual in a long white medical coat. He looked up at them and then at his wristwatch.

"I'm almost ready to close. This had better be a simple one, or you'll have to return tomorrow."

Harry took the lead.

"Now, my dear chap, I say, haven't we always been expeditious when we are trying to have one of your guests identified?"

The man in white gave Harry a complacent stare.

"And I say to you, when have I ever not cooperated to the fullest? And please stop referring to these bodies as my guests. I take exception to the inference."

Harry smiled and then gestured to Jim and Barksdale to follow them down along a row of vaults in the wall. Apparently Harry had been there many times. Jim surmised that when you are working homicide, you get to visit the morgue regularly. He was glad that homicide wasn't his sole territory. A place like this could become very depressing. About midway down, the gentleman stopped, checked a tag on the vault drawer, and pulled on it. Slowly the drawer opened, and it was obvious that there was a body in it, covered with a sheet. You could make out the feet at the far end and what must be the head at the near end.

At this point even Jim felt a bit of discomfort. Though he had done this before, he had never quite gotten used to it. The man in white announced the name of the occupant.

"This is Richard Barksdale."

You could see the shocked expression on Barksdale's face at that announcement. His tan took on a paler as he gave Jim an inquiring glance.

"I'm sorry, Mister Barksdale, but I haven't had time to notify the morgue of the change of name."

"I understand. It's just that hearing your name in a place like this gives you the creeps. I'd almost expect to see myself under that sheet."

Harry and the mortician laughed quietly to themselves. Harry did note that Barksdale was taking all this in rather calmly, in spite of his "inexperience" with dead bodies. The sheet was then pulled back to expose the head of the corpse. To Jim's surprise, Barksdale looked it straight in the face, and then lifted the sheet himself to examine the remainder of the naked body. An act that even Jim wouldn't do voluntarily. Barksdale grunted, placed the sheet back over the body and shook his head.

"Sorry, but I have no idea who this person is. He appears to have been meticulous about his health. He must have worked out in a gym with a build like that."

My, thought Jim, *he certainly took a lot in for someone who was nervous about viewing a corpse.* Harry showed no sign of any kind of reaction. Harry was very practiced in the art of self discipline. In no way could anyone read the man's thoughts. Harry and Jim thanked the mortician for his time, and left the morgue with Barksdale at their side. Once back on the street, they thanked Barksdale for his trouble and then headed back to headquarters. Jim was dying to hear Harry's opinion of Barksdale. He had some opinions of his own, but wanted to hear from Harry first. Finally, Harry spoke out loud as they drove.

"Wouldn't you expect someone green at viewing cadavers to be a bit fearful of getting so close to one? And the way he took hold of that sheet and looked the whole body over; that was a person that had not only seen dead people, but I'll wager he has handled dead bodies before."

"Maybe that one in particular?"

"That would be speculation, Jim. Too risky to make that speculation at this time, but definitely a maybe."

They rode in silence for a while. Then Harry looked at Jim.

"Did you sense anything when he first introduced himself? Anything strange?"

Jim thought for a moment.

"Yes I did. He held his hand out to me and addressed me by name. Up to that point he had never seen or spoken to me."

"Astute observation, my good man. How did he know you? Someone had to tell him what you looked like, being black I mean. Or…"

"Or he was at the scene the morning after the accident and saw me."

Jim sat up, an expression of awe on his face.

"That two-faced bastard knows what I look like because he had seen me before. He's covering up something big. I have this gut feeling about it."

Jim recalled the example he had given Officer Benson about questioning the people standing around the crime scene. A pyromaniac would appear at the scene just to observe reactions over his crime. Maybe this Barksdale was like that, only he wanted to witness when the body he had placed at a scene was discovered. Or even help things along to be sure it was discovered.

"Possibly; or someone at the crime scene told him. It is possible that there are more than one person involved in this, you know."

Jim pondered that one. Who would have not only seen him, but would have heard his name mentioned? Only two people at the scene that morning were told who he was; the tow truck driver and Officer Benson. Of course, either one could have mentioned that to someone in conversation. Yet there seemed little likelihood that his name would be a topic for conversation. Except for the rookie. Jim almost could hear him telling his peers of how Jim had talked him through his first crime scene, and how clever Jim had been regarding evidence and the discovery of a body. Jim shook his head.

"Harry, there's no way of knowing how he found out. Do you think that by his knowing, he becomes implicated?"

"It's hard to say. I knew who you were without ever seeing you at first. But then, your reputation preceded you."

Jim gave Harry a sharp look.

"Very funny!"

Harry smiled and said what he always said after giving Jim a jab.

"Pity."

Then the two of them laughed as they neared headquarters.

Again, a piece of the puzzle was sitting on Jim's desk when he walked in. It was the report from the lab on the paper with the poem on it. And again he needed Harry's reaction, so he called Harry and asked him to come to his office.

"What's up?"

"This."

He handed Harry the report. Harry read it and looked at Jim with a questioning stare.

"That's not possible."

"It is Harry, if you take Barksdale's entire statements and throw them into the waste basket. That man has done nothing but lie to us."

The report showed three sets of blurred and unidentifiable fingerprints. The key here was that there were only three sets.

"If I remember, we know that you, I and Debra handled that paper. Barksdale said he and his secretary handled it. Assuming the author wore gloves, there should be five sets of prints on that paper, identifiable or otherwise. But there are only three, which leaves us with a paper that has been deliberately made void of any fingerprints when placed in that glove compartment. Harry, that poem is still a link in this murder."

"I have to agree with you this time. Jim, why put the name of someone still alive on it? What purpose does it serve?"

"Harry, you said it yourself. The killer is challenging us. What if he put the name on it to deliberately throw us off track?"

"A fair assumption. But, if Barksdale is involved, why should the killer put the name of himself, or an accomplice on it?"

"Who is to say that old adage of throwing someone off track by doing what is obviously stupid wasn't the intent. 'I'm innocent because I wouldn't point the finger at myself.' Right?"

"Maybe, then maybe not. What about the date on it?"

"Just a piece of nothing to spin our wheels on."

Harry nodded his head in agreement. The obvious was most definitely not the right place to hang your hat. Jim tapped the paper and began to read the poem aloud. This time he placed more emphasis on the intent rather than what appeared to be evident. As he started, he heard a familiar voice call to him from the doorway.

"Jim, you have such a perfect speaking voice. Too bad it's wasted on that silly poem."

Jim smiled. He had missed the usual daily heckling that Debra provided. Perhaps Harry was right. She had him in her control.

"Just in time to hear me read. Maybe you can add some ideas to this stupid case."

"Probably hand you the answer is more like it. Good morning Sergeant Mansfield."

Harry turned, smiled at Debra, and gave her a wink.

"Try calling me Harry. I feel intimidated when a beautiful woman calls me by my official title."

"There, hear that Jim? Take some tips from Harry on how to woo a woman off her feet."

Jim just ignored the remark and waved her into his office and began reading the poem.

"'There once was a man that thought he knew every answer.' Who has an idea as to what man is being referred to in the poem? We originally thought it was the victim, but now we must consider other possibilities."

"Why don't you put the whole idea together? I think the entire statement of lines one and two should be read as one concept. Try it."

Jim read the rest of line two.

"'But alas, he knew too few.' You know, it almost sounds as if the writer was describing the futile attempts we've made at solving this case."

Harry and Debra spoke the same words simultaneously.

"That's it!"

Harry and Debra laughed at the incident. Debra motioned for Harry to continue.

"The man refers to us as the investigators. We keep thinking we have the answers, but we don't. The murderer already knows what we'll think and do. He or she is making a mockery of our efforts even before we started."

Debra chimed in at this point.

"And Jim, if you read the last two lines together, the murderer continues in the same vein. He's mocking you; taunting you with a suggestion."

"I get it. 'So now he' meaning us, 'resides where only angels roam and all the answers are now at home.' It's telling us that we have a body and all the answers we need, we just need to put it together properly."

Harry scratched his chin.

"How do you come up with that analogy, old chap? Where does the reference to angels fit in?"

Debra had that one figured out.

"It's simple, Harry. The angels referred to here are the avenues of guidance. There are any number of ways to direct this investigation. They're all good ways of solving the crime, but it's up to us which one we put our efforts into. It's much like life itself. You can fulfill life by taking the best and shortest way, taking little time and effort. Or you can take all sorts of wrong turns that will eventually lead you to fulfillment, but it takes stress and forever to accomplish."

"What Debra is telling us Harry, is that we can drag our feet and eventually solve this thing or start off with a strong objective and get the answer to our questions fast. It's up to us."

Harry continued concentrating on his goatee, as if to smooth it to a point on the bottom. Then he shook his head.

"If this is the intention of the poem, then in essence we haven't a clue here, just someone toying with our minds and telling us nothing that isn't already a known fact."

Jim sat back and placed his hands behind his neck.

"That's it in a nutshell. Now we start looking for what we already have."

Harry looked at Jim.

"Which is? What do we have?"

Just then one of the uniformed officers entered and handed Jim a piece of paper. Jim thanked the officer and read the paper. Then he stood up and stretched.

"Right now, all we have is a dead John Doe. His fingerprints were not in any records in Washington or the state."

Harry picked up the paper Jim had set down and shook his head as he read it.

"You two have forgotten one very important fact."

Jim and Harry looked at Debra. She smiled at the two of them and raised her head as if to boast as she spoke.

"You have an accident that appears to be in question as to whether it was done deliberately or if it might truly be an accident. You have two people that could have been involved. By the way, what happened with your meeting with the real Mister Barksdale?"

Jim explained.

"That meeting turned up the fact that Barksdale lied to us about everything. He has to be hiding something; I say it has to do with John Doe."

Harry turned towards Jim.

"Damn it Jim, that's speculation! I told you before what that's worth."

"It's worth pursuing, gentlemen. Rather than setting things like that aside and waiting for something to happen, why don't you force something to happen?"

Jim and Harry looked first at each other, and then at Debra. In unison they asked the inevitable.

"Like what?"

"Like something you did with that automobile accident case when you interviewed that Tate woman. You remember Jim, when you said you already knew about Patrick O'Connor when you actually didn't. You led the woman to believing something that forced her into reacting in a manner that gave away her involvement. You also made the truth come out a lot sooner than anticipated. Maybe telling this Barksdale a little white lie might force him to say or do something that will bring you closer to the truth."

Jim shook his head in amazement.

"Debra, now I know why I like having you around. You think just like I do."

Harry chimed in with a helpful suggestion.

"Since we all are bloody unscrupulous, how about a big lie instead of a little one?"

Jim smiled. He was really getting to like Harry.

"Have you something in mind, Harry, or are you just speculating?"

"I don't speculate!"

Again Jim smiled.

"Pity."

"Touché, old chap."

The two laughed, while Debra was left wondering what that was all about. Not wanting to know, she decided to tell Jim why she had stopped by in the first place.

"Jim, I have the answers about the car. First, Robert Thomas is not the original owner of the car. A Frank Spencer originally bought it. He sold it privately to Thomas after it had been in an accident. It was easy enough to find out, since my insurance company was involved in both ownerships. Apparently Thomas was able to have it restored to its original condition cheaply due to the fact that his brother owns an auto collision shop. Here's something you'll find interesting about the first accident. The car was stolen by some teenagers for a joy ride and at the end of it they decided to send it off the side of the bridge that crosses Tonawanda Creek at Campbell Boulevard. The car seems to be destined to go swimming in that creek."

Jim found that piece of information very interesting. He also had an idea.

"How about if we tell Barksdale that our John Doe's name is Frank Spencer and see if he reacts to it. I know it's a long shot, but if Thomas is so close to Barksdale, like 'brothers,' it may set something in motion. Barksdale may even know of the original owner. But I'm sure they most likely would have never met."

The three of them agreed that the idea had merit, and that they would implement it first thing tomorrow morning. Then Debra reminded Jim of their plans for the evening, said she'd keep in touch to Harry, and then left with Jim for an evening of dining and romance. Harry stayed for a while longer, reading the poem a few times to himself. He still wasn't quite convinced that their interpretation of it was completely accurate. He was, however, now positive that it was in some way connected with their John Doe. Harry was not happy with the fourth line. He wasn't sure if 'home' was their office or somewhere else that they had yet to discover. Finally tired of trying to glean insight from the poem, he placed it on Jim's desk and left for the day.

The morning brought another development. Robert Thomas called to inform Jim that he had arrived home a day early and was available to speak with him. Jim asked if he would meet Jim and Harry at the morgue to try and identify the body. Thomas agreed, and hung up. Jim called Harry and asked if he was free to meet with Thomas and if so, they would need to leave in thirty minutes. Harry said yes. Then Jim asked Harry to bring the poem to him when he came to Jim's office so they could give it more thought. Harry's response was confusing to Jim.

"It's right there on your desk. I left it there when I went home."

"Well, it's not here now. Are you sure?"

"Quite, old chap. I say, something seems amiss here. Let me come over right now."

Jim went to the file to retrieve the original paper with the poem on it. He was really puzzled to find the original paper missing from the file. However, there was a paper with something unexpected on it. A new poem. Just then Harry entered Jim's office.

"Harry, you're not going to believe this. The poem's missing. Both the original and the copy I made are gone."

"That's impossible. Only you and I would know of the existence and location of the poem. It's just been misplaced."

"Guess what is here. A new poem; someone has found access into our offices during the night. This murderer not only challenges us but also has a set of brass balls. Entering a police headquarters and tampering with evidence in a crime. Damn it, this person is beginning to give me the creeps."

"Jim, let's have a look see at the new poem. And I wouldn't be concerned about fingerprints. I would wager my paycheck it's clean."

Jim handed him the paper, holding it at the edge.

"None-the-less, let's have it checked before we assume that. But read it out loud first."

**I GAVE THE MAN WHAT HE NEEDED TO KNOW
IN THE HOPE THAT CORRECTLY HE WOULD GO.
BUT AGAIN I SEE THAT HE FALTERS AT WILL,
WHEN THE ANSWER HE SEEKS IS AT HOME STILL.**

"Damn this character! Harry, I can't believe the murderer was standing right here, in my office. And he or she is making a mockery of this entire case, to say nothing of how foolish we look."

"I notice, Jim, that the reference to 'home' is made a second time. Yesterday I kept pondering over the word, trying to decide if it was this office or somewhere else. Now I'm almost positive that 'home' is not here, but somewhere that we are aware of, but haven't looked at as yet. My problem is, where the devil is this bloody place?"

Jim decided to hold off his call to Barksdale and head over to the morgue. He and Harry dropped the paper off at the lab for analysis and headed for the street and a car. As they drove, the two bantered back and forth as to the meaning of the use of poetry in the first place and if the poems themselves weren't designed to throw them off the track rather than giving direction. Both agreed to make inquiries once they returned at headquarters; someone must have seen a person in Jim's office. It was inconceivable that anyone could blatantly go into the building and remove evidence in a case and do so completely unnoticed.

They arrived at the morgue shortly after nine and walked the familiar corridor heading towards the glass doors. A man greeted them. He was in his late twenties, with dark brown hair that was shoulder length and styled to meet the current trend. He sported a full mustache and was impeccably dressed in a gray business suit, white shirt and maroon tie. Thinking about Barksdale's age and ponytail, apparently being an investigator seeking unknown wealth required a person somewhat unique in character.

"I'm sorry, but might one of you gentlemen be a Lieutenant Hargrove?"

"That would be me," Jim said as he extended his hand.

"And you must be Robert Thomas."

"At your service. I hope I can be of some help. This entire accident situation has me quite upset. Telling me I lost a very good friend, then finding out it was a mistake. Losing my car to the creek and a murder investigation. It takes a bit of adjusting to cope with it all."

Jim said he understood as he opened the glass door. The same mortician was sitting at the desk. Harry waved a hand at him and asked if they could see the cadaver. The man shook his head as if in disbelief.

"How long do you think I can hold onto a body in here? Forever? You just made it under the wire. I was about to have the body embalmed and sent off to the main vaults for disposition. You know, this is the first time I have ever seen such a perfect specimen. Too bad you can't find a relative of some kind. Sooner or later he's bound to be missed. His relatives will never know what happened to him by that time."

"Yes, my good man. Pity."

Harry always displayed that devilish grin when he said that word. Pity, to Harry, was anything whether or not it had serious connotations or very little hope. It was something to be taken lightly almost to a point of being humorous, whether it was a person or a thing. Englishmen had a strange sense of humor.

Again Jim watched as the drawer with the body of their John Doe was pulled out and the sheet taken off the head. Jim was watching Thomas's expressions very closely for any signs of recognition, whether voluntary or otherwise. Unlike Barksdale, Thomas was not as venturesome about seeing the physical attributes of the body.

"He certainly looks like someone I have seen before, but I can't quite place where."

This was a break that neither Jim nor Harry had expected. Jim asked some questions, hoping to jog the man's memory.

"Was it in regards to your line of work perhaps? Maybe a client that you may have seen at your office recently. Or someone you met as part of your investigations."

"That's it! I saw a picture of this guy in one of the file folders on my supervisor's desk. I think he was a relative of one of our clients. I have no idea what his name is or why he would be in the trunk of my car, but I'm almost positive he is part of one of our investigations."

Terrific. Jim could hardly believe his ears. Harry had a question.

"He wasn't involved in one of your investigations?"

"No, or I would know his name. If you'd like, I'll ask my supervisor who's case it is so you can talk to whoever is handling the investigation."

"Please yes, my boy. And if you could give me the name and phone number of your supervisor, I'd like to speak with him first, so he understands what is happening here."

"Fine. Oh, and by the way, my supervisor is a she, not a he."

"Jolly good! I'm impressed by women that can take charge."

"Oh she takes charge all right. But I wouldn't recommend you treat her with anything less than kid gloves. She can be the most stubborn person when it comes to giving information to anyone about our clients. If she tells you to go to hell, don't be surprised by it."

"Sounds like a delightful woman. I can't wait to speak with her."

Harry was obviously being facetious. Jim could hardly wait to hear how Harry handled her. Harry thought of himself as a lady's man. This sometimes came back at him in some form of debacle that left Harry looking for somewhere to hide. But he was persevering; Jim had to give him credit in that respect. Unlike Harry, he was content to have a date and sometimes a little passion. He never strove to take control of a woman. Of course, now that Debra had entered his life, he was definitely never in control of things. He didn't really mind it, and given any set of circumstances, he wouldn't dream of changing anything.

Thomas apologized for not being more help and excused himself for not staying, stating he had not reported into his office as yet and there were urgent things that he needed to do. Harry and Jim had no further questions, so the trio split up. Before leaving, Harry asked if the body could be left for just one more day since there was likelihood that a positive identification might be imminent. The mortician just shrugged, told Harry to wear a mask the next time or the odor might overtake him.

Once the two were back at headquarters, Jim decided to be the first caller. He wanted to hear Barksdale's reaction to his identification rouse before Thomas let the cat out of the bag. This time they used the speakerphone connection. However, it never came to fruition; Barksdale had left and was out of town for the rest of the week. So much for plans, and besides it seemed fruitless at this stage of the game to pursue. Harry was more fortunate. He was immediately connected to a Dorothy Maguire, who had one of the sexiest voices that Harry had ever heard. However, the vocabulary on the woman left much to be desired. As predicted by Thomas, the minute she heard that Harry was looking for some information on someone that they were working with, she turned into a tiger.

"Go to hell! That's privileged information. Not even you are entitled to know."

"We will have no problem obtaining a warrant to see your files, since this involves the identification of a murder victim. Of course, once we have that warrant, say within the hour, we may as well take a look and everything you're working on; just in case there is something not right with your operations."

"You bastard! That's extortion! I'll have your badge for that one."

"Not until you've surrendered your files on all your cases. After all, I am entitled to prove I am within my rights to find deliberate misuse of your company's privileges. And I dare say, unless you are the Immaculate Mary Herself, you have made a questionable entry or a false placement of funds somewhere. I guarantee if it's there, I'll find it."

"You come on over, right now. I want to see the miserable bastard that thinks he's King of the Hill. I'll bet you look like an asshole. You sure as hell talk like one."

Harry said he'd be there within the hour, thanked her, and as Dorothy Maguire started in on Harry again, he hung up. Then he looked at Jim, who was wearing the biggest grin he could muster.

"That is by far the most obnoxious woman I have ever come across in my twelve years on the force. I can't wait to meet her. I'll bet she's in her fifties, ugly as sin and never been laid in her life."

"Harry, I think you have finally met your match. You couldn't get to first base with her if your life depended on it."

Harry never let a challenge regarding the opposite sex go undefended.

"I'll bet I get into her pants. What will you wager, old chap?"

"Twenty bucks says you never do; not tonight, not ever."

"You're on! Now I have a definite goal for this morning. To win over Miss Dirty Mouth."

"Harry, you look horrific when you can see defeat ahead of you. You're speculating that she even gives a damn about sex."

"No woman is too great an obstacle for me. And stop saying I'm speculating. You know how I hate that."

"Pity."

That broke the confrontation between them. Harry smiled and stood up.

"You come along now, my friend. I'll show you how a true man takes charge."

"Oh? Who's going to be there besides you and me?"

"Very funny!"

"I will admit one thing Harry. You were able to get an audience with her without the warrant. I commend you for that."

"Perseverance. That's how it works."

"Sounded more like persistent threats to me."

Harry looked at Jim, who started to say something else but was cut off by the wave of Harry's index finger.

"Wait and see, Jim. Then you shall believe."

With that said, the two headed downstairs for their meeting with Dorothy Maguire.

Chapter 4

The offices of Unisearch were housed in a modern industrial park that had just been built off North French Road in Amherst. As Jim and Harry entered into a waiting area, it was obvious that the company spared no expense to decorate the entrance. The carpeting was plush; the furniture was solid wood, not the veneered particleboard that was so popular. The chairs were so comfortable; once you sank into them you didn't want to get out of them. A receptionist welcomed them, took their names and who they were there to see, and asked them if they desired anything to drink.

"A good shot of scotch would be nice."

Harry thought he was being cute, but when asked if Chivas would be acceptable, Harry mentioned he was on duty and courteously declined. Jim asked if coffee with sugar would be a bother, to which the receptionist smiled pleasantly and said that would not be a problem. Backing down, Harry asked if he could have some tea with lemon, no cream and no sugar. The receptionist smiled and said she would return with the coffee and tea within a minute. Harry avoided Jim's apparent delight in the whole episode.

"You have to be aware Harry that these people cater to the wealthy, whether it be newly obtained or just the addition of even greater wealth. Nothing is too great a request for them."

"Don't rub it in, Jim. I realized it the minute I walked in, but still, the urge for a little fun got the better of me. Sorry for that."

The receptionist returned with their beverages and told them that Miss Maguire would see them shortly. She then placed a small dish with a few delicate looking cookies between them and went back to her desk. *My,* thought Jim, *I could learn to enjoy this type of living very easily.* He tasted the cookie and found it delicious. He gestured to Harry to take one.

"No thanks. I never eat anything with my tea. I enjoy the taste better without the condiment."

After a few minutes had past, a tall and very attractive woman came into the area and approached the two of them. She excused herself, said she was Miss Maguire's secretary and would they please follow her. Harry thought to himself *Baby, I'd follow you anywhere*. He suppressed the urge to say it out loud. As they walked past row after row of small individual offices, Jim could not stop wondering what it must be like to be wealthy. Every office was completely outfitted with computer, desk, file cabinets, coat racks and at least three chairs. All of it was top of the line quality. But when he entered Dorothy Maguire's office, he became totally awed by the majesty of the room.

A huge mahogany desk surrounded by three armchairs facing the occupant was the first thing your eyes picked up. Along the side was a large leather couch with end tables at either side. A tall brass pole lamp adorned the nearest corner. A small rack for coats was set next to it. Before Jim could take in any more of the room and its furnishings, his eye caught the figure of a woman sitting behind the desk. Her head was bent down obscuring her face from view. As the two approached the desk, the secretary announced their names. The woman behind the desk looked up. She was absolutely beautiful!

As she stood up and extended her hand to Jim, it was impossible not to stare at this woman. She must have been at least thirty-five years old, with dark brown hair cut in a fashionable style, just about at necks length. Her figure was perfect and the complexion of her skin smooth and olive in color. Jim had seen many mulatto women before, and all of them seemed to be a product of a mix that brought out the beauty in them. But this one was stunning. He could hardly take his eyes off her. Jim tried to act nonchalant as he smiled and extended his hand to her in return. As they shook, he could sense that she was feeling friendly towards him, and her smile revealed a set of the whitest teeth. But as she faced Harry, her facial expression changed, as did her demeanor.

"I guess you must be the wise ass I spoke to before. Let's get something straight right now between you and me. This is my turf and whatever I agree to or disagree to is final. I won't take any sass from you, and let me see your ID."

While taking in all of the fancy surroundings, both Jim and Harry had forgotten to show anyone their identification. As Jim reached for his badge and card, Dorothy looked at him and smiled.

"No need for you to do that. I can tell an honest and truthful person when I see one. I'm sure you're who you say you are."

Then she turned and looked at Harry, who had also stopped reaching for his badge and identification.

"I didn't say I believed you, though. Let's see it!"

By the look on Harry's face, Jim could tell he was becoming agitated by the discriminatory treatment he was receiving. After producing the badge and ID, Dorothy asked them both to sit down. She looked at Jim and suggested he call her Dorothy. Then she turned to Harry.

"And you can call me Miss Maguire."

Harry could not restrain himself any longer.

"Now see here! I object to your treating me as if I were some sort of—"

"Plague? That would be putting it mildly. I abhor you."

Harry could see he would get nowhere by pursuing any line of conversation, so he sat back and let Jim take over.

"Miss Maguire, I mean Dorothy, we are here to speak to you regarding a body that was found in the trunk of one of your investigator's car two days ago. He carried no identification on him. We have been led to believe that he may be related to one of your clients."

"Whose car did you say the body was found in?"

"I didn't. It was in the trunk of Robert Thomas's car. In fact he went to the morgue this morning and recognized the corpse as someone he had seen in your files. We thought maybe we could, with your cooperation of course, have a look at the file in question and see if we can put a name to the victim."

Dorothy smiled. She addressed Jim totally, and completely ignored Harry's presence.

"If I can be of any help, I certainly will try. Let me call Bob in and find out where he saw the picture."

She called for Thomas, found him in, and asked him to step into her office. When Thomas entered the office, he acknowledged Harry and Jim, and when asked where he had seen the picture, went to one of the file cabinets and opened one of the drawers.

"I was in here to get out one of my files because my own file was missing two pages. I must have made a mistake when I copied them the other day. Anyway, I pulled the wrong file out initially, and when I opened it and saw it wasn't mine, I returned it to, ah, here it is."

Pulling the folder out of the draw, Thomas handed it to Dorothy. She thanked him and with that asked him to leave.

"It's not that I don't trust Bob; it's company policy. Only the investigator on a particular case is privileged to know the information regarding that case."

Jim told Dorothy he understood and fully agreed with the policy. Dorothy smiled, opened the folder and glanced through it. Then she produced a photo from the folder and showed it to Jim. Jim looked at it and handed it to Harry, who had been sulking to himself the whole time. Harry was not a happy camper. However, duty comes first, so he took the picture and looked at it.

"That's him Jim. I'm positive that's the man. Can we have the name, Dorothy?"

"It's Miss Maguire, and yes, the Lieutenant can have the name. I'll give you the address and phone number of his family. I'm sure they will want to know what's happened."

As she wrote, Harry decided to eat crow and beg for recognition. He needed some firmer ground to stand on than Dorothy had extended him thus far.

"And I am sorry Miss Maguire for the impression I gave you over the phone. I am really not the bad person you seem to have pictured. I want only what it takes to help solve this case and put the right people in jail that deserve to be there."

Dorothy handed the paper to Jim and then turned to Harry.

"If you think that speech will get you in my good graces, forget it. You've burnt your bridge."

Jim interrupted the conversation, which was definitely all down hill for Harry.

"Dorothy, you don't have to tell me, but it might be helpful. Whose case is it-which investigator I mean?"

Dorothy looked at the top of the inside flap of the folder and then at Jim. "Richard Barksdale."

Jim decided to be evasive and play dumb. For some reason he felt uncomfortable letting anyone know of his acquaintance with Barksdale. Harry apparently felt the same way. Neither said anything that indicated they knew Barksdale. Having gotten what they needed, Jim thanked Dorothy for her help and shook her hand. Harry tried to do the same but was totally ignored. They left Unisearch and headed back to headquarters. As they drove, Jim extended the open palm of his hand to Harry.

"You owe me twenty bucks, my friend. Cough it up."

"Not yet. I'm not through with Miss Holier Than Thou just yet. Anyway, the bet is 'not tonight, or ever.' Well 'ever' hasn't happened yet."

"Harry, do you think she's in her fifties and ugly?"

"Bloody glad I was wrong on that! She is going to be one challenge I will enjoy conquering."

They rode in silence for a few minutes. Finally, Jim couldn't stand prolonging his curiosity any longer.

"What's your conclusion regarding Barksdale?"

"Say what? You must have the same opinion as I do, no?"

"The man is in this murder up to his eyeballs. Can you beat that? Looks at a body he knows and plays dumb. He's hiding something; most likely he's our man, wouldn't you think, Harry?"

"Quite possibly. He's involved, yes; but the murderer—I couldn't say at this point."

"Then you think he's just an accomplice? How many people do you think may be involved?"

Harry rubbed his chin.

"More than one; maybe two. Barksdale is smart; why would he kill a relative of his client? The more relatives he turns up, the smaller the monies divided amongst the client's relatives. I'll wager the cut for his company is averaged so that they end up with more based on the number of people they seek out and find. That creates incentive to the investigators, more profits, and ultimately better salaries wouldn't you say? They may even work on a bonus system. No matter, the idea of killing a client's relative doesn't make good business sense."

Jim took the paper Dorothy had given him and opened it.

"Harry, our John Doe's name is Harrison. William Harrison. Does that name ring a bell?"

"William Harrison. William Harrison. You couldn't mean Senator William Harrison from Nevada?"

"That's exactly who I mean. This murder is going to be big time news. I wonder how much money Unisearch's case involves. If I were to venture a guess, I'd say we're talking millions. It is certainly going to be a big factor in developing motive for our murderer. Which brings me to our other investigator, Mister Thomas. Harry, wouldn't it make good sense if there were two of them working as a team on this?"

"Yes, but remember Jim, it was Thomas that came across with the recognition of the body. Why would he finger Barksdale if they were partners?"

"Maybe by elimination, he gets a bigger piece of pie."

"Sure, as long as Barksdale doesn't name Thomas as his accomplice. That's highly unlikely. Besides, Thomas seemed sincere in not knowing who the case investigator was, in which case, he couldn't have known who the cadaver was in the first place, which eliminates him as an accomplice. We're plucking at straws at the moment."

As soon as they arrived at headquarters, Jim made some calls to Nevada. The end result was being told to keep the body on ice and someone would be there to identify the corpse. Within an hour two FBI Agents were led into his office. Once introductions were made, he requested Harry be included, and as they waited for the sergeant, Jim began to give a narrative of the events of the past two days that had led to the discovery of the corpse's identity. As he reached the visit to Unisearch, Harry entered the office. Jim introduced everyone and then continued.

"So you can see from what we've uncovered so far, it is imperative that we know what the senator's role in this case is, so we can determine why someone felt it necessary to kill him."

The FBI agents agreed to let Jim and Harry know what the senator was doing in Buffalo. In exchange, Jim and Harry agreed that any leak to the press about the death would not come from them, and if approached, they would not divulge any information to the public. With that agreed upon, all four left for the morgue and a hopeful positive identification.

As predictable, the mortician was the same as earlier, and Harry had to calm him as he digressed on how unethical keeping a body this long was, to say nothing about the sanitary codes he was violating by not having the corpse embalmed by now. The drawer was opened and the agents looked and identified the body as definitely that of Senator William Harrison. Harry had to admit that there was now a distinct and unpleasant odor being emitted by the cadaver. The mortician just shook his head, muttered a few profanities about policemen, and thanked them for finally giving the corpse a name. The FBI agents signed an authorization on behalf of the senator's wife to embalm the body while arrangements would be made to transport it back to Nevada. Having accomplished that piece of the case, Jim and Harry now had a name for the victim and a possible motive to the murder. They thanked the agents for their help and headed back to headquarters.

"Well Harry, what do you suggest we do next?"

"That thought earlier about scotch is beginning to sound inviting. I have a bloody headache."

Jim looked at his wristwatch.

"Not quite yet, but soon, very soon. I might even buy."

"Jolly good of you. You're on."

"But right now, what's a good direction for us to head? Shall we ask Dorothy to have Barksdale report on what he has to say about this, or do we surprise him at his home with a warrant?"

"God no, man! That's way too premature. What have we for evidence? A liar? On what motive? A bigger share? A bigger share of what, and with whom? Too many holes to fill in, Jim. If Barksdale is our man, or an accomplice even, the last thing we want to do is give away our hand. Right now he thinks we have no clue as to his lies. Let's leave it that way for the moment."

"But Dorothy is bound to mention our visit. That's going to give it away."

Harry smiled.

"Leave Dorothy to me, Jim. I'm not through with that cutie just yet. Harry's charm will prevail. Trust me."

"Well, so far I'm not impressed. Maybe you've lost the old charm and don't know it."

"Jim, I'll have Miss Maguire eating out of the palm of my hand. You touch base with Thomas to make sure he keeps quiet. Those two are the only ones that could hinder things."

The two had arrived back at headquarters. As they walked towards Jim's office, they were stopped by a lab technician and given the second poem back. As Harry predicted, it was clean. Then they went to the people around the floor nearest Jim's office and asked who might have been around last night to witness someone in Jim's office. No one offered any help. In fact, Jim was informed that last night had been set aside for a special meeting at the union hall, to which everyone had either gone to or had used as an excuse not to be in the office. As a Lieutenant, Jim no longer shared the privilege of being a union member, so he was unaware of the meeting. Harry apologized to Jim; he had completely forgotten about it.

Do to a lack of personnel, it was easier to envision someone getting the chance to swap poems in Jim's office, so the hope for some identification went down the tubes. The more Jim worked on this homicide, the more he realized that finding clues, tracking down information and having a standard procedure to follow was much more difficult than accident investigations. There was something to be said for homicide detectives; they required a lot more intuitiveness and patience than most investigators. Harry left Jim to start his planning for the "conquering" of Dorothy Maguire.

Jim called Robert Thomas and asked if he would cooperate by not mentioning his recognition of the corpse, just in case it should become a problem amongst his fellow workers that information about identities involved in their cases were being given out. Jim was very careful not to divulge the fact that the victim was a part of one of Barksdale's cases.

Jim tried to reconstruct the first poem from memory. He called Debra to see if what he could recollect was in any way inaccurate. He was immediately the target of criticism.

"Jim, you are becoming careless. Why don't you leave your wallet on your desk when you leave your office? Maybe someone will make it a little lighter for you."

"But I didn't leave that poem on the desk, Harry did. Besides, where else can I leave information on a case if not in my files? It almost seems that the person knew exactly where the file to this case was."

"Think, Jim. Who was in your office when you either took the file out or put it away?"

Jim thought for a minute. Then he shook his head.

"No one but Harry. I don't think he would have done it. That and the fact that his abilities with poetry stinks."

Debra listened to what Jim had put together, made a few commentaries and additions, and said what he had was about right. Then she reminded Jim about dinner, told him she loved him, and hung up. Deciding to make a clean break and start fresh in the morning, he began looking through the case files that had accumulated in his incoming basket. He spent the next two hours doing what he felt more comfortable with, accident cases. Just as it seemed the end of the day had finally arrived, Harry walked into Jim's office, a grin on his face.

"Old chap, I believe you will shortly be twenty dollars poorer. I have cajoled Dorothy into having dinner with me tonight."

Jim raised his eyebrows.

"It's Dorothy, is it? Dinner tonight? How did you manage to talk her into doing that?"

Harry had that devilish look on his face as he smiled.

"I told her you wanted me to make up for my rudeness and that my promotion was in jeopardy if I didn't fess up and make things right."

"You what? Thanks for making me the fall guy to your impetuous desires for physical satisfaction. Next you'll be telling her I was the one that put you up to the threatening approach this morning."

"How'd you guess? You weren't listening in on my conversation, now were you?"

"Harry! Don't push this. You didn't, did you?"

Harry laughed as he almost seemed to lose his breath.

"Of course not! But you should see the look on your face as I said that I had."

Jim was not amused by Harry's use of humor. But he quickly turned the conversation around by reminding Harry that the purpose of the dinner was to befriend Dorothy and obtain her trust in not mentioning their inquiry about the correlation between the corpse and the photograph. Harry said he understood.

"But I'm also serious about what I have in mind for after dinner. Do be sure and have that twenty handy tomorrow."

Jim waved Harry out of his office and departed for home and then his own dinner engagement. He hoped that Harry, as good a homicide detective as he was, didn't botch things up in his mad attempt at being Casanova. Jim had to admit to himself that if Harry did turn things around, and Dorothy became affectionate towards Harry, that he would have to acknowledge Harry's prowess in the field of love. Tomorrow should be a very interesting day.

The evening with Dorothy started out with the usual amenities. Harry wanted no stone left unturned when it came to protocol. He picked Dorothy up at her home and did his best to keep from sounding insincere. The worst thing he could do at this point was to over kill his desire to flatter her.

"I have to admit, starting off on the wrong foot put me at a disadvantage. I wasn't sure you would take me at my word, but I have never met such an attractive woman as you in my entire life."

"Then you've lived a sheltered life, Mister Mansfield."

"Not so, my dear. And please call me Harry. I have seen many beautiful women before, but none as stunning. And may I call you Dorothy?"

Harry could tell that some of Dorothy's hard demeanor was more of a veneer rather than engrained within her. She turned her head to look at Harry, a small smile on her face. He was sure she appreciated the compliment about her beauty.

"I really don't believe you're being honest by flattering me, but I accept it as a token of peace between us. I do want this to be a pleasant evening for the both of us."

"Then I may call you Dorothy, correct?"

"Yes, Harry, you may call me Dorothy. But don't think for a minute that letting you do that in any way entitles you to getting any special liberties with me."

Pity! Harry smiled and spoke like a true gentleman.

"I wouldn't even harbor a thought that was in any way disrespectful. On my honor as a born Englishman."

Harry hoped he wasn't being too boastful about his thoughts. One shouldn't overplay the part of innocence when the evening's end was to make passionate love to this gorgeous damsel. The rest of the ride to the restaurant was spent talking mostly about current events and the upcoming elections.

The restaurant Harry had selected was one he frequented often when he was courting a young lady. He liked the food and the service, and the prices were not too exorbitant. His only hope was that it would meet with Dorothy's expectations. They both settled for a moderate selection of appetizer, salad and an entrée that Harry found delectable; Dorothy seemed to enjoy her selection as well. He did get a bottle of wine for the dinner, which he normally didn't indulge in. But he wanted to spare no expense. Besides, the cost would be defrayed by Jim's twenty dollar contribution. And Harry also hoped it would dull Dorothy's sharp witted mind enough to be less resistant to his amorous advances later on.

They topped the dinner off with an after dinner drink of Tia Maria. Harry suggested they stop at his place before calling it an evening, just for a drink of some very special liquor that he had received from some relatives in England. He was shocked when Dorothy suggested he stop at her house instead. Without hesitation, Harry accepted the invitation. He could see victory close at hand. As they drove to Dorothy's place Harry seized the opportunity to mention the need for silence regarding the body found in Thomas's car and the photograph in Barksdale's file.

"It is wise that no one, not even Mister Barksdale, is informed about our discovery of the identity of our cadaver. We have asked Mister Thomas to do the same. It's just precautionary mind you, but we feel the less people know the easier it will be to extract the truth about this murder. It has also been requested by the FBI that as little as possible become public knowledge as to the unfortunate circumstances surrounding the senator."

For some unknown reason, Harry could feel a sudden chill in the air. It wasn't anything physical; it was more like a sense of apprehension had suddenly entered the car. Dorothy looked at Harry, her eyes showing signs of interest in what he had to say.

"The FBI? What do they have to do with a local murder?"

"They are involved with anything that has to do with a member of Congress or the Senate."

"How did they find out?"

"As soon as we placed a call to the senator's family, we were informed that there was to be an investigation by the FBI. This will eventually end up as a national event. Be prepared somewhere down the road to be questioned by the news media. That's inevitable."

Harry had reached Dorothy's house at this point. He turned into her driveway and shut the ignition off. As he was about to get out and go around to open the door for Dorothy, he felt her hand on his arm.

"I hope you'll forgive me, but I have suddenly acquired this awful migraine headache. I do hope you will forgive me for asking that we end our evening so prematurely. I promise we will have another chance to spend an evening together."

Harry's heart dropped down to his lap. This couldn't happen to him; not when he was so close to success. Damn!

"I hope it wasn't something I did or said."

"No, Harry, it wasn't anything you did. I think it's the wine that is affecting me. I'm not used to drinking like we did tonight. I'm truly sorry."

Damn it! Overdid the alcohol. Oh well, there's next time. Harry could sense that the opportunity was definitely still open for him.

"Let me at least walk you to your door."

Smiling, Dorothy nodded her head yes and Harry got out, walked around the car and opened the door for her. As she got out, Dorothy reached for Harry and as he pulled gently at her arm to help her out, she stood up for a moment and without warning kissed him on the lips. It sent Harry into orbit. Her lips were soft, her mouth moist and full upon his mouth. It was definitely a kiss of affection, not of courtesy. Harry's heart began to race and he could feel a flush of energy pass through his entire body. He threw caution to the wind and returned her kiss with one of his own. She did not reject it. Harry was in heaven.

Then as suddenly as the moment had begun, it ended.

"Harry, we really shouldn't start anything now. It's too premature. Please, I need to think about this. Let's call it a night for now. I promise to be a better date next time. Really."

Harry contained his frustrations, walked Dorothy to the door, kissed her again and stood there as the door closed. He was definitely a contender for her affections. He just wasn't prepared to stand at a door and watch it close and not have been a victor. He knew he would have to wait. Unfortunately, patience wasn't one of his virtues. Neither was eating crow, which was what he would have to do tomorrow when he faced Jim with his tale of failure.

Chapter 5

Jim was in his office earlier than usual again. His evening with Debra had ended splendidly, with him sharing the entire night with her. He knew that this woman was becoming so much a part of his life that being with her was utmost in importance. As he smiled to himself, he wondered how Casanova had done last night. He also wondered about what he was going to do regarding his handling of Barksdale. With the FBI involved, anything he did would have to be filtered through them; yet he wanted to be free to do things his way without being dictated to as to method. This case was becoming more than just complicated. It was becoming a nightmare. What a way to get your feet wet.

As he pondered over his next move, the telephone rang. On the other end was Special Agent Michael Anderson of the Federal Bureau of Investigation.

"Sorry to call so early Lieutenant, but I needed to know what your itinerary was for the day so that we could get together and start at the same place in this investigation."

This statement puzzled Jim.

"I'm sorry, but I don't quite understand what your intention is. Why do you need my itinerary?"

"Oh, didn't they tell you? I'm assigned to work with you on this case. Almost like a partner in a way. I hope that isn't going to be a problem, is it?"

Damn bureaucracy. This was going to be a royal pain in the ass. Jim could already feel his freedom of movements being cramped by outside influences. He sighed and gave in to the situation.

"Sorry, I didn't mean to sound unappreciative. Right now Agent Anderson, I have no 'itinerary.' I was just starting to decide on my next moves when you called."

"Excellent! Then we can both be on track together. I'll be at your office within the hour. You can start making a list of priorities while you're waiting for me. And please call me Mike. This one is going to take us many places together, so we might as well start on a first name basis now."

Crap! Getting orders already. Jim knew he was not going to be happy with this arrangement. But outwardly, for the sake of everyone, he would give it his best effort.

"Fine. And you can call me Jim."

"Great! See you in a jiff, Jim."

From the way this Mike talked, Jim was sure he was some sort of young smarty-pants with a fancy position and all the glory of the Agency to flaunt. He needed that. As he gloated over his newfound 'partner,' Harry interrupted his reverie as he walked into the office.

"Top of the day to you, Jim. How's it going?"

"Don't ask. And the top of this day is falling downhill rapidly."

Jim proceeded to tell Harry of their new partner on the case. Harry was equally unhappy about that. Then Jim reached for his wallet and started to open it. Harry, with a great deal of obvious discomfort, stopped Jim. He was about to eat crow.

"Uh, say old chap. You might want to hold off on that for a short while."

Jim smiled. He needed this moment to break the disappointments of the start to his day.

"So, our lover boy struck out? My goodness, what will the world say about this sad turn of events?"

"Now Jim, it's not all that you're thinking. I almost was there, if it weren't for me giving her too much booze."

"Bull, almost only counts in horseshoes and hand grenades. You botched it, my friend. Admit it."

As Harry was about to defend himself, the phone rang. *Saved by the bell*, thought Harry to himself. It was Debra, and she sounded angry.

"What's going on? I came into my office this morning and was greeted by the FBI. They took all my files regarding Thomas's car and told me to stop any further investigation regarding the accident. No one tells me to stop doing my job. No one."

"Now calm down. It has to do with our victim, and for some reason there seems to be an air of mystery regarding our dear senator. I have been the recipient of a new partner this morning, a Federal Agent. I don't know what's happening yet, but I intend to find out. Harry's pretty upset as well."

He made sure that Debra was consoled by the fact that everyone was in the dark, then hung up. He called his superior, Captain Hopkins, and asked what was going on. The captain apologized to Jim for not getting with him in time for the transition that was taking place.

"Please bear with me on this, Jim. I know it's an invasion of your way of working, but quite frankly the choice is not mine. The matter is out of my hands."

"Who's pulling the strings on this, Frank? The chief? The mayor?"

"I can't tell you that, Jim. I'm sorry. Just do the best you can under the circumstances. And be sure that anything you or Harry do is kept secret. That's a must."

Jim was uncomfortable. Frank's answers were not consoling at all. But he agreed, said he would cooperate to the fullest, and hung up. Harry gave Jim a questioning stare.

"No one will say anything, not even Frank. Suddenly everything we do, Harry, must be kept secret. That's orders, not advice. This is beginning to smell of a national problem and we are getting our asses tied up in it."

Harry saw that Jim was concerned.

"Maybe we should bow out; ask for another assignment?"

"Do you really mean that? I don't know about you, but I am so damned interested in seeing this through, I wouldn't miss it for the world."

"Oh, I'm bloody ready to stick my bloody ass in as deep as it needs to be. Just thought I'd throw that option out for you're benefit."

Jim loved to hear Harry when he was angry or excited about something. His language dropped into the English manner of speech, and Jim always thought of it as very colorful. As usual, for kicks Jim resorted to a response that was always unexpected and indicative of Harry.

"Pity."

Harry let out a burst of laughter that was so sudden it even startled Jim. At that moment a man of medium stature, with only a ring of hair around the sides and back of his head and graying at the temples entered the office. He wore a shirt that looked as if he had slept in it, and a pair of slacks that appeared a few sizes too big for the occupant, held up by a pair of suspenders. He was about the most unkempt person Jim had ever seen. But as soon as the man spoke, Jim knew who had just entered his office.

"Hey guys, is this Lieutenant Hargrove's office?"

Harry turned to look at the man. Still trying to control a lingering laugh, he spoke to the new arrival.

"It might be. And who might you be?"

Luckily Harry had not said the comments that crossed his mind. It was their new partner.

"I'm Special Agent Anderson with the Federal Bureau of Investigation."

Harry suddenly turned somber. Jim stood up and extended his hand towards the agent.

"Hi, I'm Jim Hargrove. Welcome to our community."

"I got here quicker than I expected. Say, you happen to have coffee? I need some java before tackling the day."

Jim would never have expected what he saw and heard to be one of the elite FBI Agents. This one must have slipped by the screening somehow. Jim could see this case was going to be an even bigger challenge than he had ever dreamed of. Further observation had Jim convinced that this agent wasn't carrying a weapon; at least Jim could not figure where such a thing could be since his clothing was in such a disarray.

"May I see some identification? Just for security purposes, of course."

The agent shrugged his shoulders and reached first into his right pants pocket, then his left pants pocket. Shaking his head he finally reached behind and produced a crumpled handkerchief and a wallet.

"Not a problemo!"

He started to hand his wallet over to Jim, thought better of it, and opening it produced a badge with an ID card, both of which became immediately obscured by the used handkerchief. Apologizing for the handkerchief, he tucked it back into his back pocket and once again opened his wallet. Jim had a hard time holding back the urge to burst out in laughter. He could see Harry, who was now behind the agent, was having similar problems.

"Thank you, Agent Anderson."

To himself Jim was wondering if this man came from another world or if he was really an agent. This case had better not be as complicated as it appeared to be. The agent was not showing much promise in the way of help. Maybe it was better he had no weapon. He'd probably shoot himself by mistake if he were called upon to use it.

"Call me Mike. Please. And I presume you are Sergeant Mansfield?" Mike said as he turned to face Harry. Harry smiled and held out his hand.

"The one and only, and please call me Harry."

"Glad to meet you. Come, close the door and sit down. We have a lot of strategy to plan by the end of today."

Harry looked at Jim, then at Mike and tried to excuse himself gracefully.

"Why don't you two start without me. I have a few other cases that need my attention at the moment. I'll stop by later and you can bring me up to speed."

"Oh, didn't they tell you? You and Jim have been relieved of all other assignments. Your other cases will be taken over by someone else. You are to devote your entire efforts to this one case only."

Jim stared at Harry, who returned the stare. Both were totally amazed at the priority that this murder had taken. Jim had this premonition that he was about to embark on a journey into the inner workings of the federal government. Harry closed the door and taking a chair and placing it on Jim's side of the desk off to the side, sat down to hear what was in store for he and Jim. Surprising both of them, Mike began to explain what the purpose of his investigation was in a very thorough and professional manner. This "misfit" was more than met the eye.

"Please be aware that everything you are about to hear is top secret and completely confidential. You are not to speak to anyone outside of the three of us about anything you see, hear or do. My task is to set up a home base of operations. Much like a command post, all information and direction filters through this home base. No one decides to make a move, ignore something or decide on anything without contacting me first. Any questions so far?"

The whole thing was intriguing Jim. He felt like he was being briefed for a secret mission against some unknown force that was about to exterminate the population of the Earth. He looked at Harry next to him and saw that he too was fascinated by what was taking place.

"No questions? I was expecting the two of you to ask why the secrecy about a murder. Not interested?"

Jim had to respond and did so just as Harry started to speak. Harry gave the floor to his superior.

"Mike, what the hell is this all about? I realize the victim is a senator, but I can't see how this becomes such a covert type operation."

"My sentiments exactly, old chap."

"Good. I'm glad you are being open. We will need to have complete understanding and trust of each other during this case. The answer is, I can't tell you that just yet."

Jim frowned.

"What kind of answer is that? Trust in each other is what you just said. That's not what I call trust."

"All in due time. Please bear with me. All good things come to those that sit and wait. Let's start first with some basics. You have a body that has fallen in harms way at the hands of someone you haven't uncovered as yet. But you do have suspects. Let's look at those suspects. Jim, who have you narrowed your list of suspects down to?"

Jim chuckled and leaned forwards on his desk.

"My long list is comprised of just two names, and one of them is suspect. But we believe more than one person is involved."

Mike looked disappointed. He shook his head and lapsed back into his former personality.

"Hey guys, that's bad news. We've got to get moving, or something. Two names; one suspect. That's not good."

Harry decided to defend their progress.

"Say what? Good God, we've only been on this case two days. No clues, no name for the victim until yesterday afternoon; what can anyone expect?"

"Results, Harry. Fast and accurate results. How'd you come by the senator's name?"

Jim and Harry alternately described the events as they unfolded, from the first call about the accident to the identification of the photograph in the Unisearch files. All the time they talked, Mike listened without any interjecting comments. He also wrote nothing down. This, both Jim and Harry would learn, was the only way to conduct business until a formal report done weekly was written for the Bureau. No notes, no chance of information getting into the wrong hands. Jim would have trouble with this system. His notepad was an integral part of his method of investigation. He had some hard times ahead of him. Mike was intrigued by the use of poetry by the killer.

"Is the killer a good poet?"

Jim and Harry smiled. Harry answered.

"More like a bloody mystic than a poet. You have to guess at what the real intent to every word is, and at that you can't be sure you're right."

"Maybe there is no 'right.' There just a ruse to confuse the issues."

Jim nodded in agreement.

"We've come to suspect that may be the truth. But having had the opportunity to get in here and switch poems undetected has me baffled."

"That will end. Your office is off limits to everyone but the three of us. Not even the cleaning lady gets in. Your captain has promised severe penalties for anyone violating that order. It also means we do our own cleaning, so try not to make any excessive mess in here. The door will have a lock and only we will have the key. Now, about this Debra Simms person. Where does she fit in at this point?"

Jim shifted in his seat, while Harry showed a big smirk on his face.

"That's the auto insurance investigator slash Jim's lover."

Jim gave Harry a look that could kill.

"She's an invaluable asset to our investigative work. I rely on her and her opinions a great deal."

Mike paused and scratched his head. Jim didn't like what he saw coming next.

"Mike, she is very important to me and to this case. I can't tell you how many times in the past-"

Mike cut Jim off.

"The past is to be buried. She is not a person to be privy to this case. I realize you can't just shut her out, but you will have to exclude her from any further direct involvement. And again, I remind you, everything we say and do is privileged information. She cannot be included in the loop."

Jim knew he was in for hell when this news reached Debra. Mike addressed Harry.

"This Maguire woman. Does her information seem accurate and trustworthy?"

Jim jumped in with a retort to Harry's previous comments.

"How can you ask him that? His sole objective is to get into her pants."

Harry's eyebrows went up in astonishment.

"Why Jim, I do believe you are trying to get even with me. Shame, shame my dear fellow."

Mike gave out with a loud sigh.

"Hey guys, this kind of bickering won't fly here. We are a team; let's behave like one. Now, since we have a couple of names, what about a motive? Any ideas?"

"Greed! Someone is looking for a big or even bigger piece of the monies involved."

Jim agreed with Harry's analysis.

"And how much money is involved?"

There was silence. Mike continued the query.

"Well Harry? Jim? Did either one of you ask what was involved?"

Jim gave it his best defense.

"Not yet. We haven't gotten to asking Miss Maguire or Mister Barksdale about their case as yet."

Mike smiled.

"I know that. That's why there are two agents at the office of Unisearch this very minute with a subpoena to obtain all files and documents pertaining to that case, just so you understand we at the Bureau leave nothing to chance in our investigations. That means, gentlemen, nothing gets left for tomorrow. That eliminates the chance of someone destroying possible evidence. Those files should have been in your hands yesterday."

Harry objected to that line of thought.

"Dorothy was so contemptuous of our presence, she would never have agreed to that. And as for a subpoena, we hardly knew what we were looking for until late yesterday, too late to get anything from the courts."

"Dorothy is it? I see Jim wasn't too far off base with his comment. I suggest any amorous intentions for this woman be put in abeyance. As of yet you have no idea if she is involved in this murder or not. In our eyes, everyone that made contact with Senator Harrison is a suspect until proven otherwise."

Harry objected.

"You sound more like an Englishman than I do. Innocent until proven guilty, isn't it?"

"Not when the FBI and national security is involved."

For a moment silence filled the office. Mike had made a slip of the tongue, and both Jim and Harry had caught it. Mike shook his head and decided it was time to let them in on the big secret.

"I goofed. I guess it's time to let you know what this is all about. I had hoped to wait a little, but now is as good a time as any. Senator William Harrison is not the man you have found murdered."

Both Jim and Harry were now totally confused. It was Jim's turn to object.

"But the body has been identified; his family acknowledged his existence here in Buffalo, and your agent made positive identification of his body at the morgue. I smell a rat here. What's up?"

Mike figured it was all or nothing at this stage of the game.

"The man you found is a double. He has been impersonating the real Senator Harrison for almost two years. The resemblance was so uncanny that even his wife was amazed at it. For a reason I cannot disclose, the real senator is on a secret mission. To accomplish this, his look alike took his place. Everything went well until this Unisearch Corporation found that the real Senator Harrison was a distant cousin to someone that had amassed a considerable amount of money. That person never had a will, or so the family thought. It turns out there was a will, and the fortune that was inherited by the children now was legally to be redistributed. Naturally, to continue the deception, our double came to Buffalo at the request of Unisearch to complete the paperwork and redistribute the monies. Unfortunately, he got murdered. Why, we don't know."

Harry needed clarification.

"So why this cloak and dagger routine?"

"Because we cannot publicly say the senator is dead. If we do that, the real senator's life will be in extreme danger."

"Then why identify the body in the first place?"

"Simple, Harry. Remember our operation here? Think of an even tighter operation involving the senator. The double is a perfect double. Our agent had no idea of what was happening. He truly thought he was identifying the real senator."

Jim looked down at the top of his desk and shook his head.

"So now what, Mike? How do we find out who murdered this guy without saying whom it is? We do have our own forms and reports to fill out. And how do we keep Miss Maguire and her two investigators from talking about it?"

This was the part that Mike dreaded to reach.

"By arresting all three on suspicion of murder."

Jim and Harry were awed by the lack of candor that Mike showed when he said that.

"You're nuts! Harry and I have dedicated our lives to being honest and fair, and to protecting the people. To arrest someone just to cover someone's senatorial butt is unconscionable. It's also unconstitutional."

"But Jim, you admitted it yourself more than one person is involved, and that one of them is definitely suspect. Who can say that all three aren't in it together?"

Jim couldn't believe what he was hearing, or that he was expected to be an accomplice in this travesty of justice. He shot a quick look at Harry who was sitting still and staring at Mike with a look of astonishment on his face.

"And on what charge? I mean murder of whom? Mister X?"

Mike knew this was going to sit hard on the two detectives.

"Jim, you're being facetious. No, not Mister X; for the murder of Mister John Smith. That's our new name for the victim."

Harry grunted in disbelief.

"How original!"

"Exactly why it has to be John Smith; it's so common a name it will not attract media attention. When the media wishes to check on this, they will not be at all impressed, give it minimal coverage, and the story will disappear within a day or two. Remember, we want a very low profile for our work on this case. It will even throw the real murderer off, unless of course we already have the murderer. It may make an accomplice relax and trip up. There are many advantages to this approach."

Jim was almost feeling convinced that the scenario he was listening to had merit. Almost.

"Then in what direction do we head in our investigation? Having three people arrested, what do we do?"

Mike looked at Jim with a small grin on his lips.

"I hear you are an expert at interrogations. I mean the kind that makes even the hardened criminal sweat."

Jim looked up sharply at Mike. Harry was grinning.

"How did you come by that information?"

"A little birdie told me. That and a reference about your method of questioning a Patrick O'Connor on one of your past cases appearing in your personnel files."

"Who the hell gave you the right to see my personnel file? That's an invasion of my right to privacy."

"Your life is an open book when it involves national security and our bureau. I'm sure you realize that whatever I see and know about the two of you never leaves my person. I'm sworn to secrecy on such matters."

Harry shifted in his chair with an obvious sign of discomfort. Mike saw the move and, looking at Harry, made his assurance again.

"Trust me on that one, Harry. I have an automatic self destruct if I even think of opening my mouth about anything in those files."

Jim looked at Harry and wondered what could possibly be in those files that would make him so uncomfortable. Jim would have to remember to ask Harry after this case was over. Meanwhile, it was back to the situation at hand.

"So I got carried away, Mike. Are you expecting me to repeat those tactics with our three 'suspects'?"

"Yes. And this time you will carry it to fruition. Have each one thinking the other is pointing the finger at them as the murderer. I want them shitting in their pants, Jim. Make them wish they had never heard of Detective Hargrove."

Harry interrupted.

"And what am I doing while Jim is playing Gestapo? Using a whip on them?"

Mike was apparently annoyed at Harry's use of words.

"Harry, I'm disappointed in you. We are not trying to coerce them into submission, just scare them into slipping up if they are guilty and providing us with some leads, which at this moment seem to be nil. I have to apologize if I come across as a ruthless individual. I am sensitive to people's feelings, and that you will be doing what is normally unethical procedures. But this is an unusual circumstance and warrants unusual methods. Harry, while not actively involved in the interrogation, you will be reviewing the files provided by Miss Simms and Miss Maguire, trying to glean some correlation between the two, and possibly some leads."

Harry and Jim sensed that their country and the democratic ways were never compromised, but the methods of acceptable procedures and rules invoked were definitely not cast in stone. What was not the right method for Jim last year was now 'in' for this year. Mike projected a plan for implementation of the arrests, each one to be followed exactly as he recommended and to be set in motion on a scheduled time and place.

As Jim and Harry listened, both became keenly aware that their first impression of Mike was completely unfounded. The clothing and mannerism displayed at the onset was merely a veneer to ward off any thought that Mike could be dangerous. He was cunning and a genius. They both would come to learn that in order to achieve his goals, Mike could also be ruthless.

By afternoon the strategy and schedule of events had been determined. Nothing was written down, but all three knew what to do and when. For Jim, this was to be his biggest challenge. No notepad and a list of things in a specific order and time were in his head; at least they were for now. Hopefully they would still be there later. Once the office had curtains installed, a blackboard would be used to initially write things on and then quickly erased. Some visual aids were helpful, and Jim looked forward to the help. As they continued with the plans, Jim's phone rang. It was Dorothy looking for Harry. With a look of consternation, Harry took the receiver handed to him. Mike placed a finger over his mouth to signal that Harry was not to mention anything about the FBI involvement.

"Hi, Dorothy. Say what? No, I don't have the foggiest idea what that is all about. Would I lie to you? Now stop being nasty. You know I care. Well, I'm not sure when tonight. Yes, of course I meant it. I'll call in a bit. I do too. Bye."

Jim could only surmise what Dorothy was saying, but it sounded as if Harry was not fairing too well with his new love in life, especially in light of recent events. Mike had a look of concern on his face.

"Harry, you are going to be able to function on this case without your desires for Miss Maguire getting in the way, aren't you?"

Jim, for the first time that he could remember, saw Harry looking a bit pale. But as always, when called upon, Harry was true to the cause.

"Yes, good fellow. Quite with it on this case, no matter the sacrifice."

Mike accepted the response as genuine. Jim knew, however, that when Harry used his very very English use of phrases, that all was not well. Harry was actually showing signs of interest in Dorothy that Jim thought Harry could never have for any woman. The lady's man was harboring serious feelings. Jim was beginning to see a twenty-dollar bill changing hands from him to Harry.

Mike proceeded to lay out in detail how and when the arrests were to be made. They would start by arresting Robert Thomas on suspicion of aiding in the murder of John Smith. This would take place in Thomas's office. Jim was perplexed by the choice of location.

"Why so open and in plain view of his coworkers?"

Mike smiled and raised his eyebrows.

"To entice anyone whose involvement we aren't aware of into panicking. If there is someone out there that we don't know of, they will most definitely come from within Unisearch. Richard Barksdale will not be back until tomorrow - yes, no?"

Both Jim and Harry shook their head. They had no idea as to when. Only Dorothy would know.

"Well, then it behooves us to 'boldly go where no man has gone before,' to coin a phrase, and arrest Dorothy while she is still in her office. That will be certain to shake up the troops. It will certainly get to the ears of Barksdale before his return. It may force him to expose the others involved by calling them or even going to them, since he is our principle suspect."

Jim could see the paler in Harry's face turn to a flushed shade of red.

"See here, do we have to be so brazen? Dorothy will cooperate, I'm sure of it. Do we have to embarrass her in front of her staff like that?"

"Part of the territory, my friend. Again I ask, are you up to this case? If so, I suggest you become completely impersonal regarding Miss Maguire. And since you wish to handle her with kindness, I think you should be the one to make the arrest on the same charge as for Thomas."

Harry was definitely not comfortable about this.

"When do we make the arrests?"

Mike looked at his wristwatch.

"Within the hour. While we were taking a break for lunch, I took the liberty of calling a colleague and obtaining the warrants. They should be here momentarily."

"You knew that this was your plan hours ago and never said a word? That's not working as a team, Mike."

"Sorry Jim, but sometimes it is easier to do it first than to explain why it has to be done. Now that we all agree to the strategy and the plan, it becomes a mute point; see what I mean?"

Jim saw, all right, but didn't agree with the analogy. Harry grumbled under his breath something about cocky blokes with egos and then shut his eyes. He was preparing for the inevitable confrontation with Dorothy. Mike ignored Harry completely. At that point a figure appeared at the door and then knocked. Harry said to come in and was greeted by a stocky man in a blue tweed jacket, a striped tie opened loosely at the collar, and hair that looked as if it had been through a tornado.

"Sorry it took so long, but the judge was in a pissy mood and wanted more information than we wanted him to know. I had to call the chief and get him to talk to the judge. With some coercion, the warrants are in hand."

And with that said, he handed Jim three papers, excused himself and left, closing the door as he walked out. Jim opened each one, examined them and handed one to Harry. A second was placed in the top drawer of Jim's desk. The third he pocketed. Picking up the phone he dialed, talked to someone about two teams of deputies that were needed immediately in his office, hung up and looked at Mike. Mike shrugged, raised his hands towards the two detectives and smiled.

"It's all yours, gentlemen. I'll be at home if you need me."

Mike gave them his home number, thanked them for their cooperation, and said he'd follow up on the locks and drapes so that they would be installed first thing in the morning. Then he got up and left. Jim and Harry stared at Mike's back, and then at each other.

"Jim, I liked that bloody bastard when he looked like something out of never-never land. Seeing him for what he really is, I think we are in for one hell of a time working this case together."

"I agree, Harry. But let's not lose sight of the reason we are working together. We all have the same goal, and that's to bring a murderer to justice.

71

We don't necessarily have to agree as to the methods used, just the results."

Even though Jim had said that, he didn't feel the statement was a true reflection of his opinion. Mike was a calculating individual that apparently stopped at nothing to achieve his goals. Jim and Harry didn't quite travel on those same paths. Somewhere down the road there was bound to be friction and confrontation. It was inevitable. But for now, he had to admit that the forthcoming arrests were a shrewd move and could produce some much-needed leads. Harry, Jim was certain, didn't see it that way. As Jim was about to give Harry some encouragement, a knock at the door produced four deputies ready to assist in the arrests.

Jim told them where they would be going and suggested that they not park close to the Unisearch offices until they saw Jim approaching the entrance. He wanted to minimize any chance of anyone forewarning the targets of the arrest. They nodded their understanding and left. Jim got up and suggested to Harry that they both use Jim's car for this, as he wasn't sure as to how much Harry would be concentrating on the road as opposed to his impending confrontation with Dorothy. Harry agreed and the two left for Unisearch.

Thirty minutes later everyone was in place for the moment of surprise. Jim looked at his watch. It was almost five o'clock. Jim and Harry got out of the car and walked towards the Unisearch entrance. As they arrived at the door, the uniformed deputies were just behind them. The time had arrived for the show of authority. Jim and Harry entered the reception area, produced their identification and badges for the receptionist to see, and asked her to lead them to Robert Thomas's office. She was reluctant to move until Jim produced a warrant from his pocket for Thomas's arrest. Rather pale at the sight of the legal paper, she reluctantly started down the long corridor, followed by Jim, Harry and the deputies. As they walked, they were met with stares and amazed looks by the people moving about. Jim could see that Mike's evaluation of what would take place was accurate.

After a few turns, and many glaring eyes, they entered an office that was well equipped with files, computer and chairs. At a desk in the center of it all was Robert Thomas. He looked up and had a look of confusion on his face. As he stood up, Jim held up the papers and told Robert he had a warrant for his arrest for the murder of John Smith. You could hear a pin drop as Robert stared at Jim.

"That's crazy! And who is John Smith? I don't know any John Smith."

As the deputies proceeded to handcuff Thomas and read him his rights,

Harry produced his warrant for Dorothy, showed it to the receptionist, and asked for her to lead them to her office. Again the receptionist walked down the corridor, followed by Harry and two of the deputies. When they arrived at Dorothy's office, Harry could hear a commotion coming from inside. Apparently some of the workers had run to her to inform her of what was going on. Harry took a deep breath and entered the office. The people surrounding Dorothy stood back from Dorothy's desk as Harry approached. Dorothy looked at him with an expression of outrage.

"What the hell are you doing here? Your presence and conduct is an outrage. How dare you disrupt my people with your stupid Tom Foolery."

Then Dorothy stopped as she realized that Harry was not alone.

"Dorothy, I have here a warrant for your arrest for the murder of John Smith."

Harry fumbled clumsily until he had extracted the papers for the second time from his jacket. Dorothy stood silent, but only momentarily.

"You bastard! You befriended me only to get me cornered by your little scheme. I should have known! And who the hell is John Smith?"

As the deputies handcuffed and read Dorothy her rights, Harry tried to explain about the body in Robert Thomas's car as being identified as John Smith.

"You are a goddamned liar! You already know it was some damned senator's double who was involved in one of our cases. Where did this change of name occur? In your fucking imagination, or what?"

When Dorothy was mad, her language could hardly be described as less than crude. Harry felt like shit. But he knew that the people in the room were eating up every word she had just said. This was exactly as Mike had planned. He hated to admit it, but the strategy was working. But his newfound relationship was also rapidly disappearing.

"You stupid twit! Wait until my lawyer gets a hold of you. You'll wish you had become a farmer instead of a goddamn cop."

As the deputies escorted Dorothy through the offices and out of the building, all Harry could hear was his name being mingled with a great deal of profanity and threats. As he walked towards the reception area to leave he could feel the stares as the onlookers watched him. He felt alone and naked. A chill went down his back and for the first time he realized that what he had just done was tearing at his heart. He had only met Dorothy and had made her a target for a bet as to his virility with women. Now he felt a warm desire for her in his heart, but that was being destroyed, with no chance of fulfillment.

Harry wondered if Dorothy weren't right about his mistake at being a cop. Right now, all he wanted to do was crawl into the nearest corner and hide.

Harry's thoughts were broken by a voice behind him. It was Jim, bringing up the rear.

"Well Harry, it looks like Mike's idea is going well so far. How did you make out with Dorothy? I think everyone in the building knows your name and what she thinks of you."

Jim chuckled. Harry found nothing amusing in Jim's remark. The two headed back to headquarters hoping to delay any interrogation until morning. Today had been a busy one; full of surprises and action. Tomorrow would be an even busier day.

Chapter 6

Jim arrived at headquarters around eight o'clock. As he approached his office he was greeted by a flurry of activity, as people were moving in and about the office area installing blinds and a new lock for the door. Just outside stood Mike, watching the people going about their tasks. Spotting Jim approaching, he smiled and extended his hand.

"Good morning. As promised, the lock and blinds are being installed. I trust everything went as planned yesterday?"

Jim shook Mike's hand and nodded.

"As expected. Today should produce some interesting results, or so we hope."

Placing his finger to his lips, Mike indicated that the conversation be put on hold until they were alone. Jim was amazed that Mike trusted just about no one. As the work was nearly finished, Jim suggested some coffee in the break room. Mike eagerly agreed and the two headed down the corridor. Entering the break room, the two were met with the somber face of Harry, who had just made himself a cup of tea. Harry looked as if he had gotten very little sleep, and his mood verified it.

"Well, if it isn't the master himself. So, old chap, I presume you had a restful evening and a good night's sleep. It's easy when you have no conscience."

Mike extended his hand in a friendly greeting.

"Now, now Harry. I have to say the evening was quiet, and the sleep restful."

"Pity."

Jim knew the significance of that comment. Harry nodded to Jim and headed for one of the unoccupied tables. Once Mike and Jim had gotten their coffee, they joined Harry, who indicated in no uncertain terms that he was not pleased. Mike tried to appease Harry with some words of praise, but that fell on deaf ears. Jim knew Harry well enough to keep clear of him when he was in one of these moods. But Mike was a glutton for punishment.

"Come on Harry, cheer up. All this will soon be behind us and I will be eternally grateful to you and your lovely Dorothy for allowing justice to prevail."

"You can take your blooming gratefulness and shove it! It wasn't you that lost a night of what was to be the greatest sex of all time."

"To say nothing of making a twenty-dollar bill."

"You can keep your bloody twenty, Jim. I don't care about it. I do care about Dorothy. Right now my ass is grass to that precious woman. Thanks to the likes of Mike."

Harry had turned to Mike for that last address. Mike seemed to totally ignore Harry's rage and smiled.

"I'm glad to hear we are all on the same track this morning. If you two will excuse me, I want to make sure everything's as it should be at my office. I'll be back shortly."

Harry finished the dissertation.

"Don't hurry on my account."

Jim shook his head as he continued to sip his coffee.

"Harry, let it be. You're just aggravating yourself. Mike isn't at all touched by your feelings. I'm beginning to think that being an FBI Special Agent requires that you relinquish your heart and conscience for the sake of the job."

This, for a moment, seemed to ease the emotions Harry was feeling. He smiled and finished his tea.

"Thank God, Jim, I never went into that branch of law enforcement. Can you picture me having no heart? It would have destroyed my love life."

"I'm not sure if you have one, Harry. I still think you're all talk and no action."

"To hell, I am. And that will now cost you dearly, my friend. The twenty is still ongoing."

"My, aren't we fickle this morning. Pity."

This brought a chuckle out of Harry. Jim finished his coffee and the two headed back to Jim's office. They arrived just as everyone was cleaning up and preparing to leave. The locksmith that had installed the lock handed four keys to Jim and assured him that there were no others like them in existence.

Then he turned and, as he left, bumped into Debra Simms as she strolled into the office.

"Well, fancy this. We are getting up in the world, aren't we. Blinds, a nice new lock, and possibly carpeting?"

Jim smiled at her.

"I thought blue would go with the décor. What do you think?"

"I think something is afoot here, and I'm not being let in on it."

"And you won't be, Miss Simms is it?"

Mike had returned. Debra turned to Mike and, in her usual frank way, responded.

"And who the hell are you?"

Mike was quite calm as he spoke with authority.

"I'm FBI Special Agent Michael Anderson and in charge of this investigation that you have apparently been privileged to have been a part in up to this point. I must inform you, however, that your assistance in this matter should no longer be of any concern to you."

Nicely put, thought Jim. *Mike, my boy, you are about to learn about Debra.* Jim was right.

"Concern, my butt, Mister FBI whatever. When someone takes my files by court order and gives no explanation, leaving me to cope with my superiors, I'm very much concerned. If you think for one minute you can commandeer your way through me without so much as an ounce of consideration, you are very mistaken. I am involved by the fact that it was my client's car that housed the body of your precious senator. If I start to put the pressure on the FBI for the return of classified material, and the obvious violation of constitutional rights as afforded my client, I could put a nasty crimp in your investigation. And I mean business!"

For the first time Jim could see concern cross Mike's face. Jim was sure Mike had never expected this type of reaction from Debra. He gestured for Debra to enter the office, closed the door and locked it. Then he closed the blinds, forcing Jim to turn on the lights. This was something he would become used to in the following days. He also knew that Debra's reference to the body as a senator meant she had information that Mike was very fearful of having become public knowledge. He sensed that Mike was suddenly aware of just how much involved Debra really was. He invited Debra to sit down and scratching his head, decided to be up front with her.

"Look Debra; I may call you Debra?"

"Only if you are going to speak to me in a civil manner."

"Of course, Debra. I'm a hard man to convince when working a case, but you have seemed to make an exception to that rule. I underestimated just how involved you are in this case."

"To say nothing of how important I am as well" Debra interjected.

"Oh, absolutely! I know how instrumental you have been while working on this, and many other cases, with Jim."

"And tread carefully; don't be condescending."

Mike was realizing by now that Debra was indeed a challenge for his prowess. Taking a deep breath, he opened up to Debra. Jim was watching and listening with amusement as his favorite girl took charge. Harry was trying to glean as much as he could from all of it so he would be better equipped at handling Mike's demands.

"Look Debra, I requested your files, as well as the files from Unisearch, in order that Harry might read through them and find some possible link between your client, Unisearch's client, and the murder victim. I must tell you now that what I am about to say is classified information and never leaves this office. If you are to continue to help on this case, total secrecy is a must; do you understand?"

Debra's eyes opened wide.

"Then you accept me as one of the team?"

Mike shot a glance at Jim, who could only nod in agreement, especially if he wanted Debra's affections. Mike looked at Harry, who only shrugged his shoulders to indicate total indifference one way or the other. Then Mike looked at Debra as if he were eyeing her up as to whether she was sincere and if she would actually be an asset to the team. Keeping her quiet, if nothing else, seemed to make sense to him.

"Then it's settled. Welcome to the team."

Mike smiled and extended his hand towards Debra, who shook it with no reluctance.

Jim thought how fortunate that the locksmith had given him four keys. Now he wouldn't have to decide what to do with a spare. With the keys coming to mind, Jim interrupted and handed them out. He placed his own in a special place with his identification, which he knew he would always have in his possession. Mike then proceeded to bring Debra up to speed as well as letting her know the rules pertaining to the room and how things were to be conducted during their meetings. Debra understood, agreed and then excused herself, as she had a full day of work ahead of her. She knew she would be called to attend whenever there was a need for her input. This pleased her, and she winked at Jim as she left.

Mike seemed pleased that he had resolved a potential problem with Debra. By bringing her into the team, he was assured her silence, her cooperation, and above all his presence of mind. She would be let in on certain things as needed. Other than that, she would have very little to do with current operations. Which brought Mike to the tasks at hand. He needed to know where they stood regarding Dorothy and Robert. But before he could begin, a knock on the door produced a deputy with two sheets of paper. One from the attorney representing Dorothy, and the other from Robert's attorney. Both wished to speak to the man in charge.

"Well gentlemen, where do we stand regarding Miss Maguire? I assume Harry that you had little trouble in arresting her?"

Harry gave Mike a demonic glare and grunted.

"And Jim, what have you gotten out of her at this point?"

Jim looked quizzically at Mike.

"What do you mean? I haven't questioned her as yet."

Mike shook his head.

"Jim, I thought I made this perfectly clear. We do not wait for opportunity, or postpone something very important, like questioning someone. By now, if she were guilty of anything, she has already formulated a way of concealing things. We have got to think differently now. This is not a simple murder investigation."

Jim had expected this reaction, but he was not about to give away more of his attitude towards moral obligations to a suspect. They were, to his way of thinking, still innocent until proven otherwise and deserved to be treated that way. In any case, by the time she had been booked, fingerprinted, photographed and issued a cell, it would have been well after nine before he would have been able to speak with her. He tried to explain that to Mike, who only waved his explanation off.

"Not acceptable, Jim. We all have to make sacrifices if we are to succeed at getting this case off the ground."

Harry spoke at Mike in a defiant voice.

"I suppose going home and leaving us here to do the dirty work is your idea of sacrifice. It sounds to me like the bloody case, which is not only ours but yours also by your own actions and admission, should have had your ass bearing some of the load right here as well. Where's your sacrifice Mister Anderson?"

Mike was silent for a long time. Then he surprised Harry by speaking in a soft and lighthearted voice.

"A valid point, I must admit. I should have set a better example by being here while you went after our suspects. And by doing that I would have inspired Jim to stick around for the questioning. You do realize Harry, that by not talking to Miss Maguire last night, she now has council to run blocker for her. Also, she had the answer as to when our Mister Barksdale would be returning. We still have no clue about that, now do we?"

That reminded Jim about finding out that answer. He excused himself, picked up the phone and dialed Unisearch. When the operator answered, he politely asked to speak to Mister Barksdale. When asked for his name he responded that he had an anonymous tip about someone involved in a case that Barksdale was handling. There was a pause, and then Jim hung up.

"He's back."

Mike smiled.

"Very clever. Nice thinking, Jim. Not only have you found out his whereabouts, but also you now have him very worried as to what's going on. That's a plus for us. Since he is our truly number one suspect, I'd say let's go get our suspect before we question anyone."

Harry had an objection to that move.

"Why? I thought you wanted to see if he exposed anyone as an accomplice or something. Why arrest him? Why not watch him first, then arrest him?"

Mike was quick to respond.

"Excellent! That's an excellent method of gleaning some leads. Since that was your idea, why don't you get out to Unisearch and see what is happening? I knew you would be a participant and not an onlooker, Harry. This pleases me."

"Thank you, my lord!"

"Now now, Harry. Let's play by the rules. Your idea, your move."

"It was your bloody idea, not mine. Why don't you go watch the bloke?"

"Because I must maintain a low image in this operation, remember?"

"Says you. Can we check this with your superiors?"

"Now Harry, must we bicker amongst ourselves? I think you will do a marvelous job."

With a disgruntled attitude, Harry rose from his seat, saluted Mike in effigy, said goodbye to Jim and was about to leave the office when Jim stopped him.

"Why don't you take the warrant with you in case the opportunity for an arrest presents itself. Just be sure to call for a back up before making any moves."

As Jim had been talking, he had opened the top drawer of his desk to remove the warrant he had placed there the afternoon before. Jim shuffled his hand around, gave a look of being perplexed, sighed and opened the drawer to its maximum. Then he shook his head in bewilderment.

"I don't believe it. Our phantom has struck again."

"What's wrong Jim?"

Harry suspected the answer.

"It's gone. The damned warrant is gone."

Mike remembered the incident with the file cabinet and the poem.

"Just proves my point about the lock. This character must make a daily cruise through your office just looking for information like that. I'll have my colleague get another. It will be embarrassing, but too late to avoid. Harry, forget the warrant for now; just cover Barksdale. We'll let you know when we have another one."

Harry nodded in agreement and left. Mike settled back in his chair and looked at the ceiling.

"What do you think Jim? I mean really think. Am I being wrong in my approach to this case? Harry is a good cop, but he has a closed mind. You seem to be more open. I need an honest input. What's your evaluation?"

Jim was silent for a while. He had to reflect on the case as it had unfolded and what had transpired up to the point of the FBI's involvement. How far had he been able to proceed and what had he accomplished? In all honesty, very little. Since Mike's arrival, things had begun to move rapidly. Jim did not like a lot of what Mike did, but he had to admit that much of it produced results. And the ability of someone to enter his office annoyed Jim. If nothing else, Mike had foresight, and it was apparent that secrecy was a dominant factor from now on.

"I'm sure you realize I'm not an advocate of a lot of your tactics. But in all honesty, this case was going nowhere until you stepped in. I have never worked a homicide and relied solely on Harry's expertise. You are right about Harry; he has tunnel vision about the way things ought to be done. I am open to suggestion only because of my lack of experience in these matters."

Jim had to admit that Mike was getting to the heart of the case at a very rapid pace. Of course, a lot of it was due to the clout the FBI had, especially in this particular situation. He would have eventually gotten to the matter at hand, but it would have taken a lot longer. Jim's thoughts again drifted to the missing warrant. How could anyone go unnoticed like that? There wasn't any union meeting last night; he was sure of that. How is it someone could walk into a police headquarters and not be questioned? He decided to ask Mike for his opinion.

"Mike, how could anyone defy their surroundings and steal material right from under our noses? And what good is a warrant in the hands of a murderer? It's both tragic and senseless."

Mike pondered what Jim was asking. He had no real feel for the why, but the how was almost evident.

"Maybe the warrant was a delay tactic to give Barksdale enough room to hide something, or cover something up. It will rear its ugly head somewhere down the road. But as for the how, I can only envision one way that anyone could go unquestioned here at headquarters. The someone has to be in uniform or known by everyone as belonging here."

"You aren't suggesting one of the accomplices or even the murderer is one of us, are you? I've known almost every detective and many of the uniformed deputies around here for years. I couldn't even dream that any of them would steal from my office, let alone be involved in a murder."

"Now who has tunnel vision? I didn't say that it was definitely the answer, but it is a logical one. Who else comes and goes around here unquestioned?"

Jim stared blankly ahead, his eyes making hardly any motion. He had a hard time coping with Mike's analogy, yet he had to admit it had merit. And only someone close would know where he kept his files and how he organized his desk and drawers. This was not something Jim easily accepted but, as a detective, had to scrutinize carefully. The possibility was unavoidable. As Jim sat pondering this new concept, the phone rang. It was Robert Thomas's lawyer. Jim asked if he would hold for a moment, covered the mouthpiece and whispered to Mike.

"Think I should set up a meeting to question Thomas?"

Mike reflected on this for a moment, and then nodded.

"Mister Trent, I need to question your client regarding his involvement in this case. Can you be available say, oh, around one thirty today? Fine. Yes, the conference room at the Holding Center. One thirty. We'll talk there. Thank you. Goodbye."

"How'd he sound, Jim? Angry? Matter-of-fact? Nervous?"

"Sounded to me like he was ready to call us idiots and have our badges for this one."

"Good. That means there is a good possibility that Thomas is really innocent of any involvement. Either that or he has his lawyer fooled and on a high paying retainer. I tend to believe the first choice."

Jim was impressed at how Mike could come up with an evaluation of a suspect without even seeing him or talking to him. But then, the arrest was a rouse in and of itself, so anyone innocent would be outraged at the insinuation, to say nothing of the defamation of his or her character. Jim could see Mike's analysis and agree with it.

"And what about Maguire? Shall we tackle her as well this afternoon?"

"No, we'll tackle her this morning. With Harry out traipsing the town following Barksdale, it will provide uninterrupted questioning. And I want you to have the momentum on that one. Don't give them much time to consider their responses."

Jim nodded, picked up the phone and dialed the number of Dorothy's lawyer that had been given to him earlier. After a few moments he was connected to a Mister Sexton. Jim told him he needed an immediate meeting with his client regarding her arrest. Jim held fast to the immediacy of the meeting, even though he was hearing a lot of flack about improper procedures and other similar stall tactics. Finally he acknowledged a meeting at the Holding Center for eleven o'clock, thanked the lawyer, and hung up.

"Well?"

"A combination of matter-of-fact and some pompous comments. This guy is from a law firm that seems to deal with corporations, not individuals."

"Hmm. That could have several implications. But the most immediate is that you will be bombarded by all kinds of bullshit to keep you off track and confused. Any direct answers will be accidental, if you hear any at all. This Maguire woman, what did you think of her when you met?"

"Quite affable towards me and our investigation. Harry had a little difficulty communicating at first. But things changed as things progressed. She has got quite a vocabulary for cursing, though. She seems to prefer the use of crude words when she wants to appear tough."

Mike smiled at Jim.

"That's a great character read. You do have a handle on evaluating people. That will be a definite plus with the questioning. I won't lie to you; this will not go smoothly. We will probably have more than one session with her. Sometimes that breaks the tempo set by the lawyer and gives us a chance to catch them in a conflicting statement. Contradiction can be a terrific tool, Jim. Look for it."

There conversation was interrupted by a knock at the door. Then they heard a key being inserted in the lock, and the door opened to reveal Harry.

He did not look happy.

"Back so soon? What's our Mister Barksdale done to deserve our having your presence here?"

"The bloke hit the road, he did. I got there only to be informed that Barksdale took a sudden day off and left no word as to his return. Looks like he's our man for sure. He's running, and he's scared."

Mike rubbed his chin and hummed to himself. Jim would observe that on many occasions; it meant Mike was thinking. Harry sat down and asked Jim what was happening. Jim told Harry about the meetings set for their suspects. Which prompted Jim to phone the Holding Center to arrange for a conference room and have the suspects brought there when he arrived. Harry was intently curious about the one for Dorothy.

"Are you going to give Dorothy that Gestapo tactic crap like we discussed? I wish you wouldn't; she's not deserving of it."

"That method is passé, Harry. With a lawyer present, we would never accomplish anything using that approach. That was for yesterday. Today is a new strategy."

Mike had come back into the conversation. Harry looked relieved at hearing this, and said how grateful he was to hear that from his lord and master. Jim just smiled at Harry's comments. Mike ignored them. Walking back and forth in front of Harry and Jim, Mike proceeded to describe exactly how he wanted the questioning to go. Jim would have to stretch their position a bit, and definitely avoid discussing what evidence they might or might not have. The lawyer would be concentrating his effort at proving there was no cause for the warrant and providing some threats of suing any and all parties involved. Jim would have to be very evasive and vague when responding to the lawyer's allegations.

"And what shall I contribute during all this?"

"Nothing Harry. You won't be there."

"I bloody well shall be! I have a stake in what goes down at that meeting."

"Your stake is a personal one. Can't have you in there getting all emotional and screwing up the pace."

Harry began to protest the decision, but was quickly put on hold.

"Just calm down. There is something far more important than sitting in on that meeting. And it will help to clear your Dorothy of suspicion, hopefully. You need to put out an APB for Barksdale and follow up on any information regarding his whereabouts. First I suggest obtaining his home address and going there with the warrant and two deputies. If he isn't there, you and the deputies stick together like glue and cover all the possible places he might have gone. Airport, bus terminal; check on where his car was last seen. He is a major key in what took place and who is involved. Are you with me, Harry?"

"I hear you. I'd rather be at the meeting, but I guess you have a point. Incidentally, where's the new warrant?"

Mike snapped his fingers and shook his head.

"Sorry about that."

After placing a quick call, he hung up and looked at his watch.

"Give it about an hour and it should be here. While your waiting, use your expertise and get the ball rolling regarding the deputies and the home address. Jim and I are heading to the Holding Center. You're in charge here, Harry. Make the best of a bad situation."

Harry waved his hands in a gesture to signify pushing them out the door and made one last comment in his very quaint English.

"Jolly good. The task is in good hands, my lord."

Mike gave a sigh and summoned Jim to join him as he opened the door to leave.

"I will return in about thirty minutes. Jim's running the meeting and I have other things to do."

"Pity."

Once the door was closed Harry immediately set himself to the chore of locating Barksdale's address. Having the files from Unisearch that belonged to Barksdale and pertained to the senator, Harry thumbed through it to see if he could glean a reference to residence or phone number. He didn't see anything other than the business address and phone number, which was to be expected. But it was a long shot not to be overlooked. Just as Harry was about to close the folder his eye caught a document that made him reopen his interest in the folder. It was a paper with the letterhead of Senator William Harrison and the government seal on it. It was addressed to Dorothy.

As he started to read it, a strange awareness came over him. Why would a case file from Barksdale, who was the representative and investigator for the client, have a letter addressed to the head of the operation? One might think any correspondence would not deal with the manager, but with the party handling the case. But as Harry read on, it became apparent that there was more to it than met the eye.

The letter was referring to some contact made by Dorothy personally with the senator. It also was written in almost a personal way; as if it were being written to a close friend rather than a business acquaintance. What caught Harry's interest the most was that it made reference to an earlier arrangement made by the two of them.

Just then he heard a key being placed in the door lock, and then the entrance of Mike, which made Harry realize that he had been looking through the files for nearly a half hour. Harry felt sure he would be catching hell from Mike. But surprisingly, when he told Mike he had been engrossed in the Barksdale folder and hadn't located an address as yet, Mike seemed eager to hear what Harry had seen so far. When Harry mentioned the letter from the senator, Mike asked to look at it.

"Hmm. You might get the feeling from reading this that Dorothy was doing something above and beyond the standard investigative work. And I'll wager this letter was placed there after Barksdale gave her a copy of the files for her records. I wish Jim had known of this before he started his questioning of Miss Maguire."

Mike looked at his watch and shook his head.

"I could try to reach him, but he's probably already met up with her lawyer by now, which means he won't be near a convenient phone. Guess this one will be left for meeting number two."

As Mike looked at the letter again, he seemed to focus on a particular spot on the letter. Harry looked at Mike and decided to ask what was so intriguing.

"What's got your eye, if I may ask?"

"It's the Capital Seal. That's what's wrong here. The Senate has a slightly different arrangement surrounding the seal. This letter was written on stationary that came from the White House. What the hell was our senator doing that gave him access to the White House stationary?"

Harry was becoming alarmed at what the implications of all this were leading to. His mind began to project thoughts of secret meetings between the senator and Dorothy; meetings that might even involve national security. He could feel the adrenalin starting to give him a rush as he pictured his newfound romantic interest becoming an accomplice to something sinister. Ultimately, it would place Dorothy very deeply within the realm of involvement regarding the senator's demise. This Harry did not find good.

Mike took the initiative regarding Barksdale's address, made a couple of calls, the second producing an address and phone number. The replacement warrant for Barksdale arrived, and Harry called for two deputies to meet him in the office. All that Harry could think of was how the meeting was going between Jim and Dorothy. Was she guilty of some shady dealings? Was she involved with the murder? Was he ever going to be able to hold her in his arms and make passionate love to her? His trance was suddenly interrupted.

"Harry! Can you hear me?"

Fumbling to cover his trance-like thoughts, Harry responded with some semblance of logic.

"Sorry, Mike. Just plotting my strategy when I approach Barksdale. The bloke is likely to resist arrest, now don't you suppose?"

Mike saw through Harry's ploy, but said nothing. He was sure Harry was concerned over Dorothy and the questioning she was going through. It was only natural.

"If he's even home, that's probably the truth. But looking at it realistically, if you thought the police were after you, would you go home?"

"Bloody unlikely. That's the first place they'd check. So why are we wasting time looking there?"

Mike had to laugh at Harry's frankness.

"Just in case he's stupid."

Harry had to laugh at Mike's thoroughness.

"Pity."

"What's this word 'pity' that you keep using? It gets used in so many instances, it makes no sense as to the meaning."

"Precisely! Mike, I'll make an Englishman out of you yet."

Their rhetoric was interrupted by a knock at the door, and Mike let in the two deputies. Harry instructed them as to what the arrest was all about, and that if by chance Barksdale was home, to be prepared for possible resistance. With that said, Harry and the deputies left.

Once Harry was gone, Mike started to look through the file that Dorothy had provided in the hopes of linking that letter to some other paperwork, but found nothing. Again, he read the letter written on White House stationary. It referred to a previous meeting. What previous meeting and where? As Mike kept reading it over and over, it suddenly occurred to him that the letter was dated earlier than the rest of the paperwork in the file. Damn! If that meant what he thought it meant, this letter had nothing to do with Barksdale's case. That indicated it had been misfiled. It also suggested Dorothy knew the senator before the case had ever been started.

Then it hit Mike even harder as he pondered this discovery. Looking at the date of the letter, it jolted him upright. The year, stupid! It's dated almost a year before the phony senator was ever involved. Dorothy knew the real senator. This changed the whole viewpoint with regard to Dorothy. She not only knew the real senator, but she might have also known that the victim in the car wasn't the real senator. That made her a prime suspect. Why was she quiet about the truth? When did she discover the switch? After the picture was added to the file, or before? Or did she already know about the switch?

Mike shuffled through the papers once again. Damn! The picture was no longer in the file. That picture might have spoken louder than a thousand words. Was it of the double, or the real senator? And why isn't it still in the file? It did explain the White House stationary. The real Senator Harrison had spent a number of months working closely with the President on something that resulted in the switch. He had corresponded with Dorothy while at the White House. It meant she had met with him prior to that. For what purpose? *The waters were becoming very muddy*, Mike thought.

Mike hadn't noticed the time passing. A key in the lock and the opening of the door interrupted him. He half expected it to be Harry or Mike. It was Debra Simms.

"Oh, I'm sorry Mister Anderson. I was looking for Jim. Is he around?"

"No he's not, and please call me Mike. Maybe I can help you. Have you uncovered something?"

"Not really; at least I don't think so. In my search for a connection between the owners of the car belonging to Robert Thomas I had told Jim that a Frank Spencer was the original owner and also was insured by my company during his period of ownership. I also mentioned that the car had been in an accident earlier involving it going into Tonawanda Creek. Jim thought that was a humorous coincidence. But the other day, I ran across the file on Mister Spencer. I'm usually efficient and file things promptly, but for some reason missed doing so with his file. Anyway, I opened it to be sure all the paperwork was in it and noticed something I hadn't seen before which might be interesting."

Mike waited a few seconds as the room fell silent. Then Mike spoke.

"And? Don't leave me in total suspense, Debra. What did you discover?"

"That Frank Spencer was an employee of Unisearch at the time of his accident."

Without another word, Mike offered Debra a seat.

"Debra, I already see the merit in having you as a member of this team. Now, was there anything else that might tie the owners and the car to Unisearch? Anything similar, or maybe different?"

Debra seemed to be holding back something as she glanced around the office.

"When is Jim returning? I need to speak with him."

Mike openly looked hurt as Debra asked about Jim.

"Debra, I get the uncomfortable feeling that you seem to distrust me. What is it that only the ears of Jim can hear? We are a team, aren't we?"

Debra was not one to mince words.

"Until yesterday, you didn't exist in my world. I trust Jim; I don't know you well enough to trust you as yet. But I'll keep an open mind. It wouldn't have any meaning for you anyway. It's something only Jim and I are aware of."

"Oh? Give me a chance to prove I'm worthy of your trust. Jim won't be back until after two o'clock, so it may serve us both to give me a shot at it. Please."

Debra was not convinced at Mike's sincerity, but she also wasn't able to stall until after two, so reluctantly she gave Mike the information.

"When Jim and I were at the scene of the accident with Thomas's car, he found that a nail had been driven into the accelerator floorboard. Jim suspected that the car had been deliberately sent into the water without anyone driving it. It appears that a similar suspicion was noted in the records relating to the accident when Spencer owned the car. Only they couldn't prove it, so the accident claim was honored. I thought Jim might have some ideas regarding that aspect. My files are still open regarding the recent accident."

Mike rubbed his chin and looked at the floor. He was positive there was a definite link between the first accident and the second, and the fact that the same company employed both owners.

"It seems that Miss Maguire hires some unscrupulous people with similar motivations. You wouldn't happen to know how long both Spencer and Thomas have been employed by Unisearch?"

Debra gave Mike a smirk and spoke in a soft tone.

"I don't usually investigate things that aren't in my realm of jurisdiction. However, since you allowed me the good fortune of being a team player here, I went beyond my usual investigating and checked on that very thing. And guess what?"

Mike looked back at Debra and gave her a big smile.

"What have you uncovered?"

"That Spencer left the firm at exactly the same day that Thomas was hired. It happens to be the same day that the ownership of the car was transferred between the two. If they knew each other, it wasn't because of a mutual employer."

Debra impressed Mike. He had thought when they first were introduced that she would just be a bothersome individual to be tolerated or ignored. This woman had definite investigative talent written all over her. He was glad he had not stood firm and rejected her help.

Mike made a mental note to have Jim check with Thomas regarding his relationship with Spencer, thanked Debra for all she had reported and promised to convey the information to Jim before Jim met with Thomas and his lawyer. Debra smiled, said she was only too glad to help, asked if Mike would tell Jim to call her later that afternoon and left.

Having a deep desire to find out the outcome of Jim's encounter with Dorothy, he decided to head over to the Holding Center and catch Jim between meetings. The first half of this day was turning out to be very interesting and informative. Mike only hoped the rest of the day would follow suit.

Chapter 7

As Jim entered the Holding Center reception area he deliberately headed to the reception desk and asked one of the deputies if he could have Dorothy Maguire brought to the conference area for the meeting with her lawyer and himself. The officer looked at his computer and told Jim she had already gone into Conference Room C at the request of her lawyer, who was already with her. Jim thanked the officer and headed towards the conference area. He had been in the conference room area only once before and was not certain of where he was headed. After a few wrong turns, he finally found Conference Room C. He identified himself to the deputy stationed outside the door, knocked on the door and entered the room.

As he stepped inside and closed the door, his eyes fell on a rather well dressed gentleman in his early thirties, who rose and extended his hand out to Jim.

"I'm Roger Sexton, Miss Maguire's attorney, and you must be Lieutenant Hargrove."

"That's me, and please call me Jim. This get together can be quite tiring if we all seem tense over each other's purpose and titles. I for one feel we should relax and get some questions out of the way without the usual fan fair. That is, if we all agree; do we have an agreement?"

Jim could see some of the tension in Dorothy diminish, but there was no evidence of change in her lawyer. He did however concede to dropping some of the formalities. Jim sat down across from Dorothy and her lawyer and greeted Dorothy as best he could without arousing any adverse reaction from her. He was sure she was dying to let loose some of her anger on him.

"Now Dorothy, I need for you to answer a few simple questions. They may seem either unimportant or insulting to you, but they need to be answered.

Please, and I'm sure your lawyer has already told you, consult with Roger on any or every one before you respond. Even though you are not under oath as you would be if in a courtroom, you will be held liable for the answers you give here. Do you understand?"

Dorothy nodded yes and tried to give Jim a half-hearted smile.

"I'm glad it's you asking the questions, and not that bastard that works for you."

"Please Dorothy, let's not get into any comments about individuals that have no bearing on what we have to find out here, and that is, why is Dorothy under arrest for murder? Do you have concrete proof she did any such thing?"

The lawyer had now turned to Jim with a question. *Very sharp*, Jim thought, *but not very appropriate for an opener.* The lawyer was trying to take charge and lead with his own questions first and not giving Jim the chance to present their case against his client by asking the questions. Jim anticipated the lawyer's next response.

"This will turn into a big lawsuit if there isn't some proof to the allegation."

Jim smiled at the lawyer.

"Are you suggesting that we just arrested your client for kicks?"

The lawyer immediately backed off and let Jim take the lead.

"Of course not. Please don't misunderstand, but it is important that we know where the charge originates from. Please proceed with your questions, Jim. I will hold any criticism in abeyance."

Jim could feel the emotions of the moment straining at Dorothy. Good, he was definitely the one in charge of the meeting from this point on, thanks to her lawyer. Jim sat back and thought out his first question. He was used to using his notepad to scribble things down as a reference. Mike's new method of carrying everything in his head was still very new, and the task of doing an investigation out of your head was very taxing.

"Dorothy, I know you have been with Unisearch for many years, am I right?"

"Are you asking my client for information, or do you know the answer to that question and want to trip her up?"

"Oh Roger, stuff it! If I need your advice, I'll ask. Otherwise just shut up."

"Now Dorothy, I'm here to be your council. I can't if you want me to be silent through this meeting."

"Then council me when I need it. How long I have been with Unisearch is not a threatening question; and the answer Jim is yes, almost ten years. It was my first and only job since graduating college."

"Don't add any information to an answer that wasn't specifically asked of you. He didn't ask if it was your first—" Dorothy broke the statement.

"Roger, will you please shut up. I know what I can say and what I shouldn't; do you think I'm stupid?"

Jim could see the other two were not going to be a smooth team. Good. Jim's task would be much easier.

"That makes you a very young and successful executive. You've accomplished your goals rather early in life. I take it then that you were used to supervising men over the past few years. Did any present a problem to you that was beyond your control?"

Dorothy smiled. The lawyer tried to signal her not to answer. She ignored him.

"I'm not well liked because of my quick rise to where I am, but so far I haven't met any man that I couldn't handle. I've always been a take charge individual and strong willed. You have to be if you are half black and half white. You're never accepted by either racial group."

Jim could empathize with some of what she had said. He would have loved to say to her that the mix rendered her beautiful as a consolation, but he knew that would be out of place for the moment. Jim had also caught her lawyer shaking his head in disbelief at what he was witnessing.

"Jim, what has the employment history of Dorothy got to do with her arrest?"

Jim deliberately sat silently, only moving his head as if to relieve stiffness in his neck. He wanted the moment to build a possible uneasiness in Dorothy. To his surprise, the uneasiness came from her lawyer.

"See here, Jim. Can't you just come to the point? It almost appears you haven't prepared for this meeting, or maybe it's that you have no just cause for Dorothy being here after all."

Jim smiled at Sexton again.

"Roger, why are you so pushy? Relax. I'll get to the point, but in my own way."

Jim refocused his look to Dorothy, who was now showing signs of a restless nature, her fingers taping on the table in front of her. This was good. Maybe a quick response without thinking may be in the offing.

"Dorothy, why was there a picture of the victim found in Robert Thomas's car in Richard Barksdale's file case folder? Do you often take pictures of clients and their relations?"

Dorothy sat back and for a moment seemed unsure of what to say.

"The senator is not related to the client."

The lawyer winced. Dorothy reacted, as she realized she had admitted to knowing the victim. Jim was not shocked, as he had suspected she did during their conversation in her office the other day.

"If you knew the victim, why didn't you say that when I asked you about the picture the other day when I was in your office?"

This time the lawyer was not going to sit still and see Dorothy succumb to Jim's interrogation.

"Dorothy, you've said more than you need say at this time. Jim, are you searching for answers to build a case against my client, or do you have proof she committed the crime?"

Jim had gone further than he had anticipated. But he needed a couple of questions answered before he would call an end to the meeting.

"Dorothy, I must have your honest answer to the next question, and your full cooperation."

Dorothy looked inquisitively at her lawyer, who shook his head in a very adamant no, and responded.

"I'll listen to the question Jim, only because I trust you. But I will refuse to answer it if it in any way is going to incriminate me."

The Fifth Amendment. She was not a stupid woman.

"Fine. If I were to tell you that the body of the victim was not who you think it is, what would you say to that?"

Without hesitation, Dorothy answered.

"Then I'd say you're lying."

"That's it? That's all? Nothing suspicious about the question or my inference?"

"That's it!"

The lawyer threw his hands into the air in total frustration.

"Dorothy, what are you doing? I'm wasting my time even being here if you don't consult me before you answer."

Jim had done the damage needed to keep Dorothy overnight. This would break up any plots between Dorothy and her lawyer and give Jim a shot at a more structured second meeting, just as Mike had wanted.

"Roger, I do not understand why your client was charged with murder. However, since without ever seeing the body in the trunk of that car or at the morgue, she can be positive of the victim's identification gives me just cause to keep her detained until we can sit down and talk again. The charge should rightfully be suspicion of murder. I shall make sure the court is notified of that adjustment. In the meantime, I will leave you two to discuss your position and set a time for our meeting tomorrow. I thank both of you for your time."

Dorothy was obviously rattled.

"But Jim, I was honest about my answer. Please listen to me. I didn't kill the senator!"

"I'm sorry Dorothy, but that's not for me to determine. I'm just doing what I have to do under the circumstances."

Dorothy's demeanor became belligerent.

"God damn you, you're no better than Harry. I hope you both rot in hell!"

Jim knocked on the inside of the door, and when it opened to let him out, he informed the deputy that the prisoner was still under arrest. Then he walked towards the reception area to regroup his thinking for the next session with Robert Thomas. He was not happy with what he had just done, for he liked Dorothy. But he had settled one thing from this meeting; Dorothy was not all innocent of the crime.

Now even Jim had a feeling that Dorothy was somehow involved. She had been too quick to respond and had implicated herself. There was no way she could have been so positive that the body was the senator's unless she knew about the crime. What did puzzle Jim was her response about the senator being a relative. It had almost sounded as if the picture wasn't meant to have been taken, or maybe it wasn't even suppose to have been in the folder at all.

As he entered the reception area he spotted Mike hurrying through the door and head in his direction. He was walking in short but fast paced steps as he approached Jim; his cantor definitely one of haste.

"Am I glad I reached you before the next meeting. I have a few tidbits of information that will curl your hair."

Jim smiled at Mike's referral about curly hair. Mike realized what he had said and was quick to apologize.

"Sorry Jim, I guess it's already curly, isn't it."

Then the two of them laughed.

"Enough said about hair. What's the big news you have, Mike?"

Mike gently took Jim's arm and led him to a corner where no one could hear them.

"One. The file folder we got from Unisearch on Barksdale's case had in it a letter from Senator Harrison addressed to Dorothy and dated prior to the start of the case Barksdale was on. I mean it was from **the** senator, and it indicates that they knew each other even prior to that. I'd say this gives our

Dorothy some serious involvement, seeing she acted as if the victim was just a person that was part of a case they were handling."

Jim's eyebrows went up. That fit the idea Jim had about her knowing who the victim was and trying to conceal that knowledge. Jim told Mike about what had transpired in the meeting and of his discovery. Mike nodded in agreement.

"It fits a profile, Jim. And I'll wager the letter wasn't suppose to be in that file folder, but misfiled. As for the missing picture, I haven't figured that one out as yet."

"It's simple, Mike. It too was misfiled. Or it was placed there for a purpose only known by the murderer. Tomorrow's meeting will be a lot more informative than today's. Now I have some ammunition to work with."

Mike congratulated Jim on being successful and that they now had a legitimate reason for detaining Dorothy. Jim wasted no time in asking Mike to talk more.

"That was one. What's two?"

Mike told Jim about Debra's visit and her discovery regarding the other owner of Thomas's car. Jim understood and promised he would throw some questions in regarding Thomas's knowledge of Frank Spencer. He also made a mental note to ask Dorothy about Spencer at tomorrow's meeting as well. Jim looked at his watch and told Mike he had to excuse himself as the time for the meeting with Thomas was nearing and he wished to prepare a bit for this one. Mike agreed, wished Jim another success, and turned to head back to headquarters.

"Jim, just a word of caution. Thomas may be in on it, and maybe he isn't. Use discretion. If you really don't see Thomas fitting into the picture, don't detain him. If you're wrong, we can retrace our steps later. It is best that we don't appear out to get just anyone for the murder, but the actual culprit. Down the road, it will help the cause when we try justifying our actions today."

Jim said he understood and left for the reception desk again, this time to notify the deputy he wished to have Robert Thomas available and brought to the conference area as soon as he or Thomas's lawyer said they were ready. The deputy told Jim to use Conference Room D and that a deputy would be posted there as soon as Thomas was brought from his cell to the conference room. Jim acknowledged the deputy and headed for Conference Room D. He needed a few minutes alone to collect his thoughts and strategies. Working out of your head instead of a notepad was more stressful, but Jim was slowly developing the skill. Still, it took longer to prepare for something like this.

Jim found the right conference room, went in and sat down and stared at the table in front of him. Then he noticed the room had a blackboard in it. That was great, having a place to jot down some thoughts, and have an agenda for the meeting. This was going to be a definite help.

Jim must have spent about twenty to thirty minutes at the blackboard developing his agenda. Just as he had completed his list, the door opened and in stepped Thomas followed by a portly gentleman brandishing a burly mustache on a rounded face that was topped by a very sparsely and disarranged growth of hair. The man was breathing heavily and his forehead had beads of sweat on it. This had to be Oscar Trent, Thomas's lawyer, and he appeared to be straining under the effort to move all his weight around.

The deputy that had brought Thomas to the room nodded and after the two men had entered the room, closed the door. Jim knew he would be standing outside in case of any problem. The three of them sat down at the table, with Jim on one side facing the other two men. After introductions were made, Jim pointed to the blackboard and indicated that on it was the basic agenda he was going to follow, and asked if there were any additions they would like to make. Thomas spoke up first.

"Lieutenant Hargrove, I thought I had been very open and helpful regarding this unfortunate incident. How could you even suggest I killed that man? I wasn't even in town."

"My client has bent over backwards in an effort to help the police. Is this how appreciation is shown? By drumming up some mumbo jumbo and arresting him?"

Jim could see the adamant position developed by Thomas's council. No accusations, but definite criticism.

"I'm sorry for the appearance of accusation in our methods. We have been working on the evidence presented to us, and if that is in error, I will be the first to make the wrong into right. I think, Mister Thomas, you have seen that I am a fair man in whatever I do."

"Then let's put the cards on the table. You show me what makes you think Mister Thomas is guilty of murder, and I'll show you how this will become a matter for legal restitution against this county."

Jim stared at Oscar Trent. He was amazed at how strong this unkempt individual stood up for his client. Jim liked the man's zealousness in his job. Jim said he hoped to clear everything up at this meeting and started to proceed with the list he had prepared on the blackboard.

"Now is it all right if we use first names here?"

Everyone agreed.

"Good. Robert, when you first discovered that your car had been driven into the creek, did you make any arrangements with the party that you had loaned your car to have it removed and towed to a shop for examination and repairs?"

"No. Richard, the man I had given the car to use, said he would take care of everything and cover any costs not covered by insurance."

"Did he mention or infer that anything out of the ordinary was involved in his so called accident?"

"No. He sounded a bit shaken, but nothing unusual or suspicious was said."

"What do you mean by shaken? Was he stammering, hesitant, speaking incoherently?"

"Kind of in a hesitant manner more so than nervously."

"Shouldn't that have given you an indication that something abnormal was involved?"

Jim could sense the next move before it started.

"Now see here, Jim. My client is not a psychologist or an expert at interpreting people's behavior. And besides, what the hell has this got to do with my client and a charge of murder?"

"True Oscar, but it seems that anyone hesitating when he speaks is suspect to choosing his words carefully, possibly to conceal something. You don't have to be an expert to deduce that. And yes, if what Robert says is true, then he has deliberately held back information that would indicate foul play by Barksdale, making Robert a possible accomplice."

"Jim, that's ridiculous! Not seeing things as if he were a professional investigator like you doesn't make him guilty of any cover up."

"But Robert is a professional investigator by profession. Am I not right, Robert?"

There was a moment of silence, broken by an attempt at sarcasm from Oscar.

"And because I enjoy playing Santa Claus for my company's Christmas party, that makes me capable of going up and down chimneys."

Jim had to smile at the thought of Oscar in a Santa suit. No need for padding, that was for sure.

"A point well taken. Incidentally Robert, what was your relationship to Frank Spencer other than the fact that you bought the car from him?"

Jim had slipped that in at a moment when it was least expected, hoping for a candid response. He got one.

"Just a good deal. Spencer was leaving the company for another position, and his car was in need of repairs that I could have made through a relative for next to nothing."

"Did you work with him long?"

"Not at all. I was just hired as he was leaving."

A bewildered Oscar interrupted.

"What the hell has that got to do with anything? And who's this Spencer person?"

Jim was satisfied with Robert's answer. He was also beginning to feel that Thomas was unaware of what the victim was doing or how the body got into the trunk of his car. His answers thus far were convincingly open and honest.

"Did Spencer ever say how the car had gotten into the condition it was in when he sold it to you?"

"No, just that it had been in an accident and was under water for a couple of days."

"Nothing else? Like if it had been involved in a crime of some sort?"

Oscar Trent's cheeks puffed out and turned a shade of red.

"Hey, what gives? Are we here to resolve the accusation of murder against my client or are you two going to rehash old stories?"

Thomas broke the conversation.

"Oscar's right. This isn't helping my cause, and it really is not part of that list you have up there."

Jim liked Thomas's candor. It helped to give a more comfortable resolve to his feeling of Thomas's innocence. Jim proceeded to run through the questions he had jotted down.

One by one, Thomas answered them. Each one was followed by some rhetoric from Oscar. Even Thomas was becoming vexed at the lawyer's persistent demand for the proof of his client's guilt. At the end, Jim was satisfied that if Robert Thomas had anything to do with the murder, then he was one of the smoothest con artists he had ever run across.

He made some fumbling excuse for what apparently had been a mistaken interpretation of Thomas's actions, apologized for the inconvenience the county had imposed on Thomas, and told the two to remain in the conference room while he went to fill out the necessary paperwork for Thomas's release. The lawyer made the expected threat of suing the county, and Robert Thomas tried to explain that he wasn't interested in restitution, just peace of mind.

By mid afternoon, Thomas had been released, Dorothy had been returned to her cell in the Holding Center, and Jim had returned to his office to brief Mike on the results of the day. Harry was not present, and his whereabouts were unknown.

"So what do you think, Jim? Do we have enough to put Dorothy in the prime suspect category, or should we see if we can nail Barksdale for it?"

Jim didn't like Mike's use of the term 'nail'. It sounded like he was picking the sacrificial lamb without a care as to innocence or guilt. Jim, no matter how he perceived the need to find justice, would never succumb to looking for a person to hang for a crime regardless of whether they deserved to be the accused or not.

He remembered his case against Claire Tate and Patrick O'Connor almost two years ago. As much as he knew that they had been guilty of causing a major accident that had disrupted many lives and killed one person, he never once stooped so low as to create false evidence to create a conviction. On circumstantial evidence, he had presented his case to the judge in the hopes of a conviction. It was a tough way to go, but it was the only way Jim's conscience would allow.

"I'm for waiting to hear what Barksdale has to say for himself. Mike, there's just too little credence in Barksdale's stories, and a lot of suspicious moves in his actions to hold Dorothy accountable as the murderer. She may be an accomplice in this, but not the prime suspect. Which brings to mind our other partner; where's Harry? He was with you looking at the files from Unisearch, or was there a change in plans?"

"He went to check out Barksdale's residence along with a couple of deputies. He hasn't called in, so your guess is as good as mine."

Just then a key in the lock and a movement of the door produced the figure of a very tired looking Harry.

"Well Jim, look at what the cat dragged in. Greetings Harry."

"Greetings my bloody ass! I've just spent a couple of hours chasing the devil himself, at least that's how it feels."

Closing the door, Harry quickly sat down and slumped into it, almost extending himself beyond the seat. Jim could see that Harry was breathing irregularly, and his hair was in total disarray. Mike broke the picture by offering a calming and reassuring word of sympathy.

"Bet Barksdale wasn't there. Trying to track someone on the run can be frustrating, so don't take the defeat to heart. We thought it was a useless move, but we had to follow through."

"Oh, he was there all right. He was one of the stupid ones that run home when they feel the police are looking for them. It doesn't fit his profile, Mike, but the stupid bloke was there."

"Great! And where is he now? Do you have him in the Holding Center?"

"No, unfortunately."

"He got away? Harry, don't tell me you let him slip through your fingers."

"No, not bloody likely."

"Then where is he?"

"In the morgue. Mister Richard Barksdale is very, very dead."

Both Jim and Mike stared at each other in total disbelief. The room became silent except for the heavy breathing coming from Harry.

"Harry, you didn't shoot him in your attempt to arrest him, did you? God, man, he was the prime suspect! If you killed him—" Harry cut Mike off.

"I didn't do any such thing. He was already dead when we got there."

"From?"

"Two bullets through his bloody head. The second was done from the mouth. It blew his bloody brains all over the place. God, what a mess!"

Now Jim could see why Harry looked the way he did. The sight must have been gruesome, and would shake even the staunchest of people. Jim asked, though he already knew the answer.

"Was it suicide or murder?"

Harry looked at Jim, and the frustration of even having to answer the question was evident in his voice.

"With two bullets, suicide is impossible Jim, you should know that. Either shot was deadly. And besides, there was no weapon at the scene. Damn, I wish we had gotten there sooner. We not only could have prevented the thing from happening, but maybe we could have come upon the real murderer, face to face."

Mike nodded in agreement. He was as guilty as Harry, since he had not obtained the replacement warrant earlier in the day, and the longshot that Barksdale would head home made him lethargic in making the trip to Barksdale's house appear urgent. Mike began to feel dismayed at his inefficiency. He was normally not like that, and it may have cost Barksdale his life. Jim interrupted Mike's thoughts.

"So are we to assume that Barksdale was guilty of being a party to, but not the prime suspect in the murder?"

Harry reached into his pants pocket and produced a paper that he had obviously hastily shoved there and, opening it, handed it to Jim.

"There back. See what you make of it, my friend."

Jim looked at the paper, shook his head, and handed it to Mike. It was poetry time again.

YOU HAVEN'T FOLLOWED AS YOU WERE TOLD.
THE PATH IS THERE, AND THE MESSAGE IS OLD.
AGAIN I SAY TO THOSE WHO HEED THE WILL,
THE ANSWER YOU SEEK IS AT HOME STILL.

"Shit! Here we go again. Interpreting this crap is not easy. We thought we had it figured out once, but this 'at home' has us stumped. Mike, if it's OK with you, I'd like to get Debra involved in this poem. She's been pretty sharp on the last two, both of which have disappeared, as I told you. The last line rings a bell, though. I think it's the same line from the second poem. Apparently, whatever we devised as the meaning may require some fresh considerations."

Mike consented, Harry applauded the idea, and Jim called Debra. He was told she would be gone for the rest of the day, so he hung up. Jim told the others he would be seeing her that evening and would bring the poem with him to go over with her. Mike did not like the idea of the poem leaving the office, but through perseverance Jim convinced Mike it would be safe with him. Just the same, another copy would be made to ensure it didn't disappear like the other two. Everyone agreed it had been a hell of a day, so they decided on an early break, and left.

Jim went home, showered and then left for Debra's house. He made sure he didn't forget the poem, or the flowers he had thoughtfully bought for Debra just on the chance that she would not be receptive to a little police work on her own time. He felt confident that between the two of them, a solution to the poem and its intent could be resolved.

He was greeted at the door by a woman who had obviously gone to a lot of trouble to have herself a picture of perfection. Jim had recently noticed that Debra was going to great measures to please him. He had the feeling that the thought of wedding bells might be in her mind. Jim wasn't sure he was quite ready for that, but he didn't rule it out either. Jim handed Debra the flowers, complimented her looks and kissed her.

After a round of small talk and a cocktail, Jim approached the subject of the new poem. Debra gave Jim a look of impatience and spoke out her feelings about work after hours, but reluctantly said she'd overlook it, but just this once. Jim graciously thanked her and, as he handed her the paper with the poem on it, gave her another kiss.

"Now that, Mister Hargrove, is not going to admonish you from this intermingling of work with pleasure. You owe me for this."

"Another kiss, perhaps?"

Debra smiled.

"Hopefully more than just one."

Jim knew he was captured by this woman's beauty and charm. He would give her anything she wanted. Debra opened the paper and read the poem. Then she read it again, then a third time out loud.

"Jim, I remember that last line as the last one in the second poem. By repeating it here, I'd say it is the key to what is being told to us."

"And?"

"The key here is to determine what 'home' is, and that will give you the answer."

"I already figured that out, Debra. What I need from you is some idea of what this 'home' is that we are seeking. It was thought that it was somewhere that we knew and were familiar with, and not necessarily my office. But then, maybe I shouldn't rule my office out either. What's your thought?"

Debra mulled over that viewpoint. She also recollected that not too long ago Jim would never have conceded to seeking her opinion on anything. Now she was his pillar for advice. That gave her a warm feeling. She and Jim had come a long way in their relationship. From adversary to admirer. Suddenly an idea focused her attention back to the poem.

"Jim, has anything happened, or even been said by Harry or Mike, that ever made you feel that there was something or someone at headquarters allowing things to happen without being questioned? Like, for example, when the first two poems disappeared?"

Jim looked upwards towards the ceiling and took a deep breath. As he pondered those questions, he remembered he had asked several times how anyone could come and go without being questioned. Having access to his office; knowledge of his files. Then he remembered what Mike had suggested as a food for thought idea. It was conceivable that the person doing those things was someone from within; someone that wouldn't be questioned regarding his or her presence or actions. He mentioned this to Debra.

"You know Jim, that's exactly the idea that crossed my mind. And if that is true, this 'person' is right where the poem puts the murderer. Right under our very noses. In our 'home,' if you care to choose that word."

"But it isn't saying that it's the murderer, but a source for answers. It may be another accomplice."

"Or the murderer. Why is it so hard for you to consider that another policeman could be a murderer? It wouldn't be the first time, or the last unfortunately."

"Because that leaves just a handful of people, all of whom I respect, including Harry."

Jim fell silent for a few minutes as he placed his arm around Debra's shoulders. Then the two looked at each other and smiled. Debra ended the talk.

"That's enough business tonight. Now, where are those kisses you keep talking about?"

Jim wrapped himself around Debra and for a while let the evening become a symphony of passion. He became lost in time, and he knew that whatever came out of their talk that evening would be looked at seriously in the morning. The rest of the evening was for other matters.

Chapter 8

Jim arrived at the office the next morning to be confronted by Mike and Harry in a heated argument over something. Closing the door quickly so as not to attract attention to the shouting, he went over to his desk, sat down and calmly asked for some silence. Getting none, he decided to shout.

"Will the two of you shut up?"

Harry, who had not seen Jim enter since his back was to the door and the desk, looked around and with a startled expression on his face, uttered what only Harry used so well to sum up any situation that he had no justification for or answer to; his one word covers all expression.

"Pity."

Mike, who had deliberately avoided Jim's glances as he had entered the office, now looked straight into Jim's eyes and made a sound that was a cross between a deflating balloon and someone passing wind. The room fell into silence. After a moment Jim looked at the two and made quick pickings of the situation.

"You two are acting like a couple of kids. What the hell is going on? This is an office, **my office**, and not the local gymnasium. If you want to spar, do it elsewhere."

Mike was the first to speak up.

"Sorry, Jim. I got carried away by the discussion I was having with Harry."

"My ass, Jim! This bloke is bloody irritating. He thinks he can come in here, change policy, change people's lives, change—"

"That's enough, Harry! You and Mike aren't going to resolve your differences by shouting at each other and calling each other names. You should see the looks on the faces of those outside this office as they hear your ranting. Mike, you made access and visibility to this office secure, but it isn't soundproof. Every individual passing by knows whatever you've been yelling about. Some security."

Mike ran his hand across the top of his head, looked at the ceiling, and took a deep breath.

"You're right, Jim. I apologize. I should know better. I let the anger of the situation take charge. That's not the way I was trained, and it certainly isn't the way to achieve top performance and a well oiled machine as a team."

Harry just grunted. It was his way of agreeing with Mike. Jim sat back in his chair, looked at the two of them, and decided to let it lie.

"OK. Enough said. Now, what the hell started all this in the first place?"

The two immediately started to talk at the same time, and both began to accelerate the speed and tone of the words as they flowed out at Jim. Jim raised his hands and took charge.

"Stop! One at a time, and slowly; no shouting. Harry, you first."

"Well Jim, I came in this morning expecting to find that Dorothy would be considered innocent of being the murderer and that after you questioned her, she would be released. Mike tells me he intends to charge her as an accessory to the act and will request a hearing before the courts."

"I didn't say that, not exactly."

"Mike, it's not your turn. Please hold it until Harry's finished. Harry, is that it?"

"Not all of it, Jim. You know that third poem that I found on Barksdale? We copied it and left it on your desk, seeing as the room is now secured. Well, it's missing and Mike says I had to be the one that took it. Bloody stupid, and wrong, wrong, wrong!"

Harry was now glaring at Mike and starting to shout again.

"That's enough, Harry. Let's calm down. Mike, what about Harry's statements? Are they true?"

Mike crossed his leg and leaned back so that the back of the chair rested against the wall.

"Somewhat. I said that I wanted Dorothy detained for further evaluation, which might lead to her being held over for a hearing. I didn't say that it was cast in stone. If her answers make sense today, she will be released. But it isn't an automatic done deal."

"That's not how you put it, Mike! You're covering your blooming ass, you are!"

"Harry, cool it! What about the missing poem, Mike?"

"All I said was that since I know I don't have it, and we all know you don't have it, not the original at any rate, then the only person that could have taken it was self evident."

"And what do you call that, Jim? Who could he mean but me? Who else?"

"Mike, it sure sounds like you meant Harry. Did you?"

Mike let the front legs of his chair come down to rest on the floor. He placed both feet squarely in front of him and, placing his hands on his knees, leaned forward in Jim's direction.

"I meant if it wasn't any one of us, then we have an intruder that can access this office with the cunning and the means. That's all."

Jim rubbed his chin and looked straight at Mike.

"Sorry Mike, but it still sounds like the finger points at Harry. After what I tell you regarding the evaluation of the poem I made with Debra yesterday evening, it may surprise you to know that there may indeed be an operative from within, possibly even the murderer."

Jim could see from the reaction of both men that he had their complete and undivided attention. After giving an in depth description of the thoughts expressed by he and Debra, it appeared almost a certainty that there was someone within the building that knew the movements and locations that were needed to be so successful at removing and adding evidence from Jim's office. Harry was the first to make a comment.

"Great! Now even you seem to want me as guilty."

"Not so, Harry. All I said was the person has to be an insider. It's the only explanation of how they can operate without notice. But the fact that the door is under lock and key, with only four keys to be accounted for, it does place you in an uncomfortable light for the moment."

A knock at the door interrupted the conversation. Mike got up, unlocked the door and, after opening it was handed a folder. He thanked whoever was outside, closed the door and relocked it. Then Mike opened the folder and skimmed its contents. Grunting, he closed the folder and sat down.

"Sorry for the interruption. I asked for this yesterday, and I'm surprised it got here as quickly as it did."

Jim sat for a moment, then raised his eyebrows and made the obvious request.

"Well, what is it? Or are you going to keep us in the dark?"

"I requested a check on our Frank Spencer from Washington. I have it, and what it says is amazing, even to me."

Mike opened the folder and placed its contents on Jim's desk so all of them could see the papers at the same time. It identified Frank Spencer as a former Navy Seal that left the service and became an investigator for Unisearch. Spencer spent two years with Unisearch, and during those years worked on three cases, all of which produced a series of accidents and the death of one or more of the clients or their relations as part of his work. Then he suddenly dropped from sight. Presently his whereabouts were not known, but there were indications from reliable sources that he was involved in some covert operation under an alias. Jim and Harry were impressed.

"Mike, I'm amazed at how much you have on this fellow. Does Washington keep records of everyone as detailed as this?"

Mike smiled and looked at Harry, who was showing signs of discomfort at Jim's query.

"Heavens no. Big Brother exists, but he is not watching everyone. The reason for the detail here is that Spencer was a Navy Seal. That means he was privileged to a lot of top secret information about our government. Due to this, he is constantly under the watchful eye of our people in Washington. Just a precautionary measure, I can assure you. What has amazed me about this report is that they have no idea as to his activities lately. It's not the usual scenario, and could mean he has gone under cover in order to avoid being discovered in some illegal behavior. Seals are very well trained to survive and can do many things the ordinary individual would be incapable of."

"Such as cold-blooded murder?"

Harry had come to life. Mike answered in a matter-of-fact manner.

"Unfortunately, yes."

Jim pondered on that remark.

"Then it is possible that Spencer's cases involving murders could be linked directly to him, if one were to find the evidence to prove it."

"Oh, most definitely, Jim. And his profile would fit perfectly in our situation if it weren't for the fact that Spencer is no longer with Unisearch. But see here, Jim? The part about his leadership as a Seal? He was a member of a team of five men. Look at member number three."

Jim focused on the list of the men in Spencer's team. Harry let out an audible gasp.

"The man is Richard Barksdale!"

Jim couldn't believe his eyes.

"You're right on the money, Harry. Damned, this case is turning out to be one hell of a complicated list of people and events. Give me my simple accident investigation; that is where I want to be. This homicide business sucks."

Another knock at the door interrupted the discussion. Jim shook his head. "This morning is a flurry of activity for this office."

Jim got up, went to the door and opened it. Outside was one of the detectives from down the hall, and in his hand was a piece of paper.

"Sorry for the interruption, Jim. I found this in the copier last evening. I think it belongs to you."

He handed it to Jim, apologized again for the interruption, and walked away. Jim closed the door and locked it. Then he chuckled and handed the paper to Harry.

"Harry, you're getting careless in your old age. I suggest you calm down and get some needed rest."

Harry took the paper, opened his eyes wide, and let out with a hearty laugh. Then he shoved the paper at Mike's face.

"There, you bloody fool! Accuse me of being a murderer, will you? Here's your bloody poem!"

Mike took the paper, turned a shade of red, and placed it on Jim's desk.

"I guess I made a bad call on that one. Sorry Harry. I have to apologize to both of you. I have never made so many wrong assumptions, or accused someone so wrongfully as I've been doing on this case. I may be a hard-nosed individual, but I've always thought of myself as fair. I've not been very fair lately. Maybe I'm not the sharp agent that I used to be. Maybe I'm getting too old for this line of work."

Jim couldn't believe his ears; Mike admitting fault. It looked like even Harry was surprised to hear Mike's admission. Though only a team for a few short days, Mike had appeared invincible, until now.

"We all make wrong assumptions from time to time. I'd go easy on myself if I were you. And besides, it is a fact that there appears to be a strong chance the murderer, or an accomplice, is amongst us here at headquarters. Debra and I are convinced of that. But who is anybody's guess. Harry, maybe you should sift through the files from the auto insurance company and see if you can turn up some sort of link between Spencer, Unisearch and someone here in this building."

Turning his head toward Mike he continued.

"And Mike, I think that the missing photo from Unisearch's file folder and that letter from the real senator were both misfiled and belong in another case folder. That file must be relatively near the one for Barksdale's case file to have been placed there accidentally. I'd say it may behoove you to get to Dorothy's office while we still have her detained and snoop through to see if the picture is now where it should be, and let's see what that file tells us."

"Great idea, Jim. I'll have a search warrant issued and we can check on that fast. And thanks for taking charge this morning. It just proves that we can be a successful team if we put our minds to it."

"And it also proves you don't always have the right answers."

Harry had to throw that one in, just to give the ending a little zing. Mike did the usual with Harry's innuendoes; he ignored it. Jim kept silent just to keep the peace. The phone rang, giving Jim a perfect reason to get off the subject. He picked it up, listened for a few seconds, then said he understood and hung up.

"Your wish came true, Harry. Dorothy's free."

Mike jumped to his feet. His face grew red as he raised an alarming protest at the ceiling.

"No! That's not possible! You've done me an injustice."

Then Mike caught himself, held back from showing his rage, and looked back towards Jim.

"How?"

"Early this morning, around five. It seems our Dorothy knows a few people and by pulling a few strings had her lawyer get an injunction against Erie County for unlawful detainment. One of the judges is her uncle's good buddy at some club they belong to. We let the momentum fall through the crack. I failed to let the court know about the change in the charge against her. My mistake, Mike. Sorry."

"Damn it! There goes all the effort to get something positive in leads. I'd bet my weeks salary Dorothy is in on this, somehow. Today, we would have pinned her with a charge she deserves, I just know it."

Harry didn't cover the fact that he was elated at the news. Even Jim, though embarrassed by the fact that it was his error that precluded her being held in jail, felt good that she had been able to arrange her release. He had not been happy with Mike's methods and attitude about obtaining her arrest. It just was not the ethical way to go about it. This, of course, would make obtaining that search warrant far from easy. Mike knew what was ahead for him, made a few phone calls, and after he had finished with the phone, sighed in relief.

"Thank God for people owing favors. We still can have that search warrant, but now it's me that owes a favor. I like it better the other way around. Jim, I may need you with me when we go for that search. She doesn't know me, but the FBI identification will rattle her cage. She seems to have some liking towards you and that may give us the edge we need to get that file before she disposes of it. I'm sure she will add up the facts and realize your questions about identifying the senator and that picture will inevitably lead to us looking for the picture, and that file. But we have to act fast. The warrant is on its way to us as we speak."

"And I'm going as well, chaps. To protect the interests of Dorothy, which you two seem to want to chop up."

To Jim's amazement and chagrin, Mike agreed. *What in the world does Mike have in mind?*, Jim thought. *Harry will make her go bonkers!* Then Jim changed his thoughts in mid-stream. *Of course she'll go bonkers; a perfect diversionary tactic!*

"We have one thing in our favor, Jim. She is not yet aware of Richard Barksdale's demise. She will not think about the files until she realizes he isn't around. We hope."

A knock at the door produced the search warrant, and the three of them left, Harry riding with Jim while Mike and one of his associates rode in another car. They arrived at the Unisearch offices around nine fifteen, walked in and identified themselves to the receptionist, who remembered Jim and Harry immediately. As they were escorted to Dorothy's office, a line of people gathered at their office entrances to watch the parade of men as they walked along the corridor. In the distance you could make out the voice of Dorothy getting louder as they approached. Once inside Dorothy's office, the shouting was deafening.

"What the hell do you want now! I've put up with enough of your stupid antics! If you're here to arrest me again, I'll be sure you all never see the light of day again."

Mike smiled at Dorothy.

"Are you making a threat against my life, Miss Maguire? If so, I'll call for back-up and have you dragged off to jail right now."

Dorothy was taken aback by Mike's smooth response. She also realized her comment could be taken in several ways. Dorothy was angry, but not foolish.

"Just a manner of speech. And who the hell are you?"

Mike introduced himself and his associate and yielded their identification to Dorothy, who looked at it and gave them a nasty stare.

"What the hell are two FBI goons doing with the likes of these two assholes?"

Harry took offense at Dorothy's reference of him.

"Now see here, Dorothy, that's no way to talk of someone who is here to be on your side. I came just to—"

Dorothy did her usual number on Harry, called Jim a two-faced nigger, and went on for about a minute before she realized that Mike had opened her files and was looking through the maze of folders.

"Hey! Get your God damned hands out of there! Those are confidential, buster!"

Mike let his left hand show the warrant while his right hand continued to flip through the folders.

"A search warrant gives me the right. Read it and weep."

For a moment Dorothy fell silent. Then her face seemed to loose its color as she realized he was looking for the picture. As she attempted to move towards the filing cabinet to stop Mike, his associate stepped in her path and held up his hands. Without losing a beat, Mike kept on going through the files as he spoke.

"If you so much as interrupt this search, my friend there will have just cause to cuff you and place you under arrest for interfering with the lawful search being conducted. And that charge, my dear lady, will not be overthrown."

At that point Mike raised a folder out of the cabinet and handed it to Jim.

"There, Jim. Take a look at what's inside."

Jim took the folder and opened it. On the top of all the paperwork was the photo that he had seen in Barksdale's file folder. Under it was a few letters of correspondence, all bearing the signature of Senator William Harrison. Harry saw the contents as he looked over Jim's shoulders. His hopes of protecting Dorothy were fast fading as it looked like she indeed had been concealing something.

"What's the title of that folder, Jim?"

Jim turned it so he could read the label on the folder. He couldn't believe what he saw.

"Read it, Jim. Get it out in the open so Harry will stop making a fool of himself and us."

"It reads 'Senatorial Shakedown.'"

Dorothy made an immediate retort.

"I can explain that. It doesn't mean what you think it means."

Mike frowned at Dorothy's outburst.

"Miss Maguire, what makes you think anything you say at this point will be taken as credible? By removing that photo from Barksdale's file folder and concealing that fact, in addition to failing to acknowledge your relationship with the senator makes you prime suspect as a murderer. And who believes what murderers have to say?"

"I am not a murderer! And I did not have an affair with the senator!"

Jim was beginning to think, listen and respond in his usual manner.

"Affair? Mister Anderson said 'relationship', which can mean any number of things. Why did you jump to the conclusion he was referencing an affair? Did you have an affair with the senator?"

Dorothy now realized she was not going to talk her way out of this, and decided to protect herself.

"I have nothing further to say until I talk to my lawyer."

Mike responded instantly.

"And you shall have opportunity to do just that very shortly. Jim, read Miss Maguire her rights and place her under arrest. Harry, are we together on this?"

Mike was making sure that Harry was on the same frequency and not about to do any heroics.

"Yes, Mike. Damn it Dorothy, why didn't you give us the truth? All this wouldn't be happening if—"

Dorothy cut Harry off.

"On what charge are you arresting me this time? Making love to your precious senator?"

"I wouldn't talk or act so glib, Dorothy. The charge is suspicion of the murder of Senator Harrison and Richard Barksdale."

Suddenly Dorothy's complexion went from red to pale white.

"Barksdale? Shit, when did this happen?"

Jim could sense the shock of hearing Barksdale's name as a victim was genuine. If she were the murderer, she was playing the role of innocence magnificently. Mike signaled to Jim and Harry; he didn't want any further conversation that would give Dorothy information to use in building a defense.

"I think enough had been said. Harry read Miss Maguire her rights, cuff her and let's get out of here."

Harry obeyed and within five minutes he, Jim and Dorothy were in the car heading towards the Holding Center. Jim radioed dispatch to alert the center of their arrival so there would be someone to take her into custody. Harry would file the paperwork while Jim headed to his office and a closer look at the folder he still had in his possession. Since Jim's car wasn't equipped with a shield between driver and the back, Harry sat with Dorothy, cuffed to her using Jim's handcuffs. He could hear Harry trying to talk some sense and reasoning into Dorothy, but getting silence and the cold shoulder.

They were met at the Holding Center by two uniformed deputies who took Dorothy into the center while Harry, returning Jim's cuffs, walked in behind them to do the paperwork. Jim headed back to headquarters and upon entering his office was greeted by the smiling face of Debra.

"I guess you having a key will give you every opportunity to surprise me here, just like always."

"Now Jim, is that any way to greet your teammate?"

Jim smiled, gave her a peck on the cheek, and placed the folder on his desk. Debra immediately picked it up and read the folder's tag. Her eyebrows shot upwards and an attempted whistle passed from her lips.

"My, my! What have we here? It looks like your Dorothy may be in on some shady behavior after all."

Jim sat down and asked for the folder, which Debra relinquished reluctantly. He opened it and picked up the picture, staring at it and trying to visualize the corpse. For some reason he could almost believe that, though distinctly very similar, there were slight differences. He gave it to Debra to look at and asked her if that was the person she saw in the trunk of the car. Though she had become nauseated at the time, someone that was that averse to looking at a dead body would have what she had glimpsed etched in her memory.

"It might be, but then I didn't get that good a look at him. And besides, this picture was taken a few years ago, so it could be he just aged and looks slightly different now."

Jim gave Debra a look of surprise.

"How do you know that picture is a few years old?"

Debra gave Jim her enchanting and cunning smile and turned the picture over.

"Because it has a date on the back, silly! You men never think of these things. That's one reason you need women; to be successful."

Jim chuckled, took the picture and looked at the date. It was dated five years ago. That meant it had to be a picture of the real senator. The double had only been placed two years ago, according to Mike. It also confirmed the thoughts that Dorothy knew the real senator long before the double had shown up as a corpse. It also meant there was a strong possibility that Dorothy may have known that the victim wasn't the real senator. This made her very much suspect to involvement. But Dorothy's reaction to Barksdale being dead, plus the fact that she was incarcerated at the time of Barksdale's murder, ruled her out as the murderer; a definite plus for her being an accomplice. Jim began to shuffle through the papers in the folder on his desk and was interrupted by the entrance of Mike. He greeted the two and sat down facing Jim's desk.

"So, has anyone here got any ideas on who killed the senator? Debra, I was appraised of your suspicions about an insider being either the murderer or an accomplice. Care to expand on those suspicions?"

It was obvious from Mike's questions that he was confident that Dorothy, though involved, was not the murderer. Debra was eager to be a part in this case, and responded with enthusiasm.

"Mike, it has to be someone that Jim has known for some time. Someone that Jim trusts and shares information with, otherwise they would have been questioned by now. Especially since Jim had gone out of his way to enquire about who was around after the first intrusion. I also think you can rule out Harry, since he was with you, Mike, up until he left to arrest Barksdale. I can't see him arriving at Barksdale's place with two uniformed deputies and performing the murder without being detected by the deputies. He was with them and no gunshots were heard by the deputies, so it can't be Harry."

"Not as the murderer, that's true. But he still could be an accomplice."

Jim mulled over what he was listening to, rubbed the back of his neck, and decided to make a contribution to the conversation. He felt compelled to defend his friend and colleague.

"I think he can be ruled out as an accomplice as well. Debra, remember I mentioned that the first time the poems had been tampered with I asked around for some reason why no one had seen a person in my office. It was the night of the union meeting, so some went to the meeting while others took advantage of an early quit, free time off, whatever. Well, Harry being a sergeant is still a union member. He wasn't around either."

"Nice try, Jim. A good assumption on your part, but not a guarantee that Harry wasn't here that night, just the same."

Debra was her usual thorough self. She did, however, give Jim some consolation.

"Maybe you can check around and see if he went to the meeting. Or ask Harry if he went. If he did, then you're right. But if not, then he still is suspect."

Jim knew asking Harry that question would lead to all kinds of ramifications and backlash. But he might be able to glean it out of someone that knew Harry well enough to have recognized him at the meeting. Unfortunately, attendance was not taken, only a check of membership cards was required or it would have been a simple matter to verify.

With a sigh, Jim turned his attention once again to the folder. Mike helped by reading some of the contents of the letters and records, while Debra tried to decide whether to stay or leave. She had come to see Jim about some arrangements she wanted to make for a weekend together, but now seemed like an inappropriate time. She excused herself, told Jim she would call him later, and bumped into Harry as she left. Harry had an obvious look of frustration on his face. It only took a matter of seconds before he had the full attention of Mike and Jim.

"This is turning into a bloody side show. We arrest a very dear person, then she gets released on a technicality. Then we arrest her again, and she gets released on another technicality. This is frustration with a capital F!"

"What? What the hell do you mean she gets released?"

"Just as I'm halfway through the paperwork, a phone call comes to the desk, and the officer tells me to forget the papers. Dorothy's lawyer, a Saxton, Senton…"

"Sexton?"

"That's the bloke. Apparently he had been informed by someone at Unisearch of Dorothy's arrest and was at the Holding Center minutes before our arrival. He had an order from the courts for her release based on some infringements of her constitutional rights."

Mike's face turned red, and he stood up and shouted at Harry.

"What the hell was infringed upon? We did everything by the book! There's been some royal fuck up by the courts!"

"Don't yell at me. I didn't make that decision."

Mike apologized, picked up the phone and called someone to find out what had happened. After some yes and no and so what comments, Mike hung up the phone and sat back down.

"Well, I don't owe anyone a favor anymore."

Jim looked puzzled.

"What happened, Mike?"

"It seems the judge that issued our search warrant wasn't made aware of the 'mistreatment' of Miss Maguire yesterday and claims he was duped into issuing the warrant. He feels we obtained the warrant to make an unlawful search and seizure at Miss Maguire's office and therefore illegally arrested her in violation of her constitutional rights. Now, before any warrants are issued, we have to produce hard documented proof of her involvement in any crime before we can arrest her. How about that shit?"

Jim felt it was about time. But he kept that opinion to himself. He was disappointed only due to the fact he had wanted to question her regarding the matter of Frank Spencer. Maybe there was still a chance to ask her, but Mike's next comment squelched that idea.

"And to top it off, her lawyer has requested and gotten from the courts a Limited Restraining Order barring us from contacting her either in person or on the phone unless it is a matter of personal safety or an emergency. If we don't prove that it was either one of those, we will be charged with harassment and measures taken to prevent our doing it again. We have been slapped."

Harry was amazed at the news.

"Can she force that kind of restraint on the FBI?"

Mike reached for the phone, dialed and after a few moments started to relate the situation to the other party, presumably his boss. After a few additional minutes of grunts from Mike, he hung up and uttered one word.

"Yes."

"Mike, what kind of clout does Dorothy have to be able to stop the FBI cold in its tracks?"

Mike pointed to the folder on Jim's desk.

"That kind. I have been informed that any activities that potentially alert anyone to the facts regarding the senator is strictly forbidden. It seems your Dorothy has gone to the people she knows in the Senate and screamed foul play. They bought it, and we are told to back off. Incidentally Jim, that folder is now classified information and is to be returned to Unisearch immediately. But, of course, its not our fault if we happen to have seen everything before being told that, right gentlemen?"

Jim could see the devilish gleam in Mike's eyes. Harry, Jim and Mike shared the folder's contents and set aside those documents held by the reader to be the most important. Then Mike left the office with those documents and returned minutes later with copies of all of them. Then he returned the originals to their rightful places in the folder and left with the folder in hand. He returned almost immediately, locking the door behind him.

"I gave the folder to my associate to return. Our part is done. Now, shall we see what we have in our hands?"

Jim was sure they were exceeding their authority by reading the materials, yet he was drawn by a compelling desire to find his murderer. Harry was sure he would find something to exonerate Dorothy from anything wrongful.

Mike couldn't wait to see what there was that would give him the chance to put Dorothy back where he felt she should be; in jail. With three distinctly different feelings and emotions, they set the material out so everyone could see it and pick from it the things that they felt most pertinent. After what seemed like hours, Mike made his first comment.

"Here we are. Look at this nifty piece of information. It doesn't take a mastermind to see what is happening here."

Mike was brandishing a paper on Senate letterhead written by the senator to Dorothy. It was dated two and a half years ago. In it the senator stated that he wished that his being with Dorothy over the weekend not become common knowledge. He stated he never regretted one moment of it and would do it again if the situation arose. He said he loved her, and that she was everything a man could ever desire.

Jim found nothing about the letter that gave a clue as to her involvement with the murders. Harry felt saddened by the fact that the woman he had pictured as hard to seduce was apparently very seductive herself. Mike thought it would kill the people at the White House if he made them aware of what had transpired, giving him new leverage to his operation. Regardless of the mixed opinions, it was set aside as a primary document.

The next paper startled even Jim. It was a letter of correspondence from the senator to a member of the House of Representatives. In it the senator stated that if he gave the House a favorable vote on the issue of tax relief for the people who acquire unusual wealth by unexpected inheritance, then he would like to see the bill on increased spending for research of unclaimed wealth in the country passed. Both were directly related to work being performed by Unisearch. Jim saw in it many possibilities regarding the amount of effort placed on search and the distribution of funds acquired through Unisearch. A definite link between Unisearch and the senator.

Harry saw this as a positive position that Dorothy, as a company employee, would take; an advantage in motivating her employees, not as a destructive tool but, rather, a positive tool. Mike saw the correspondence as a reason to cover and conceal the senator's personal involvement in Unisearch; possibly a reason for killing him.

Harry chimed in with a discovery of his own. A personal note on Unisearch letterhead addressed to the senator at the White House. It was dated just six months ago. It stated that even though she didn't know how to reach him, she was sure someone there would. The letter referred to a newly found wealth that was tied into the senator's family and that it was important that he contact her as soon as possible regarding the possible inheritance of many millions of dollars.

What was inspiring was the closing remark. "I wish I could be with you." A very strange closing. Jim felt that there was something phony about a statement like that. It inferred a personal association, possibly a romantic connotation. Not likely in a letter that Dorothy would send to be read by someone she wouldn't even know. And it almost sounded as if she knew the existence of the senator's double.

Harry saw into the letter a need to contact the senator on a matter of business. She could hardly be expected to just let things go without pursuing the financial gains. It was, after all, just a letter to a client. Mike found it to be the nail in the coffin. Dorothy was admitting her knowledge of the senator's special assignment, and the fact that the double that showed up was not intended to be the recipient of the grandiose wealth. A definite reason to eliminate the imposter.

As each piece of correspondence was reviewed, Jim, Mike and Harry all found something in them that fit his particular outlook on the situation. All three agreed that there was enough here to present to a judge in support of an investigation of Unisearch and their records. The problem was how to do this and not be accused of illegally acquiring the information. Then something else entered Mike's mind.

"Gentlemen, I may have a possible way for us to proceed. It is obvious that we need something that was not part of the 'classified information' file, but still a part of the picture it represents. We have it, guys. The letter in Barksdale's folder that was misfiled there. Under oath, we would be telling the truth by saying it wasn't part of the file we were ordered to return. At least, it wasn't when we read it, and kept in the file it was found in. That could help. Let's look at it and see if we can get enough from that one letter to do the trick."

Harry had removed the file in question from the file drawer as Mike was talking. Opening it, he took the letter Mike referred to out and placed it on Jim's desk for everyone to see. As he did so he accidentally shuffled the other letters, dropping one to the floor. As he picked it up, he gave one of his familiar grunts and placed it alongside of the misfiled one. Then he tapped on the date of the copy that had fallen.

"Take a squint at that, chaps. It's dated a week before the letter in Barksdale's folder. That pinpoints the exact week that the senator was replaced by the double."

"True" Mike agreed. "And it also makes Dorothy aware of the senator's whereabouts and that the senator had been replaced by an impersonator. I'm afraid you have not only found the loophole we're looking for, but a definite question as to how deeply involved Dorothy is in all of this."

Harry's enthusiasm turned to disappointment.

"Damn! Why is everything you see a building block for hanging Dorothy? The poor woman—"

Mike broke in.

"The poor woman is as guilty as sin! Why is everything you see a path to forgiveness and innocence for Dorothy? When will you admit to yourself that she has to be involved? Why else the folder marked 'Senatorial Shakedown'?"

Jim could see another shouting match brewing and looked at his wristwatch.

"Why don't we call it a day? It's already almost six o'clock. The courts will not want to hear our plea at this hour. Using this evening to ponder what we have and cool our frustrations, we will be in a better state of mind to approach the courts. This had better be done right the first time, or our jobs could be in jeopardy."

All agreed and, after placing the copies of the letters in a blank folder and filing them they left, making sure the office was secure. Looking around, Jim could see only a few familiar faces in the area. All the rest had gone for the day. He took a deep breath and hoped that tomorrow would turn out better than today. After all, what else could go wrong?

Chapter 9

"I can't believe it! This is absolutely impossible! Jim, I want every person familiar with your office questioned until we find answers. We have an infiltrator in our midst and I want that person found ASAP."

The shit was hitting the fan. Mike was in a rage, and Harry was speechless.

"But how do I do that without implying that whoever I question is suspect to a murder? Mike, these are my fellow officers; some are my subordinates and others are my peers. I can't just blatantly go to them and ask 'where were you last night, and can you prove it'. That's not ethical or sensible. I have to work with these people."

Mike sat down and was obviously trying to cool off. He muttered a few obscenities under his breath, stood back up, paced for a minute, sat back down again and placed his hands to the back of his head. While Mike did this, Harry sat and blankly looked at the file cabinet, and an open drawer which should have held the blank folder with the copies of the senator's letters in it, but which was missing. In its place was a poem and Harry knew it wouldn't take Mike long to decide to accuse him of the theft and the poem. Jim felt frustration and, for the first time in his career, total defeat. He took the poem that had been placed on his desk and read it aloud.

IT IS SAD TO REPEAT A MESSAGE SO OLD
A CLUE YOU SHALL HAVE ON HOW SO BOLD
THIS POEM REPLACED WHAT YOU HELD STRONG.
THE ANSWER YOU SOUGHT WAS HERE ALL ALONG.
NOW TO END THIS WASTED, USELESS PLIGHT
GO TO THE MORGUE THIS VERY NIGHT.
THERE YOU WILL FIND A NEW BAG OF GOLD
TO CONTINUE THIS SEARCH THAT MUST UNFOLD.

Harry shook his head in dismay.

"I suppose the bloody answer was in the file cabinet. It wasn't the folder we created yesterday. That means something else is missing from the files. Jim, shall we have a look see?"

Jim hastily got up and went to the file cabinet and started to flip through the files. Mike sat up and watched in interest. Jim's heart began to race in anticipation of discovering what he had held in the files that would point to the killer. After twenty minutes of thumbing and looking, he realized what it was. Shaking his head in disgust, he slammed the file drawer shut, walked back to his desk, sat down and began to laugh. Mike just looked at Harry with a questioning glare. Harry heard Jim utter the word to end all words.

"Pity!"

Then Jim burst into a flow of louder laughter that had Mike and Harry almost laughing as well, for what reason they had no idea. Finally Mike could take the suspense no longer.

"OK, Jim, what's so funny?"

Jim tried to contain the laughing and after several attempts to stop, finally succeeded.

"The file cabinet. It's not what's in it, it's the file cabinet."

Again Jim went into hysterical laughter. Mike and Harry were lost as to what Jim meant.

"Come, come, old chap. Make some sense if you would."

Jim lightened up on the laughter just long enough to utter 'pity' and returned to his laughing. It took Mike and Harry five minutes to finally calm Jim down enough to explain the outburst.

"It's not my file cabinet. The files that should be there aren't; and there are files that I have no idea as to who they belong to. Don't you see? The murderer switched file cabinets to provide us with documents that will clue us in on what or who the murderer is or why the murder took place. It's all right here in our hands. Now, all we have to do is go through every damned folder in the files to see where there is a clue that will lead us to the killer."

Mike was amazed at Jim's discovery. Harry was amazed at Jim's lack of concern over the horrendous task that lay ahead for them. The file cabinet must hold at least a few hundred folders. No small task to examine each and every one of them.

"Jim, this could take days, maybe a week to sift through and decipher what the clue is. We don't have the luxury of that much time."

Jim, having finally gotten his composure back, shook his head at Harry and smiled.

"We don't have to; don't you see? Once we remove what we placed there while working on this case, the rest of the folders belong to the individual that rightfully owns this file cabinet. Our task is to locate the owner of the cabinet and, I'm willing to wager, we will have our killer, or at least the clue we need to locate the killer."

Mike clapped his hands.

"Great deduction! Let's look at the folders and see if we can tie them into something or someone familiar."

Jim got up and went to the cabinet. He carefully removed all the folders he or Harry had placed there. Then all three began to pull folders out and rummage through their content. After a few minutes, Jim became acutely aware that something was amiss.

"You know something? None of these cases even remotely resembles any cases that came through this division. I dare say they don't even look like cases that the Erie County Sheriff's Department would be involved with."

"What are you implying, Jim? They may not be police files?"

"Oh, they're police files. But not on a county level. More like a local level. Look at this, for example. Here's a case involving a lost cat. And this one, an answer to a request for investigating a foul odor coming from the house next door. And this one regarding a disagreement between two neighbors resulting in some damage to the vehicles they own. They all involve small investigations of a minor nature. Harry, check the addresses of the people in these folders. See what area they belong. I suspect they are the files of a local police department. Maybe the Buffalo Police Department, since their offices are so close to us. Whoever switched cabinets wouldn't necessarily wish to travel too far with it."

Harry took a few of the folders and left to check out the addresses. Mike sat down across from Jim and looked him straight in the eyes.

"Jim, you wouldn't be faking this, now would you?"

"Why should I do that?"

"To protect Harry, for a starter."

"No Mike. As much as I want my department to have a clean bill of health, the cabinet and the files are of a local nature and definitely not mine or anyone else that works here. As a matter of fact, the owner of that cabinet most likely being a police officer, could explain the disregard for his or her coming and going around here. Since the Holding Center is just around the corner and tied into this structure, police from all over the area have been known to be in this building for one reason or another."

Mike seemed content with Jim's answer and sat back.

"Then what's tonight's visit to the morgue going to produce? The poem left little to guess about. Are we going?"

"Hopefully it will produce a bag of gold. I could use a few extra bucks."

Jim and Mike were feeling more relaxed now that something positive had resulted from the disaster of the morning. The two talked about the next move and how they were going to approach the judge now that the papers they had were gone. Suddenly Jim got up and shuffled through the files he had removed from the cabinet and produced the Barksdale folder.

"All is not lost. We still have that misfiled letter which we were going to use. At least I hope we still...yes. Here it is."

"Great. Incidentally, do you see any correlation between Dorothy's actions yesterday and the fact that the copies we made were the intruders target last night?"

Jim had to think hard before answering.

"Not really Mike. How could she even know that we had made copies?"

"Because she holds you in high regard when it comes to intelligence. She could easily have second guessed their existence."

"But the idea was yours Mike, not mine."

"She doesn't know that, and besides, if I hadn't suggested it, I'm sure you or Harry wouldn't have been far behind in coming up with the thought."

Jim's mind went back to the poem. Mike had posed a real question regarding that night. What was the bag of gold, and should they go. What if it was a wild goose chase, or worse yet, a set up to incriminate them in something that would force them off the case. That would certainly make life easier for the killer. And if Dorothy was involved in it, she was very good at twisting the truth to suit her needs.

Jim's thoughts were interrupted by a knock on the door. Mike opened it allowing Harry to enter with the folders he had taken with him, some additional pieces of paper, and a smile on his face.

"Two good things. One, the addresses are all located within the Amherst area. Two, guess what your fellow agent handed me, Mike?"

Mike took the papers and gave out with a shout of praise.

"Thank God for mistakes!"

The papers turned out to be a second set of those made yesterday.

"Your associate had misunderstood and had made another set before returning the folder to Unisearch, thinking that was your intention. Only this set was a complete one, not just the selected ones."

Jim was uncomfortable with the duplication of the entire folder. He could only hope that knowledge of the possession of these documents wouldn't lead to repercussions. Jim picked up the phone and called some of his detectives requesting they come to his office. Then he looked at Harry and made the rules quite clear regarding what Harry was about to do.

"Harry, I want you to take charge of tracking those addresses using the manpower I will assign to you. Each man is to cover an area alone, and it will be up to you to make sure they do just that. Then you will coordinate the findings, assimilate them by priority and accuracy, and report back with those findings by tomorrow afternoon."

"Jim, that's impossible. It will take—"

"I know the time is very short and the task very large. I will give you more men if you need them. I also will authorize overtime, if necessary. I can ask the captain for some uniformed deputies, if you think it's warranted."

"A damn bloody must have."

"Fine. And one thing more. Don't even suggest to anyone that we are looking to find something to force an arrest of Dorothy. We are looking for the owner of a filing cabinet mistakenly taken and placed in our headquarters. That's the story, nothing more. Understand?"

"Yes. But won't the fact that we are searching for the owner of that cabinet flag a warning to the murderer?"

Jim and Mike both smiled. Mike took the lead.

"Exactly! We sure hope so. It will let our murderer know we have solved his little game of poetry and are intending to put on some pressure. Maybe the murderer will slip up and make a foolish move. I suspect, however, that the filing cabinet is just a ruse and will be nothing more than a dead end. The murderer is buying time, thinking we will be preoccupied with a lengthy search of its contents. It's the hope for a mistake that we are looking for, not the owner of the cabinet as such."

Jim called the captain and explained what the team was about to undertake and requested some help from the uniformed deputies. He grunted several times, said yes at least five times, and hung up.

"The captain has his reservations, especially seeing that we feel the murderer may be one of his own people, but consented to giving us five men. Will that suffice?"

"Splendidly."

"And now that the captain is aware of where we stand at this moment, he wishes that none of us make any further moves without his being informed. This goes for you as well, Mike. He has spoken to your superior, and as you are our guest on our turf, you need to follow all the same rules as we do."

Mike looked peeved at the remark, but remained silent. Harry looked delighted at Mike's being told his place. Jim saw in both of his teammates that the differences they had still remained. The knock at the door produced six detectives. Jim told Harry to fill them in, wished them all good hunting, and for Harry to pick up the uniformed help on the way downstairs. Once the door was closed and locked, Jim felt it was time to get his feelings out in the open to Mike.

"I don't like being in possession of this file from Unisearch, Mike. It is a dangerous path we are walking along. If it is ever discovered that we made copies, our asses are grass."

"Then give them to Debra. Put it in a sealed envelope and tell her to keep it in a confidential file somewhere for safekeeping. Tell her it's a list of possible suspects here at headquarters. Tell her anything you like, but let her hold onto it. No one will ever think of her as having anything like that. But before you do, let's review them and pull the ones we made copies of yesterday first. And this time, let's not use the filing cabinet. Do you have another place in here that would be less likely to be the object of our intruder's interest?"

Jim couldn't think of anywhere else that wasn't subject to a search. However, he had a suggestion.

"Why not let Harry keep them in his office. The lack of security would make our intruder dismiss any thoughts of anything important pertaining to this case being kept there."

Mike frowned.

"Well, I'm sure that would be true. Unless our Harry is an accomplice. Then-"

"So what, Mike? He has the key to this place. What's the difference?"

Mike shrugged, agreed, and the decision was final. Producing the letter from Barksdale's folder, Mike reviewed it along with the discussion made yesterday on how he could use it as leverage before a judge and obtain an arrest warrant written for Dorothy.

By mid-morning Mike had worked out the details of his approach before the judge and how the judge would have to agree it was sufficient grounds for an arrest on suspicion as an accessory to a conspiracy against the senator and the United States. He would have to make the judge cognizant of the fact that the victim was a double and the real senator on a secret project, but that was a compromise that Mike had to make if he was to seem credible.

The best part was, since that would be his approach, the judge would now be from the federal courts, not the state or county. A new person and a fresh slate going into the arena to do battle. It was perfect. And no mention of the Unisearch files need ever be brought up, and if it did later on, the misfiling of the letter covered him.

With confidence Mike decided to handle this personally and left Jim to reading the files they had pulled while he went to the federal courthouse. Jim said he would let the captain know of the new move and wished Mike luck. The captain wasn't thrilled at the involvement of the federal courts, but agreed with the plan, should Mike be successful at obtaining the warrant.

It was also apparent now that the investigation was taking on a new look, with the FBI now actively participating openly and in some control of the events. Jim wasn't too happy about that, but the captain sounded glad, since the burden of responsibility was now shifting to the rightful shoulders of the federal government and not only his department. There was merit in that way of thinking.

Jim decided to take the files from Unisearch to Debra. The sooner they left his office, the more comfortable he would feel. Placing them in a large manila envelope, he closed the flap and secured it with the fastener. He did the same with the copies for Harry's office. Harry's envelope he left in Harry's desk file drawer under miscellaneous. Then on the way downstairs he stopped in the clerk's office and sealed the one for Debra with packaging tape to ensure no one could open it without destroying the envelope in the process.

Then he left headquarters and walked the few blocks to the Rath Building where Debra and her company were located. The greeting he received when he finally got to her office was unexpected.

"So what is happening? No calls, no evening plans?"

"I'm sorry, Debra. I know this case is getting in the way of our being together. But there is so much happening, I thought you'd appreciate me getting you up to speed."

Jim hoped the involvement approach would appease Debra and inflate her ego at the same time. It was only partially successful.

"Thank you for the thoughtfulness. But don't beat around the bush with me, Mister Hargrove. What about tonight?"

Jim frowned for a moment, and then delivered his cheery smile and alert response.

"We'll be together dear, only we won't be alone."

"And what's that supposed to mean?"

Jim explained the events of the day before and that morning. He mentioned the new poem and the part about the morgue and the bag of gold. Debra listened with interest, making no comments or interruptions, which for her was extremely unusual. As Jim ventured into the part about the second duplicate set of files, he could see the expression of understanding cross her face.

"And I suppose that envelope in your hands represents my part in this deal."

"Well, sort of. We, that is Mike and I, thought that it was wise to give the file to someone who could be trusted to protect its content without question."

"And that someone you thought would be me, right? Wrong! What's in it?"

"I can't tell you just yet. But it is extremely important, and you're the only one that can be trusted with it."

"If I'm that trustworthy, why can't you tell me what's in it? It's the Unisearch files, isn't it? Right?"

Jim wiggled in his seat and tried to look nonchalant, but Debra saw through it.

"I'm right. And my answer is no. That is a loaded package, and it means trouble big time to the possessor. I thought you loved me, Jim. How could you even suggest I keep that for you?"

Now Jim was beginning to feel guilty at having agreed with Mike's suggestion.

"I do love you, that's why I felt you were the only one I would ever trust with such a—"

"Bull shit! I was convenient. You and Mike don't want to be found with it, Harry can't be trusted with it because he might be in on this murder, and that leaves Miss Convenient. Did I get the picture right?"

"Yes, dear."

The silence that followed seemed to last forever. It was Debra who finally broke it.

"OK, I'll keep it. But you owe me, and I will collect. Give it to me."

Jim handed it to Debra with reluctance. He knew her all too well and the price for this would cost him dearly. As he was about to thank her for helping, she was into the next conversation.

"And as for tonight, I gather that you expect our being together but not alone means you think I'm going to the morgue tonight with you. Is that what I think I'm hearing?"

"I thought you wanted to be a part of this investigation, so naturally I—"

"Wrong again! If you think my idea of an evening with you is a trip to the morgue, you're sadly mistaken. But, seeing as how I have become so invaluable to the team, I will go as a team member. That means you owe me big time twice today. Boy, am I going to have fun when it's payback time."

And with that said, Debra sat back in her chair with a broad grin on her face. Jim was in for it. What though, he wasn't sure. But it wouldn't be good; he could sense that.

Having accomplished his mission, Jim made arrangements for picking Debra up at six for the trip to the morgue, kissed her, and left. As he headed back to headquarters, he smiled to himself. Even though he would be paying for Debra's cooperation, somehow he felt that it was bringing them closer. By being a team member, Debra was proving herself a worthy partner. He wished that there were some way to make her actively a permanent team player in his work. He'd have to think on that one for a while.

Jim reached his office within a few minutes. As he unlocked the door he heard Mike's voice behind him.

"We're in business. Get inside. We need to plan this out."

Once inside, Mike started to relate what had transpired at the federal court. He seemed to be inspired by some new achievement and eagerly ready to make his next victorious move. The judge, as it turned out, was a former member of the FBI that had worked in the legal department prior to his election as a judge. He was around when the senator from Nevada had been called to the White House. He had heard rumors of something important being done and that it was top secret. He had not heard about the double, or the fact that the double had been murdered. He was extremely interested in what Mike had to show as evidence of a conspiracy.

"And we have it. The icing on the cake."

Mike reached into his jacket pocket and produced a paper that held the word Warrant at the top.

"Let's see what Miss Maguire can do to change the mind of this judge. Jim, get a couple of deputies. We're going to pay another visit to our sweetheart at Unisearch."

Jim felt sorry for Dorothy. Even though he was now sure she was deeply involved in some way, he couldn't help feeling like that. Maybe it was the way Mike kept going after her that made Jim wish that there had to be another approach. Unfortunately, Jim also knew that there was only one course, and that was to arrest Dorothy. He picked up the phone, called for two deputies to assist in an arrest, and headed downstairs and to his car with Mike immediately behind. On this trip they would travel together, and throughout the trip all he heard was the bragging from Mike as to how he had led the team to this point, and how instrumental his leadership had been in achieving this moment of success.

Jim wished Harry were with him.

Chapter 10

The receptionist at Unisearch just shook her head in disbelief as Mike, Jim and the two deputies entered the building. Without waiting to see identification, she got up and motioned for them to follow her. As before, by the time they arrived at Dorothy's office, the corridor was lined with curious onlookers. Only this time there was no screaming when they entered and confronted Dorothy. But the cynicism still flowed from her lips.

"Are you two still playing your silly ass games? You just don't know when to quit, now do you. What's it this time? A charge of being faster than you and winning?"

"I wouldn't be so smug, Dorothy. This time you won't walk out. I'm sure you'll appreciate the advice."

"Detective, you and this asshole FBI agent will pay dearly for another arrest."

Mike smiled and interrupted the conversation.

"Miss Maguire, you are under arrest for conspiracy against the United States. A federal judge in a federal court issued this warrant. Your 'buddies' will not overturn this one; I guarantee it. Officers, read Miss Maguire her rights and get her downtown."

Dorothy was looking a little perplexed with this new approach.

"What the hell are you talking about? What conspiracy? Are you nuts?"

Jim tried to lessen the shock of the charge and also prevent Dorothy from sticking her foot in her mouth.

"Dorothy, let things be until you're booked and you've had a chance to talk to your lawyer. This has turned into a very complicated and serious charge. This time try not to fight me on what I need. Stick around for the meeting that you avoided and let these matters come out. It will be for your own good."

Unfortunately, Dorothy was not listening, and she was back to her usual scenarios. And she was once again screaming.

"You will both pay with your jobs, you fucking bastards! I'll nail your asses! You won't get away with this bullshit!"

She struggled with the deputies, but to no avail. By now the entire company had lined the path to the door as the deputies had to almost drag Dorothy along while she continued to struggle to get free, shouting obscenities the entire way. Jim felt bad that things had to come to this, but he admitted to himself that Dorothy had put herself in the hot seat. Her beauty and her intelligence was no match for the long hard arm of law and justice.

As Jim drove back to headquarters, Mike continued his boasting about what he had done, what he was going to do, and how great he was. Jim just agreed as Mike spoke. He would have liked to tell Mike to shut up, but offending him would only set him off, and he needed Mike for the visit to the morgue. There was something about the poem's message and the location that had Jim feeling uneasy. And he hadn't told Mike about Debra tagging along as yet, which he suspected would meet with opposition. He needed to be on Mike's good side for both reasons.

The rest of the afternoon went by slowly. At around five, Jim told Mike he would meet him at the morgue around six and that he had made arrangements to have someone available in case of an emergency. Harry would not be in attendance, as his present assignment would take him well into the evening. Jim had deliberately not mentioned Debra's unscheduled presence at the morgue, figuring it would be rather awkward for Mike to say no with Debra standing next to him. Not altogether honest, but one needed to play some things close in order to win in certain circumstances. In this case, it was Jim's peace of mind and a desire to keep his relationship with Debra intact.

Jim grabbed some sandwiches at the local deli and surprised Debra at her place by arriving early enough to have something to eat. Debra appreciated the gesture, as she was not fond of the thought that she would be spending the next couple of hours in a morgue. She had thought she would skip eating, but when she had finished the sandwich, she was thankful for the comfortable feeling the food had provided.

It was a little past six when Jim and Debra arrived at the city morgue. Jim had decided to tell Debra about his feeling uneasy regarding the visit. She was understanding and consoling, which made Jim feel much easier about things. As the two emerged from the car, Mike, who was sitting in his car a few feet from the entrance, flagged them down and motioned for them to get into his car. The motioning seemed extremely urgent. As they got into the back seat, Mike made a hurrying motion and quickly closed the door.

"What's up, Mike? Did you spot something?"

"While waiting for you, I saw this guy go into the morgue. He seemed nervous and kept looking all around as if trying to catch sight of someone. Then he came back out, walked to both sides of the building and then went back in again. Very strange movements."

Jim agreed it sounded very odd. As he was about to venture a guess as to what it might be all about, the door to the morgue opened and a very familiar figure emerged.

"Well I'll be damned. You won't believe this, but I know who that is."

Without another word, Jim opened the car door and waved to the man, who turned and immediately headed for the car. As the man approached, Jim caught a glimpse out of the corner of his eye of a scared expression on Debra's face as she saw Mike reach inside his jacket and pull out a gun. Jim reacted swiftly and immediately advanced himself in front of the car and greeted the man, blocking any clear shot should Mike decide to play hero. Then he reached behind and gave a thumb up signal that all was fine. Turning, he and the man walked over to the car.

"Mike, this is Robert Thomas. You remember Mister Thomas? He works at Unisearch and has been helpful in our investigation."

Mike nodded his acknowledgement but remained holding onto his gun. Debra felt very uncomfortable about her position in the car and decided it was safer outside and got out of the car. Jim turned to Thomas and asked if he carried a weapon. With a shocked look, Thomas replied he did not.

"I need to be sure. Would you please stand straight with your arms up in the air while I verify that?"

With hesitation, Thomas agreed. Once Mike was satisfied that the man was unarmed, he placed the gun back into it's holster and stepped out of the car. Thomas was now extremely nervous.

"What's going on, Lieutenant? Why did you think I was armed? And why are you here?"

"I was about to ask you the same question. Why on Earth would you be here at this time of day, or here at all for that matter?"

"I was asked to be here."

Jim stared at Mike, who shrugged.

"Who asked you to be here?"

Thomas produced a folded piece of paper. On it, in the same printing as was on the poems, was a request that he be at the morgue around six to meet with a group of people who needed the services of Unisearch.

"Didn't you think it was odd for the meeting to be at this location?"

"Sure I did, but I never ignore an opportunity to add a client to my list. It gives me more bonus money at the end of the year."

Mike was now rubbing his chin and looking suspiciously at Thomas. He introduced himself, showed his ID and then excused himself and Jim, pulling Jim off to the side.

"What the hell are you doing, Jim? This guy is a suspect. He may even be our killer. Why are you so cordial with him?"

"Because I don't see Robert Thomas as involved. He is clueless on so many issues; he would have to be the greatest actor in the world to be involved. And besides, did you see that note? It was in the same printing as our poems. Something is going to happen here, but what I have no idea. If he were involved, he wouldn't be here on our side of the fence."

"He could have made that note just so he could be with us. I don't like this, Jim. Getting his attention like you did was risky. And why is Debra here?"

Jim was all set to make light of her tagging along, but now with Thomas as a factor, it was not in Jim's best interest to defend her presence. He would have to bite the bullet on this one.

"I was talked into it. Sorry, Mike. Bad judgment on my part."

"Don't sweat it. We all do that from time to time. We'll make the best of it, and I promise not to make her feel unwanted."

With things explained, Mike walked back to Thomas and apologized for his reaction. Then he turned to Debra and smiled.

"Welcome to the world of cops and robbers. Now you see how things can get a bit sticky. I hope my actions didn't frighten you too much."

Debra looked relieved. Jim was sure she thought Mike would come crashing down on her for being there. The group then started to make their plans.

"Shall we ask Thomas to leave?"

Mike decided not to do that.

"If Thomas is the murderer or an accomplice, he will have to force our hand and we'll just have to cope with whatever happens. If he isn't involved, his presence must be required or the invitation would not have been made for him to be here."

So it stood, and the four of them talked at some length about what to look for once they were inside. Interpretation of 'a bag of gold' could mean any number of things. Mike felt it would be a lead that the murderer hoped would send them off in a false direction, thus to bide more time for covering any tracks left undetected as yet.

Jim was feeling the discomfort of the event even more so than earlier. He was almost certain that it was a set up to put them in an unfavorable light with his superiors and get him off the case, which would be beneficial to the murderer. But the how was the uncertainty that Jim did not like. Thomas had no clue as to why he was asked to be there. So the bag of gold meant nothing to him. Debra, however, had a thought that the others had not gleaned from the poem.

"What if the reference to a bag of gold was just a euphemism to cover the real object that might have made our decision to be here unfavorable?"

Jim made a gesture and shook his head.

"That would justify my gut feeling that we are walking into a trap."

"Not a trap, Jim, but a look into the past and possibly the future, both of which might be threatening to us as investigators and shocking to our way of thinking. Something so ludicrous that none of us would even venture a guess as to how something like that could exist. I think what we are going to find is going to threaten our desire to pursue the murderer any further. We are at the morgue, gentlemen. What do you find at the morgue?"

Jim could feel a sweat developing all over him as the words that Debra said sank in. He could see from the paler on Mike's face that Mike was seeing the same thing. It was Jim that spoke next.

"Dead bodies. God, Debra, you think what we are here to find is a dead body? Whose?"

"That is what we don't have a clue about. But it will shock us; I have a feeling it will not be pleasant either."

You could see an uneasiness come over Thomas. He obviously was wishing he had ignored the invitation. Jim and Mike weren't any too happy about being there either. Debra gave out a deep sigh and looked worried. If she turned out to be right, this was the last place on Earth she wanted to be.

The group decided to do the inevitable. Together they walked up to the entrance and entered the morgue.

Upon entering, they proceeded to walk the corridor towards the set of double doors that housed the refrigerated remains of the numerous victims of the day. Jim recalled the all too familiar row of chairs outside the doors and the desk with the coroner just inside them.

But this evening especially, he looked from side to side as they passed closed doors and side corridors, expecting something or someone to jump out at them and threaten their approach. Jim was not usually that unsure of his surroundings, but the words that Debra had said outside just a few moments ago kept repeating over and over in his mind. 'Something ludicrous' she had said. Jim added hideous to that, and sweat was forming on his forehead as they approached the doors.

Once through the doors, they confronted the coroner rather than the mortician at the desk. He was not the one that Jim had seen of late, and after everyone identified themselves, he asked where the other fellow that he had seen might be.

"Oh, it's his day off. We do get days off, you know. Now, I was told you needed to check around the place for something. Wasn't told what, but that it was OK for you to look around. Be my guest."

Mike scratched his head and shook it slowly.

"My friend, if I knew what I was looking for, I'd be eternally grateful."

To Jim's surprise, it was Debra that asked the question that they all knew needed asking.

"Are all the bodies in here accounted for? I mean do you know who they are? Or maybe more to the point, are there any that have arrived recently that have yet to be identified?"

"My dear, if the body is in a drawer, it has been logged in, identified by cause and, if known, named and tagged. If an autopsy is requested, that also is done prior to placement. We do not just put them arbitrarily in a drawer. It's apparent you haven't any knowledge of the system here."

"No, and I'd prefer if you would spare me the details."

Mike decided on a path of action.

"If we are all in agreement and choose Debra's theory as accurate, the obvious thing to do is look inside each drawer for "something." Can we do that, Mister—?"

"Call me Freddy, and your wish is my command."

Debra made a slight gasp.

"Good idea, but not for me. I think I'll snoop around outside this room and see if I can find something that the murderer might have left behind. Or maybe another piece of poetry."

Jim smiled. He knew it would take only so long before the existence of corpses would make Debra uncomfortable. She had reached her limit of tolerance. Without further words, Debra left the group and, while the others went through the task of checking the bodies for some clue as to what they were looking for, decided to walk down some of the side corridors to see whatever there was to see.

It was after hours for the technical staff and the office help, so the corridor was silent except for her own footsteps as she looked from side to side, reading signs on walls and on the numerous doors she passed. The sound of her footsteps echoed around her and as each step was taken, it began to take on a rhythm that etched its way into Debra's mind.

It was almost a macabre beat that caused her to slow down at first, then pick up her pace to change the rhythm as the moments started to drag into minutes, then becoming endless time. Everything became motionless and the noise of her steps even drowned out the beating of her heart as it started to race with a sense of urgency.

As Debra rounded another corner, an unresisting solid substance suddenly pelted her in the stomach, almost knocking the breath out of her. She let out an involuntary cry as she backed away from the object in her path. The cry sounded eerie and ominous as it echoed through the halls. For a moment she felt in a state of panic until her eyes focused in on the object that had struck her. It was a large portable laundry cart that had been left in the middle of the floor.

As Debra's mind absorbed what it was, she felt relieved and, at the same time angry. Not so much at the individual that had left the cart in such a dangerous place, but at herself for having gotten wrapped up in her surroundings to a point where her imagination had taken possession of her mind and body.

Smiling, Debra decided out of curiosity to look into the cart. Her eyes became riveted, and all she could do was scream at the top of her lungs. And scream and scream and scream! What seemed to her like an eternity, Debra could not stop screaming as she heard the sound of many footsteps running in her direction.

Then the sound of Jim's voice behind her broke the chain of screams. She turned and sobbed uncontrollably as Jim wrapped his arms around her trying to comfort her. It was the first time in many years, as far back as Debra could remember, that she cried so hard. Debra was shaking and her trembling went on for minutes before she could regain her composure.

By the time Debra was back in control of herself the others had looked into the cart to see what had triggered such a reaction. Robert Thomas was as pale as a ghost and had gone over to the wall to use it as a support. Mike, though not much better off, did manage to stand back without needing support, but looked dazed. The only one that seemed to be handling themselves well was the coroner. Jim decided it was time for a look.

"Are you going to be all right, Debra?"

Rather sheepishly she whispered to Jim.

"I think so. If you're going to look, prepare to see something grotesque."

Jim squeezed Debra, gave her a kiss on the cheek and walked over to the cart. What he saw was horrid. It was something straight out of some horror movie.

In the cart was the nude body of a woman that appeared to be somewhere in her mid thirties. She had been dismembered, decapitated and disemboweled. Stapled to her forehead was a piece of paper with another poem on it. The coroner seemed to be taking it all in with an air of professional interest.

"Detective, I'd say whoever did this knew their anatomy. See the way the limbs have been removed? Only a skilled person could have done it so clean. No bones damaged; clean cut through the joint. And the head—"

Jim began to feel nauseous.

"Spare me Freddy, please. I'm glad you're impressed. Do you think you could reach in there and retrieve that note for me? I don't think I'm up to it right now."

"Sure thing."

Once the note had been given to Jim, the four of them left Freddy to the task of clean up and placement of the corpse in a drawer. Walking to the entrance of the building, they stepped into the fresh evening air. Debra seemed to be adjusting and was no longer trembling. Mike had regained his color, but Thomas decided he had held back enough and emptied his stomach out near the side of the building. Jim was handling it better than even he would have expected. It took another fifteen minutes before the group could talk about the discovery. Jim took charge of the questions.

"Does anyone have any idea who the woman was?"

"I do, Lieutenant."

It was Thomas, and he seemed to be reacting more than a person would normally. It was evident that he knew the victim.

"She's Marcia Gibbs. She works at Unisearch and took over the case that is connected to the dead body found in my car. All of Barksdale's cases went to various people. She had the apparent misfortune of getting that one."

Now it was evident, Thomas was there for positive identification of the body. Debra had been right about everything. Jim felt like reaching out to her and holding her close. The bond that he felt for her had doubled in the past few minutes. He was proud of her stamina, and felt the hell he knew she had experienced in discovering the corpse. Jim was definitely feeling that this woman would be a perfect wife for him. Hearing Mike's voice broke Jim's thought.

"So we have another victim. That makes three now, right Jim?"

"The senator, Barksdale, and now Gibbs. And we know the murderer is not only ruthless, but vicious as well."

"Not really vicious so much as pursuant to bringing his point across in a manner that you will most likely never forget. Dead is dead, whether whole or in pieces."

Jim was amazed. A statement like that coming from Debra was phenomenal. She may be squeamish, but she was direct in her evaluations. Jim looked at the paper that held the new poem and decided to read it aloud.

A SHAME IT WAS TO END HER LIFE
BUT ALL IS FAIR; IT EASED THE STRIFE.
YOU NOW HAVE PROOF THAT FOR ME THE TOOL
TO WINNING THIS GAME IS MAKING YOU THE FOOL.
END YOUR PURSUIT, FOR THE GAME IS NOT RIGHT
OR THE FUTURE MEANS DEATH AGAIN ANOTHER NIGHT.

Everyone stood silent at the end of the reading. A tear ran down Debra's cheek. Mike took a deep breath and Thomas stood straight and shook his head. No one was uncertain about this message. Keep up the pursuit and someone else dies. The problem was, each one of them knew that the case would continue, and the search for the murderer would continue, and that if someone else fell victim, it was an unavoidable situation.

There was no way the case would remain open and unsolved. Too much had happened, and the government was too involved to just turn its back on the events. *Justice would be served,* thought Jim, *but at the expense of how many lives?* That was yet to be determined.

The group broke up for the night with Mike vowing to get resolution on who the murderer was before another victim was chosen. Robert Thomas would report the loss of his coworker in the morning. Jim and Debra retired to Debra's house for the rest of the evening. Though they felt the need for each other's company, the evening's emotions dampened any thought of making love. But Jim decided to stay the night just to keep Debra from remembering the details. He could still see the shock of it in her eyes; something that would remain there for quite some time.

Chapter 11

It was earlier than usual when Jim arrived at his office the next morning. Nonetheless as he approached, a light could be seen coming from within. Not believing that Mike would be there as yet, Jim figured it had to be Harry. Just as he was looking down and reaching with his key to unlock the door, the light went out, the door opened and a figure emerged that Jim could not quite make out. Before he could look up, whoever it was slammed into Jim knocking him to the floor.

By the time he was able to shake the suddenness of the event and look around all he caught was a glimpse of a tall figure in a police uniform bolting through the stairwell door and disappearing. Getting up off the floor he ran to the stairwell entered it and looked down. The figure had disappeared completely.

Jim walked back to his office and as soon as he went inside he was hit with a picture of total disarray. The file drawers were opened, his desk was in shambles with paper strewn everywhere; everything in the room had been ransacked. It looked to Jim as if he had come upon the perpetrator in the middle of a search unexpectedly. Searching for what, he couldn't even venture a guess. As he was about to look through the papers to ascertain if any were missing Harry walked in.

"What in God's name happened here? It looks like a bloody battle zone!"

"Our friend the intruder was in the midst of searching for something when I arrived. I caught him by surprise. Unfortunately, he also caught me by surprise. Knocked me down and fled down the stairwell before I could do anything. And guess what, Harry? He was wearing a uniform. I don't think it was one of ours. The color looked a bit different."

"Did you get a look at his face?"

"No, it all happened too fast. But from looking at his back, I'd say he was quite tall. That's about it."

"Not much to go on, my friend."

"But it proves something. The door wasn't damaged; the lock is undamaged. I'd say whoever it was had a key."

"But the locksmith swore there were only four keys. Unless the locksmith was lying."

"We'll have to check on him and find out if he has a record, or talk with him to see if there is some way that more keys exist than he is telling us about."

Harry grunted his agreement with Jim, and started to help put things back into some semblance of order. It was almost nine by the time Mike showed up. Jim explained what had transpired and Mike agreed to have his people check into the legitimacy of the locksmith. Then Harry was filled in on the arrest of Dorothy and what had happened at the morgue. Harry was amazed at the activities and stated his usual comment when there were no other words to cover it.

"Pity."

"I'm sorry for being so late this morning. With all that was happening yesterday, I forgot to return the warrant for Dorothy. I stopped at the Courthouse this morning to drop it off. I still had it in my jacket when I got home last night."

Jim and Harry looked at each other and spoke in unison.

"The warrant!"

"What about it?"

Jim could not restrain a small laugh over the discovery.

"That's what our intruder was looking for; the warrant."

"What would the bloke want with that?"

"He was trying to get the name of the judge who issued it. The warrant is the easiest, least conspicuous and most expedient way of finding out."

Mike was fascinated.

"That means he had to go to the Courthouse and ask for a look at it. Discovering it wasn't there must have prompted this morning's visit. He thought it would be here in your office."

"Whoever this person is, he is not only bold, but knowledgeable and resourceful. He's quite an adversary; he had to be informed by someone that the federal courts issued it. The only source I can think of is Dorothy or her lawyer. I'll check that out when I have our little talk today. How did you make out yesterday, Harry?"

Harry sat and shook his head in dismay.

"Poor. The addresses were no help. They all border along Amherst and Tonawanda. Either police could have responded to the calls, depending on the time and workloads. I need to check the names of the responding officers against the Amherst roster to see if they are Amherst police or not. This seems to be leading down a path called a dead end so far."

Mike looked quizzically at Harry.

"Why's that?"

"If this file cabinet belonged to someone, wouldn't you think they would have reported it missing by now?"

Jim pondered on Harry's comment and finally had to admit he had a good point. Mike, paying little attention to the conversation, began to stare at Harry with a look of concern.

"Jim, didn't you say that Harry arrived just as you got back here and began to straighten out the room?"

Harry gave Mike a dirty look. He didn't like the implications that Mike was leading up to.

"Now see here, Mike, don't you start on me. Just because I happened in about the time of Jim's confrontation doesn't mean a thing."

"Maybe so, then maybe not. You could have come in earlier after finding out that the warrant hadn't been turned in last night."

"Damn you Mike, you're not being fair. And besides, the bloody bastard was in uniform. You see me wearing a uniform?"

"But you do own one, don't you Harry? All detectives keep one uniform for dress occasions and special assignments. Your office is only one floor below; ample time to go down a flight of stairs, disappear before Jim could enter the stairwell, then change clothes. And you are tall, Harry."

Jim could see Harry's face becoming red and his fuse about to blow.

"Mike, let's not start accusing one another until all the facts are before us. I would question the locksmith first, then let us see where Dorothy's statements today lead. We've pointed fingers before only to be proven wrong. And really Mike, you do seem to always accuse Harry for being our enemy. He's never given you any reason to doubt him."

"Thanks Jim, but I don't need to be defended. Mike, if you insist on calling me an accomplice or a murderer, you had better have the evidence to prove it, 'cause I'll sue the shit out of you personally, then the FBI collectively, and the United States, if so be it."

"That's enough out of both of you. This is my office; this is a place of business; this is our headquarters for the investigation to which each of us is a team player. A team player; hear me? No more of this unless one is ready to place the other under arrest with cold, hard evidence. Understood Mike?"

Mike, remembering how he had backed down for being wrong and having apologized to Harry once before, nodded in agreement. Harry just sat there and sulked.

As Jim was about to proceed with the discussion on the file cabinet, the lock on the door turned and in stepped Debra. She appeared in much better shape than she had looked the evening before. She greeted Jim with a big smile, and a hello to Mike and Harry.

"I'm not too late for the big discussion on where to head next, am I?"

"Don't you work for an insurance company, or something? Don't they miss you?"

"Why Mike, how rude! I thought you wanted me as a team member on this case. And after last night, I certainly earned that right."

Jim made a soft chuckle and informed Mike of something he knew would be unappreciated.

"Debra has taken a small leave of absence from her job just so she could be with us a hundred percent of the time and provide her fair share of the work."

Mike gave Jim a look as if to say 'oh great' but without the happiness normally associated with a statement like that. Harry stood up in a gesture of defeat.

"Fine. You can take my place. I've had enough of the harassment being handed out."

"Sit down Harry! Just give the moment a little room to air and you'll see things in a better light."

"What's happened? Something happened, didn't it?"

Jim filled Debra in on the events of the morning. Debra listened intently. Then she made some remarkable evaluations.

"Listen, all of you."

She looked at Mike.

"Mike, I'm no fool. I realize you really preferred I not be fully involved. But I have the ability to compliment the three of you with direction and insight. From the perspective of a civilian, if you prefer that analogy.

"I see what you miss because I can visualize something without the clouds of regulation and experience. It is sometimes a help when you are confronted with a new situation. And it definitely helps when you get so wrapped up in using procedures and guidelines."

Mike had to smile at her. She had him evaluated fairly well. Then she turned to Harry.

"Harry, you are a bull-headed Englishman. That can be useful, but most of the time it gets in the way of your seeing reality. Mike sees you as a possible threat in this case. He is only using instinct and what he evaluates as ability and accessibility to make you suspect. If the roles were reversed, I'll bet you would be down his back with suspicions. Be open-minded; see his point of view. He didn't know you two weeks ago, and he only has his heartfelt desire to solve this case in mind. Work with him, not against him. Take the steps necessary to show Mike your position and trustworthiness. The truth always prevails. At least I hope it will in this case."

Harry admired Debra. Jim's choice of a mate was a good one. He was almost ready to eat crow. Almost.

Then Debra faced Jim. She smiled and gently touched his chin.

"And as for you, Mister Lieutenant. Stop trying to be the buffer between two rivals. Show leadership and direction instead. You have a special talent. It's time you applied it."

Jim took a deep breath and smiled.

"And what about you, Debra? What have you come up with that makes you so much wiser than us?"

Debra turned to all of them, a look of cunning on her face.

"We have here a definite case of treachery and I'm willing to bet none of you have even resolved the most obvious question. Why was the senator's double murdered in the first place? I'm not the expert, but I thought the first thing you look at is motive. So? What is the motive, gentlemen?"

For the first time all three looked at each other and realized that the question of motive had not really been answered. Why was all this taking place? Was it for money? To shut someone up who had discovered something that was not meant to be known? Revenge? Politics? Greed? An international plot? A mistake?

In disbelief, the three of them just looked at each other. It had taken a civilian to enlighten them to the fact that they had no idea why all this was happening.

Mike stood up and looked at Debra with a new sense of admiration.

"Debra, I'll be the first to admit I really didn't want a woman's presence on this case. But you have added to this team more wisdom and direction than I could ever have. From now on you are welcomed as an equal to assist us in any way possible. And I'll be damned if I know why this case ever erected its ugly head. Someone here give me an idea."

"The answer as to motive lies in the files of Unisearch. Mike, I recommend you obtain a warrant to have the files of all the cases for, oh say the last three years involving the loss of a life while the case was still active, removed from Unisearch for close review. Call it suspicion of foul play by Unisearch. I will go through the files and see if there are any similarities to any of them. I suspect the motive to our murder stems from attempts at extortion that, when fought off by the targeted recipient, ends up in their demise."

Mike's eyebrows lifted. Harry opened his eyes wide. Jim looked at Debra in awe.

"And what makes you come up with extortion as the motivator leading to murder?"

"Because, if my guess is right, all of the victims in those cases will be people of wealth and influence. Those types usually have a skeleton in their closet, making them an ideal target."

"But what about our victim in this case?"

"Since he wasn't the real senator, he was ideal for backing into a corner with threats of exposing him as a fake. The double would have worked a deal that would keep his secret and give the extortionists their booty. It must have been a real shocker when the double said he wouldn't go for the deal."

"Nice theory, Debra. It's certainly worth a look see, right Mike?"

Mike wanted to express reluctance in letting Harry run with the information they would obtain. Letting go of his feelings about Harry's possible involvement was tough. There were so many 'what ifs' that Mike decided it was best to let things happen. He would definitely keep a watchful eye on Harry. Mike faced Jim with a proposal.

"How sincere do you think you can make yourself sound when talking with Dorothy today? I would like you to give her the feeling that we have hard evidence linking her to the murder of not just our victim, but many victims."

Jim sat back and stared at Harry. Harry raised his hands in a gesture of surrender.

"I've come to the inevitable conclusion that Dorothy is in deeper than I thought. She's fair game, and I'm out twenty bucks."

As the two let out a small laugh, Debra wondered what that was all about, but decided not to ask. Jim looked at Mike.

"Mike, if it's a game of bluff you want, I can be the most convincing person on Earth. Just be sure that you don't abandon me if the tables get turned again. How far do you suggest I go?"

"All the way. I want her so shaken that you know so much that she is ready to finger the murderer just to save her ass."

"And if the lawyer calls a halt to my questions until we produce what we say we have?"

"Even more convincing than the questioning. Dorothy will interpret that as the lawyer feeling sure that we know something that he needs to be informed of. The proverbial 'catch 22' where everything comes full circle. You know that I know that you know that I know…that's pretty much the idea."

Debra sat there and reveled at what she was hearing.

"Does that kind of deceit go on routinely, or is this Dorothy a special case?"

Jim answered Debra with caution in mind.

"It's not a common practice, but if you had met Dorothy you would understand the need for such tactics."

"Can I be present at the meeting?"

Jim smiled softly at Debra. He knew how much she wanted to be a participant in the case.

"Sorry Debra, but these meetings are done in the auspices of confidentiality. You are not an official of this department, or of the police for that matter. It would not be permissible."

Jim could see disappointment on Debra's face. He would love to have her sit in, but if anyone found out she shouldn't have been there, any information or admissions made during the meeting would be inadmissible in a trial. Debra smiled back, understanding and trusting Jim's explanation.

"I need some time to organize my thoughts before confronting Dorothy and her lawyer. The appointment I set up is approaching quicker than you might think."

"Fine. I need to leave anyway to obtain the search warrant for Unisearch's files personally, especially since I have a close connection with the judge in the court."

Jim felt it would be important to the case having a second party on their side attending the meeting and invited Harry to attend. Harry was pleasantly surprised to be considered important, especially after Mike's accusations.

Debra stood up.

"And I need to take care of a few personal matters at my office. I'll return later when the files have been obtained."

Once Mike and Debra were gone, Jim and Harry spent the next hour reviewing strategy and what the hopes for the results of the meeting with Dorothy would produce.

"Harry, I feel confident I will get a confession and some indication as to the murderer's identity."

"I must reluctantly admit that Dorothy is guilty of some participation in the murder. I may be able to get Dorothy so stirred up she might slip and give some important leads in resolving the reason for the murder."

Both agreed to put on one hell of a performance in the attempt to break Dorothy down.

As the hour for the meeting approached, Jim and Harry left the office and headed for the Holding Center. They walked briskly along West Eagle and around the corner to the entrance of the Holding Center, just in time to avoid a sudden downpour.

"I sometimes wonder if Mother Nature doesn't plan these outbursts just to get people to pay attention to her."

"Bloody devilish planning, if she does. Pity."

Though a gloomy day weatherwise, both men hoped their meeting would be much brighter.

They checked in at the front desk, obtained the conference room assigned to the meeting and was informed that Dorothy and her lawyer were already in the room. As they walked towards the room, Jim could sense Harry tensing up in anticipation of confronting Dorothy.

"Thinking of what to say to her?"

"More afraid of what she'll say to **me** is what I'm not looking forward to."

"Harry, there's always a price to pay for being a romantic."

"Eh what? A hellish payment to be sure."

Jim felt sorry for his subordinate, and almost sympathetic to Harry's feelings. Harry's dream of being in a torrid love affair had been short lived.

When the two entered the room, they were greeted by an angry stare from Dorothy and a very abrupt hello from her lawyer Roger Sexton. Jim and Harry sat opposite the two and were immediately bombarded by rhetorical claims of prejudicial treatment and illegal procedures.

"There had better be something this time to back up your abuse of Dorothy's rights. She pays taxes, just like all of us. She has never been guilty of any wrongdoing. An upstanding citizen in a country that believes in the protection of everyone's privacy. And need I remind you, always innocent until proven guilty?"

Jim and Harry just sat there and let Roger spout off. After about five minutes, Roger ran out of words and sat in silence waiting for Jim to speak. Jim smiled at Roger and Dorothy and gave the first remark of the meeting that meant anything.

"I hope that the two of you have made some serious considerations as to what you plan to do regarding this case. I, that is the County and the Federal Government, have decided that with everything we have on Dorothy, the charge of accessory to murder on several counts will put Dorothy away for the rest of her life."

Jim watched as the color drained from Dorothy's face leaving a chalk like appearance in her cheeks. Roger Sexton looked like he could be on the verge of shock.

"What the hell do you mean by 'several counts'? You have arrested my client on suspicion involving one murder. I'd like you to explain yourself before we proceed any further."

Harry began to feel the pace of the conversation and picked up the next response.

"The senator was first, followed by Richard Barksdale, and as of yesterday, Marcia Gibbs. And involvement in the breaking, entering and tampering with the evidence in this case will be another charge."

"To say nothing of interfering with the due process of law and involvement in several other suspicious deaths associated with Unisearch and Dorothy."

Jim had interjected the fearful additional jeopardy. Dorothy made a gasp and, as she tried to speak, could only manage a barely audible whisper.

"What are you saying? Marcia Gibbs dead? Other cases? What else have you found, and how?"

Jim's magic touch had worked once again. Dorothy had made a concession that she had some other skeleton's to hide. Roger broke in with a blunt word at Dorothy.

"Shut up! Look, Jim, I demand to know what you have as evidence to make such an accusation. And why the hell is this going through the Federal Courts? As counselor for the defendant, I demand to be told."

Jim was feeling a sense of achievement. Even Roger was taking the bate. And Mike was right about the effect of that, as Dorothy was now totally ashen in paler. Her lips were quivering and she shifted nervously from left to right as she spoke.

"Jim! Harry! Please tell me what's going on."

Her words were choked and strained, her voice shaky. This was not the Dorothy they were used to seeing and hearing. This was a person in a state of panic. It had taken only a little over a minute to transform the arrogant and confident Dorothy into a person in obvious fear of God. Jim added the final touch to the presentation.

"Your partner in crime, the murderer, paid me a visit this morning, only he didn't expect to find me in so early. I managed to get some information out of him that was quite interesting."

Now you could see Dorothy was becoming unnerved. Roger sat back, a sweat forming on his brow. Surprisingly, it was the lawyer that added the first piece of information.

"If you're referring to the warrant not being available after Dorothy's arrest, I can only say that I enquired at the Courthouse, found it hadn't been turned in, and told Dorothy later that evening not to worry. I would find out who issued it and get this resolved quickly. I spoke to no one else."

Then a very embarrassed Roger blurted a quick cover your ass statement that Dorothy had no contact with the outside either during her incarceration last night as he realized how his comment might implicated his client. It was Harry who picked up on the next nail for Dorothy's coffin.

"How would you know that, Roger?"

Proudly Roger stated his admission to suggesting to a close contact he had in the Holding Center that Dorothy should not be permitted to use the phone or see any visitors just as a precaution. He failed to realize that this kind of a move could be interpreted as Roger not having full confidence in his client's innocence. Jim added some spice to the recipe.

"How do you know it would be someone outside of the jail that she would make contact with?"

Roger gave Jim a blank stare and just sat silently with his mouth open. Dorothy, however, made a fatal mistake by responding to Jim's query.

"He had no idea who I would talk to, if I needed to talk to someone. I swear Jim, I had no idea making conversation with that cop would lead to anything. I'd never met him before, not ever. Honest!"

The guilty, usually thinking that saying the opposite to the truth would exonerate them, was a typical and always fatal move. Jim wished he'd had more knowledge of the workings of thought processes. He would forever be fascinated by the rational of the criminal mind.

To protect her lawyer, Dorothy had admitted speaking to a cop. Then by saying she never knew the officer and would not expect it to be harmful gave away that she knew Jim's intruder was in uniform. How very interesting.

Harry, absorbing all that was being said, made a move that even Harry was surprised at, coming from himself.

"So, you know Jim's intruder was in uniform, you speak to someone in uniform while in jail who you claim not to know, and yet aren't really involved in a murder of various people within the structure of Unisearch whether client or employee. How much crap do you think we can handle at one time. You know who our murderer is, and so do we. Why don't you come clean and fess up to the bloody fact that we have you dead to rights. The bloke you paid to kill all those people wouldn't waste a minute nailing your ass to protect his."

"Is that what he told you? That I paid him to do it? That bastard!"

Dorothy had been caught up in the moment and resurrected her old self, only to realize that she had just said the wrong thing. Roger Sexton was still silent, but not for long.

"Dorothy, keep your big mouth shut! Gentlemen, I think we had better stop this meeting and reschedule after you have properly informed myself and my client of all the charges against her. Apparently you have a lot more than the original charge to place on her. And I need to have a long talk with my client before making any further conversation."

Jim tried to throw one more attempt out at getting a name.

"And how many more people will die while you wait, Dorothy? You know he's ruthless. Would he protect you like this?"

"Frank would—" Dorothy was immediately cut off.

"That is enough! Detective, you are exceeding your boundaries. One more word and I shall personally see that you are thrown off this case."

Jim apologized with the sound of sincerity and left the room with Harry. However, the damage had been done. Dorothy had given him at least the first name. She had also implicated herself even further. As he and Harry walked towards the entrance to the Holding Center, Harry smiled and turned towards Jim.

"That was a fantastic piece of work, old boy. Smooth. Polished. I shall take lesson and perfect the tactic for myself when and if I need it."

"Why thank you, Harry. I'm flattered."

The rain had let up sufficiently for the two to make their way around the corner and into headquarters. Once in the confines of Jim's office, a quick call to the locksmith that had provided the lock on Jim's office door produced a startling piece of information.

As with any special security lock, for emergency purposes, one copy is given to a central security office to hold. It is never circulated or used, just stored by number and registered along with documentation as to where the lock it fits is installed. No one has access to it but the locksmith or an official of the department or company that was issued the lock.

Jim asked if there was a phone number that he could use to call and ensure that the key was indeed still where it should be. There was, and Jim wrote it down, thanked the locksmith, and hung up. After checking the key's status using the phone number he had been given, Jim leaned back and looked at Harry.

"Guess what."

"Don't tell me. The key was picked up shortly after it had been registered by a policeman that said he worked for you. Am I right?"

"Almost. The policeman asked for it, but instead of taking it, was thoughtful enough to return it after making a copy for 'emergencies.' Wasn't that thoughtful of our murderer?"

"Pity."

"My sentiments exactly. I think he hoped no one would know the additional copy had been made. Now that we know, I suppose it best we ask the locksmith to install a new lock."

"What for, Jim? One, the murderer will only figure another way to get a copy. Two, now that we've set Dorothy into a panic course, and we no longer trust anything as safe in here, why worry about a lock anymore?"

Two valid points. But, once Mike returned and was appraised of what had happened at the meeting and about the extra key, it was decided by Mike to install another lock anyway. It was almost one o'clock, so they decided to order subs and wait for Debra before proceeding. Debra arrived as promised, and the discussion as to what to do next started off with a bang. It was from Debra.

"I had a chance to take another closer look at our files on Frank Spencer while in my office. He listed on his application for insurance that his occupation was a retired officer of the Navy."

Mike looked nonchalantly at Debra.

"So? That's true; we all know that."

"But for his present occupation at that time he didn't list Unisearch. Not originally. It was modified a week after application. You'll never guess what he had originally."

All agreed they couldn't guess.

"Law enforcement officer with Erie County."

Mike looked suddenly very interested.

"What branch?"

"Not determined. He was at the academy and hadn't selected a branch. Apparently something changed and he dropped the academy for Unisearch."

Jim snapped his fingers.

"That's the difference in color! He was wearing the color of an officer in training."

Mike spoke up.

"That explains the lapse of time between his retirement and his being listed as employed by Unisearch. And Dorothy let it slip that our murderer's first name is Frank. People, the puzzle is beginning to come together. It looks very much like our murderer is none other than Frank Spencer. Hard as it may seem, our Navy Seal is using his skills for benefiting his and Dorothy's pocket book. But what is he doing now? He's dropped out of site even from our own intelligence people. We now know it was intentional in order to commit these heinous acts of profit by murder. But where is he, and what is his disguise?"

Once again Debra had proven to the group her value. Jim was proud. Debra looked over at him and gave him a big smile. It was obvious she loved being part of the group. It was also obvious she enjoyed making Jim proud of her. Jim could visualize a future evolved around the two of them. Not only in a personal relationship, but a business relationship as well. Maybe a team endeavor in the business of solving crimes that was hitherto unsolved.

Mike broke Jim's reverie.

"Another point I've been meaning to mention is that we may have lucked out and caught our murderer on video tape. I was made aware that a surveillance system was installed in the morgue just a few months ago. The murderer may not have been aware of that bit of information."

Harry's eyebrows went up.

"Neither was I. A bit of luck may be headed our way, eh Jim?"

The phone rang bringing the discussion to a halt. Jim answered, made a few brief yes or no comments, grunted, shook his head, thanked the party at the other end and hung up. Debra was the first to ask.

"What was that all about?"

Jim looked at her and winked.

"That was the clerk at the Federal Courthouse. She was asked by the judge to inform us that an attempt by an individual in uniform to request a copy of the warrant issued for Dorothy's arrest was made about an hour ago. He identified himself as my second in charge of the murder case and that I wished to have a copy for my files. One of the judges happened to be entering the hall from his chambers and overheard the officer. Suspicious of such an unusual request, he stopped and asked for some evidence that he was working for me. The man turned and bolted through the door and into the street. He disappeared before anyone could follow and detain him."

Mike was very interested in the incident.

"What made the judge suspicious enough to confront the man?"

"Because the person was in uniform. Usually a second in charge would be a ranking officer. And my second would be a detective, not a uniformed officer. The judge was very sharp to pick up on that."

Mike stood up and turned towards the door.

"I had better get over to Unisearch and pick up those files. Debra, I'd say you can count on seeing them by late this afternoon."

Debra nodded.

"Would it be inappropriate if I take them to my house? The security here is no longer in effect. Actually, it appears it never was to begin with."

Mike began to object and then changed his mind.

"Sure, why not. Just be sure to bring them in tomorrow morning. And Jim, check and see if and when we can get a look at that surveillance tape from the morgue. I've got some things to attend to, so I'll see you all here tomorrow morning."

Jim agreed and Mike left. The rest of the afternoon was spent discussing the possibilities of who Frank Spencer was masquerading as, and why he was using so much effort to finding the name of the judge that issued the warrant.

Jim had the locksmith come and put a new lock on the door, obtained and distributed the keys, and told the locksmith to have a note left at security that no one was to have the spare without calling for personal verification by Jim. Jim held onto the fourth key to give to Mike tomorrow. Harry left around five, and at five thirty the files from Unisearch arrived.

Jim helped Debra take them to her car and agreed to meet her at her place later. Jim was confident that the evening would be wonderful, and that tomorrow would be very enlightening.

Chapter 12

Mike arrived around eight thirty to find the office locked. His key didn't work, and he assumed the lock had been changed the day before. That didn't bother him, but what did was that no one was around. It was not like Jim or Harry to be later than a few minutes past eight o'clock. He went to the break room for coffee and as he entered the area met up with Harry, who was also headed in that direction.

"Good morning, Harry. How come you're not in the office? And where's Jim and Debra?"

"I forgot to change keys on my chain. I still have the bloody old one and couldn't get in. And I haven't the foggiest idea what happened to Jim. Not like him, being late and not phoning in."

Now that it was evident that the murderer was not Harry, and that Harry was innocent of being an accomplice, Mike felt more at ease as they talked. He was glad that he had not pursued his instinct to come down on Harry the other day. Even though he knew Harry still held harsh resentment, there was a new attitude being exhibited.

Mike no longer was a threat to Harry, and a better relationship was being shared. Harry even made a couple of efforts at humor to which Mike tried showing appreciation, even though the dry English humor was hard for Mike to understand. By nine o'clock the two felt uneasy and concerned, so they headed back to Jim's office. It was still locked and unoccupied.

Harry went downstairs to his office, which he hardly occupied any longer, and called Jim's home. Only the answering machine came on line. Not knowing Debra's number, he decided to head home to exchange keys so he could open the office for Mike and make some effort at working on the case. As he was about to leave, his phone rang. Picking it up, he was startled to hear the voice of Jim at the other end.

"Harry, I'm glad I got a hold of you. Listen; there's been some big trouble at Debra's house. I can't go into details now, but grab Mike and head over here. I'll give you directions. Hurry!"

Harry wrote down the directions, went back upstairs to get Mike, and then the two headed for the street and Harry's car.

"What's happened Harry?"

"Damned if I know. Jim sounded tired and upset. He wouldn't tell me. Just said to hurry. Bloody crazy way to start a day."

Harry decided on a little fanfare and used his bubble and siren all the way to Debra's house. Harry liked using them once in a while, just to remind himself that there was at times the need for urgency. Besides, he liked the feeling of power it gave him as cars moved out of his way while he sped along at twice the speed limit. Whether it was necessary or not was irrelevant.

Arriving at Debra's house was like arriving at a parking lot full of people desperately trying to vie for the one last spot available. It was mass confusion with people lining the curb trying to make out what was happening.

An ambulance was backed into the driveway, its back doors open. No one was inside it, but the flashing of the lights indicated it had arrived for an emergency. There were a few police cars parked so as to block any cars from entering the area. One was a City of Buffalo patrol car; the rest were Amherst Police vehicles. Harry and Mike got out and headed for the front door of the house. A police officer hailed them down.

"Hold on there! Who are you people?"

"Erie County Sheriff's Department. I got a call from my superior to get over here fast. What's going on?"

"Some ID please."

Harry showed his ID and Mike followed suit.

"FBI? What's your stake in this?"

"Where checking into the efficiency of the various law enforcement groups in this vicinity."

The officer did not find the humor in Mike's remark.

"Very funny, wise guy."

Harry was becoming impatient.

"Look, I need to report to my superior. May we go in?"

"Sure, just knock. There are police officers inside. Just show your ID and you're in."

Then he looked at Mike.

"Maybe you'd better be more polite, or they may ask you to wait outside."
Now it was Mike that did not find the humor in the remark.

The two approached the door and knocked. A female officer opened it and, after showing her their ID, they were allowed to enter. What Harry and Mike saw once inside sent chills through them. As they approached a room towards the rear, they could hear the moans of someone in severe pain.

They turned to enter the room and were confronted by the site of blood smears on the walls and in the carpet. Debra was lying in a bed, the sheets covering her drenched in blood. At her side were two people in white. A third with a stethoscope was listening to Debra's chest as they held onto her wrist.

An IV was strung in a makeshift fashion next to her and was attached to Debra's other arm. Next to the IV stood Jim, his shirt covered almost completely in blood. He was looking on with a grim expression. He looked up at the two as they entered the room.

"Harry. Mike. I'm sure glad to see you both."

"What the hell happened, Jim?"

Jim started to speak, but for the moment seemed breathless. His eyes were red, tell tail signs that he had been crying a lot. Jim tried to speak again, took a couple of deep breaths, and managed a few words.

"That bastard tried to kill Debra."

Emotion set in again as Jim turned away to hide the flow of tears. Harry had never seen Jim so emotional. Jim was a seasoned police officer; tough to most anything. But having been so close to Debra, it was his first taste of being struck in a personal way. Even Harry, who wasn't close to Debra as Jim was, felt an emotional rush at seeing her in that state.

"God, man, who did this?"

"Our murderer. Frank Spencer. He tried to waste Debra while she was reading the files this morning."

With some effort, Jim related to Harry and Mike how Debra had felt restless during the night, so she got up early and began to look through the files from Unisearch. Jim had decided to dress and go into the kitchen to make them some breakfast.

As he was preparing the meal he heard a muffled scream coming from the bedroom. Thinking Debra had stumbled onto some pertinent information, he slowly walked out of the kitchen and turned towards the bedroom. He called out to her asking what she had found. There was a loud thud followed by a loud scream. As he raced towards the bedroom he saw the figure of the same man he had seen the day before in his office run out of the bedroom and head out the door, which was ajar.

Jim felt he had better check on Debra before pursuing the man and was confronted by the sight of Debra hanging backwards off the side of the bed, her breasts bare and blood flowing out from a gash in her chest. Acting quickly he ran to her and lifted her so that her head rested on the mattress. Then he applied pressure to the open wound. Finally he took the top sheet and made a makeshift tourniquet to minimize the bleeding while he got to the phone and called 911.

Then he raced back to Debra, knowing the sheet would be almost useless for any length of time, and sat there with his hands over the wound, hoping to prevent her from bleeding to death.

"He must have slipped in the front door while I was in the kitchen, not knowing I was in the house. That makes twice I've surprised him. He obviously intended to kill her and make off with the files, but my presence thwarted his getting at the files. But he did manage to stab Debra, hoping to kill her. I wonder why he was so hell bent on killing her? He had failed at his purpose for being here, so why commit the act anyway?"

"A matter of indifference. An instinct. Who knows. Remember, he is a trained killer."

The doctor that had been checking Debra's vital signs interrupted Jim.

"She's got an elevated pulse and rapid heart beat. I can't tell now how much internal bleeding is taking place, but you did a great job of preventing a massive amount of blood from being lost through the wound. We'd better get her into the hospital and surgery ASAP. I'll need you there as soon as you get yourself cleaned up. You're sure some of that blood isn't yours?"

"I wish, Doc. No, I'm OK. Give me about an hour and I'll be there."

At this point, as the attendants started to move Debra onto the stretcher, Jim caught sight of Debra moving her lips. Her eyes were still closed, but her consciousness was beginning to return. She seemed to be mouthing a name, but Jim could not quite make out what it was. He leaned over to her, placing his ear up to her lips, but by that time Debra had become unconscious again. He kissed her gently on the lips, hoping to stir her back to awareness, but to no avail.

"Sorry sir, but we had better move fast."

Jim stepped back, apologized, and watched as the attendants wheeled Debra to the door then out to the ambulance. Harry felt the horror of what had happened begin to sink in. Though Debra was a civilian, Harry thought of her only as a team player that had been violated. He took it as a personal violation upon himself as well. Much the same as if another officer had been downed, his only thought was to find the person responsible for the attack on Debra, and make him pay dearly for it.

He grabbed Jim by the shoulder and squeezed it.

"She'll make it, Jim. She's too good a person to loose her life like this. And besides, she hasn't finished reviewing those files yet. She'd better recover quickly. We need her."

Jim, realizing that this was Harry's way of consoling him, smiled and gave Harry his due.

"Pity."

Harry smiled back at Jim. He knew exactly how Jim felt. Mike began to walk around the bedroom examining the bed from different angles. Then he lifted a folder smeared with blood from where it had been beside the pillow and looked at its contents. He seemed to be concentrating on a particular part with a great deal of interest. Jim was not ready for investigating anything at this moment and made Mike aware of it before Mike got any ideas about lengthy discussions.

"I really need to stop by my place to shower and get some fresh clothing. I called on the two of you to come here so you could pick up the files and take them to headquarters. Make sure they get into no other hands but yours. Whatever is in them, it seems important enough to kill for."

Then he reached into his pants pocket and produced a key, which he handed to Mike.

"New lock. As soon as I've seen that Debra is out of surgery and any danger, I'll meet you at the office."

With that said, Jim headed out the door and to his car. Mike and Harry collected the files, including the one Mike had been looking at, and headed out the door towards their car. The officer that had met them when they first arrived walked over and opened the back door for them.

"Looks like those files are mighty important. Hard to figure what goes through the mind of a murderer. This one seems to know his stuff. Entered the house without a sound, no key, and almost got away with murder, so to speak."

Harry just gave the officer a dirty look. He was in no mood for a playful play on words. Mike, however, seized the moment to compliment the officer and simultaneously ask a question that was bothering him.

"Clever wording. Incidentally, how come there's a Buffalo Police car here. Isn't he out of his jurisdiction to be answering a call in this community?"

"Funny thing about that. When we arrived, it was parked right where you see it now. No one around to claim it either. We think it was the vehicle used by the attacker to arrive in. Neighbors say the man fleeing down the street on foot was wearing the uniform of a policeman. If it was his car, you'd think he'd use it to escape in, wouldn't you?"

"Not if he wasn't authorized to use it. I'll wager it was stolen from their garage and hasn't been missed yet."

"For FBI you're pretty sharp. As a matter of fact, it was just reported missing about fifteen minutes ago. I guess you government types aren't all that bad. Just have a bad wrap, that's all."

Mike smiled demonically at the officer and decided to bite his tongue and say nothing. The words forming in his mind would only aggravate and stir up resentment. Enough friction between agencies already existed.

Harry thanked the officer for his help, got into his car and listened to Mike cursing under his breath as he got into the passenger side and slammed the door shut.

"That guy is on my shit list."

Harry smiled.

"Pity."

Harry removed the bubble from atop the car and decided to make the ride back to headquarters in more of a relaxed fashion. It took almost forty minutes from door to door, and once in Jim's office, Harry called the morgue and asked about reviewing the surveillance tapes.

He was given the name of the security division that would have the tape from the day before, called them, and made arrangements for two o'clock that afternoon to see them. While Harry did this, Mike made use of the time by reopening the folder he had been looking at in Debra's house. He kept looking at the top paper, turning it around inside the folder in several positions. Harry noticed Mike's behavior and once finished with the arrangements, looked curiously at Mike.

"I give up. What the hell are you looking at so intently?"

"This."

Mike handed Harry the sheet of paper he had been examining. He began to read it, finding what it was about to be of little interest.

"No, Harry, not the words. Don't read it, look at it."

Harry looked at it. At first he thought Mike was going crazy. Then it struck him what Mike was talking about. There was a waving streak going around the corners of the paper, and then moving down into the text of the paper. The streak had been made in blood.

"Don't you see, Harry? Debra tried to give us a clue, using her own blood as a marker."

"A clue to what, Mike?"

"Who her attacker was. You know, the murderer we are looking for."

"You mean she recognized her attacker? God, Mike, that means we know who the murderer is, we just don't know 'who' he is."

"Exactly. We know it's Frank Spencer, but we don't know who Frank Spencer is, not in his present character. Debra seems to know him. But as who?"

"That also answers the question as to why he tried to kill her regardless of his failure to grab the files. The killer knows she recognized him. Damn, that's bad news. That also means Debra's life is still in danger. Once he learns she's not dead, he'll try again. I'd better send some deputies to the hospital right away. She'll need protection. A twenty-four-hour watch is the only way."

"Good idea."

Harry made the necessary phone calls while Mike kept looking at the path of the mark left by Debra. It circled only three quarters of the edge of the paper, and then traveled down to a point just below the list of names that apparently represented the people involved in the case folder. What puzzled Mike was why it circled first then led down through all the names on the list. It really didn't point to any one person. Harry told Mike all was taken care of, looked at the paper once again, and marveled at Mike's inept approach.

"Mike, you must realize that Debra had precious few seconds once stabbed before she passed out. Not much time to think of using her own blood as a source for writing, let alone do the graphics you suggest. She went directly to the name she recognized on the paper. You've got the trail backwards. All the rest was the result of her becoming unconscious."

Of course. Mike felt somewhat foolish, but sensed no animosity in Harry's words. He looked at the end of the streak of blood to the last name on the list. Walter Greider. The name struck no bells; sent no messages. Who the hell was Walter Greider?

"What we need to do here Mike is to look at some of the other files to see if that name appears in other cases. It has to be the common link that ties all these cases to our murderer."

With that said, the two began to furiously thumb through the other files looking for the name of Walter Grieder and the link that would place him as their murderer, Frank Spencer. As they lost themselves in the search, time flew by, and it was only the sound of the lock on the door that roused them to awareness that it was nearly two o'clock. It was Jim, looking like death warmed over. Harry thoughtfully asked the results of the surgery on Debra.

"She's strong willed, thank God! The doctor said she was lucky that the knife had barely missed some vital organs and that she would recover. When I left she was still asleep from the sedation. I thought it best to come in and see where we are with this case. The hospital will call me as soon as she awakens."

Mike gave a reassuring pat on Jim's shoulder.

"I'm glad for both of you. And just in time, as we are scheduled to view that surveillance tape at two."

The three left, headed downstairs to Harry's car, and as they drove to the security offices where the tape was, Harry filled Jim in on the blood smear and the name that Debra had indicated on the paper.

"So far there seems to be no other case file with this Walter Greider's name in it. We're baffled as to who this bloke is and how Debra recognized him."

Jim had no explanations either, so the subject was left on hold as they parked and found their way into the building that housed the security agency. Once they identified themselves and their reason for being there, they were escorted to a small room that had a large television screen against one wall and a row of seats facing the screen, much like a little mini theater.

Behind the seats was a small table where a VCR had been set up. They seated themselves as the room lights began to dim until there was barely any light. Then the sound of a tape being inserted in the VCR followed by a faint hum made the room take on a ghostly illumination as the picture began to be visible on the screen.

The three of them watched intently as the events of yesterday at the morgue were shown from several different points in the building. The tape was a composite of recordings from many cameras. The time was shown at the upper right hand corner of the picture, and the location at the lower right hand corner. Harry, being most familiar with the layout of the morgue, asked that certain corridors and hallways be specifically displayed, and to start from late afternoon, as that would be more likely to have been the time that their murderer would have brought the body of Marcia Gibbs into the building. Any sooner would have been too risky and the chance of the wrong people discovering the corpse more probable.

As the footage was scanned rapidly to the point Harry had suggested, the view of the activities of the morgue by day almost resembled an old silent film, with people's movements jerky and rapid, so characteristic of the early days of movies. Approaching the five o'clock time of day, the footage slowed to its normal pace. The people were walking out of their offices and heading for exits, some waving to an acquaintance, others ignoring their surroundings so as to avoid any delay in leaving. Within a few minutes the halls were void of activity other than the few stragglers and then, finally, no one.

The tape scanned the areas Harry had requested in a random pattern. The camera in the main corridor indicated five-fifteen PM. The shadow of a person became reflected on the wall as someone was walking in the direction of the double doors leading to the morgue's refrigeration vaults. The three onlookers sat up in their chairs in anticipation of seeing for the first time their intruder and murderer. Suddenly the back of the head became visible in the camera lens. It was the coroner. Jim relaxed back in his chair. For a moment he thought he would see Debra's attacker. He wasn't sure if he was relieved or disappointed. Mike uttered a profanity, while Harry gave his usual 'Pity' and both settled back in their seats.

More time elapsed as the view shifted from the main corridor to the secondary side halls, changing the view on a minute-to-minute basis. The clock ticked on. Five thirty. Five forty. As the tape started to change to the main corridor once again, Jim caught a momentary glimpse of what appeared to be the large cart that had held the body of Marcia Gibbs rounding the corner.

"Hold it! Stop! Go back to that hallway. Pick it up at the exact time it was a moment ago. I think we're about to meet our murderer."

All three of the men sat straight in their seats. There was total silence with the exception of the VCR as it hummed quietly and created the picture on the screen. The clock at the corner of the screen read five forty two. As the cart rounded the corner and headed away from the camera lens, the figure of a tall man in a police uniform emerged onto the screen. Jim recognized the back of the murderer instantly. He had seen that view twice before. Mike and Harry sat with their eyes glued to the screen.

Jim could now hear the sound of heavy breathing. It took only a moment to realize it was his own breathing that had become heavy and rapid. More than anything, he wanted to see the face of this master of disguise and possessor of a cold-blooded heart. A sweat had developed on his brow.

The figure stopped at the end of the hall at a corner where it intersected with another hallway. With deliberate movement he placed the cart so it would be an obstacle for anyone rounding the corner from the other hallway to enter that one. Then, backing away from the cart, the figure turned to retreat back down the hall he had arrived from, facing the camera lens. Jim's eyes almost strained and felt riveted to the image on the screen. Then a loud voice broke the silence. It was Mike.

"Freeze the picture! That's him! That's Frank Spencer. I recognize him from a photo I saw of him back at the agency."

Jim's mouth had opened in an attempt to speak, but no sound escaped from his throat. He was in awe of what he saw. Harry noticed the expression on Jim's face and made mention of it to Mike. Mike looked at Jim and began to prod Jim to say something.

"What's got your tongue, Jim. Out with it before the thought consumes you."

Jim looked at the screen, where the picture had been frozen at that spot so that all of them could see plainly the face of the man they were seeking.

"So that's Frank Spencer, is it? Well, well, well! I know him by another name. And now I know how Debra knew him. That is our rookie cop from Tonawanda. That's Officer Benson."

Jim sat back down in his seat and remained focused on the face of the man on the screen. He had not only known the murderer, but had helped him to unveil the discovery of the first victim in this case. It was ironic. And it had been Debra that had taken pity on him when Jim tried to educate him in the ways of good police work. The memory of that morning at the creek ran through his mind as the shock of this final discovery sank in.

Suddenly the lights in the room came on as a man entered the room and handed a piece of paper to Jim. He glanced at it quickly and bolted out of his seat.

"The bastard is at the hospital. They have him pinned down inside the stairwell between floors. Debra is in danger. Let's move!"

Within a minute the three had left the building and were running for the car. Harry grabbed the bubble and threw it onto the roof of the car as they climbed in. Seconds later they were speeding towards the hospital, the siren in high, headlights flashing in an alternating pattern as Harry tried to weave in and out of the mid afternoon traffic.

Harry could sense the tension in Jim as he felt his own heart racing. He never anticipated using the emergency equipment twice in the same day. He also never anticipated the emotion he felt as he desperately maneuvered around vehicles to make the trip in the least possible amount of time. It was as if the murderer were threatening his own existence and challenging him.

Without taking his eyes off the road, he tried to console Jim and at the same time convince himself that everything was in control. He was doing poorly at both.

They arrived at the hospital amidst a maze of cars trying to move away while others tried to get closer to see what was happening. There had to be a dozen police vehicles at the entrance to the hospital, from the Amherst Police to the Erie County Sheriffs Department, and even one State Police car. If Frank Spencer, or Officer Benson, thought he was walking out of this one he had to have some pretty big tricks up his sleeve.

Harry impatiently honked his horn, which could hardly be heard above the siren, as he made his way around the flow of cars and to the front of the hospital. As he pulled up, a deputy sergeant ran up to the car and waved for them to get out.

"He's in the north east stairwell between the second and third floor. We have him pinned down. I tell you, it's a weird feeling to be shooting at someone that looks like he belongs on your side."

"Where's Debra?"

"Who?"

"Debra, damn it! The woman he's here to kill."

Jim was showing no patience at all. Even Mike felt uncomfortable at the way Jim was yelling at the officer.

"Oh, her. Sorry, Jim. She's in a room on the third floor. There are two policemen and a trooper at her room to ensure the killer doesn't get to her."

"Not good enough. This guy's a Navy Seal. It will take more than that to stop him."

"What Jim means is, if this guy gets past our men in the stairwell, we will need more coverage at the room. Get some of our men up there as well. How's the civilian situation?"

"All the patients are restricted to their rooms and all hospital personnel are at their work stations, where they have been told to stay put until notified otherwise. And don't worry about me, Jim. I understand how you must feel. I'd be just the same if I were in your place."

For a moment Jim stopped and reflected on his behavior. He smiled at the officer and tugged at his arm.

"Sorry. I'll make up for this somehow. I promise."

Then Jim was back in gear with the crisis. He walked into the lobby and made his way to the elevators, Mike trailing behind him. Entering the elevator, Jim pressed three and hit the button several times.

"Damn it, move! There's no time to waste!"

"Easy, Jim. This is a hospital. Elevators here are designed to move slower than usual."

"God damned engineers! Don't they think of emergency situations like this? It should have some kind of override."

Finally the doors began to close, interrupting Jim's dissertation of engineering designs. As the elevator moved slowly upwards, passing the second floor, it arrived at three. Almost. There was a hesitation as it approached, and then the lights and power went out.

"Shit!"

As the emergency light inside the elevator cab came on, Jim shoved his fingers full strength through the rubber edging of the elevator doors and started an attempt to open the doors by using force.

"Jim, wait a few seconds. This may only be temporary."

"Forget that, Mike. Help me. I've done this before. They'll open."

Seeing how futile an argument would be, Mike began to shove with his whole body against one door. At first the resistance was tremendous, but as the two persisted, it finally moved open enough for them to see that they were almost at the floor level. Pushing further, they were suddenly confronted by a state trooper who had just opened the outside doors.

"Thought you two might want a hand."

Jim was never so glad to see the uniform of the state police as he was now.

"Thanks!"

With a little help, Jim and Mike were finally on the third floor.

"What happened to the power?"

As Jim asked, three deputies ran up to them from the stairwell at the far end.

"He got out. Don't know how, but he managed to go over the side of the stairs and just jumped all the way to the ground floor. We tried to shoot him, but he was moving too fast. We think he shot out the main power switch. Can't even imagine doing something like that and succeeding without being hurt."

"Debra! What room is she in? She'd got to be protected."

"Room 346. She's got protection; don't worry."

"From this guy I'm not so sure."

Jim ran swiftly down the hall towards Room 346. As he approached, three deputies, weapons drawn, met him. Jim flipped open his ID to flash his badge and yelled for them to follow. He shoved the badge down his jacket breast pocket so the badge remained visible. He spotted the room, which was blocked by a trooper and an Amherst officer. Addressing them as he approached, Jim could feel his heart racing, panic taking control of his mental processes.

"Is she OK? He's not here yet, is he?"

The trooper opened the door to the room for Jim.

"She's fine, sir. An officer is at her bedside. And no, our would-be assassin hasn't shown up."

"Thank God."

Jim entered the room to find Debra propped up slightly so that she was able to see her surroundings. Her eyes were wide open, and as soon as she saw Jim she produced a huge smile. Jim could see she was weak, but her stamina was top of the line as she spoke.

"It's about time you got here. I thought you'd given me up for dead."

Trying desperately to hold back the tears and emotions of seeing her alive, he walked gingerly over to the side of the bed and gave her a big kiss.

"I knew you'd be fine. It would take more than a knife to keep you from seeing this case put to rest, along with that bastard who thinks he can kill anyone he feels like."

The officer acknowledged Jim and stepped away to give Jim a little more privacy with Debra. Jim could see the strain in Debra's eyes from the ordeal she had been put through. Her breathing was shallow and rapid; she was obviously in a lot of discomfort.

"Need some medication? I'll get the nurse to give you something for the pain."

"No, Jim. I've had enough sedatives for the moment. What I need is some information. Has our murderer gotten away? What happened to the lights? Those things I need to know."

Jim gave Debra a smile and shook his head in disbelief.

"My dear, what would it take to quench that insatiable thirst for information? You never cease to amaze me."

"A big kiss. And the answers, please."

Jim satisfied request number one first, and then proceeded to fill Debra in on what had transpired since her being attacked. When he got to the last part about the shooting of the power switch, Debra shook her head at Jim.

"He didn't do that because he wanted to get to me. He's much too clever not to realize the protection I had would be increased instantly. No, he probably did it to make you concentrate on me and loose track of his whereabouts."

Jim stood back and pondered Debra's words. Then he turned and ordered one of the deputies to check on what was happening. He also asked for a check on where Harry was. Jim had lost track of the fact that Harry had not followed him to the elevator. Then he turned back to face Debra, who was giving Jim that 'I told you so' look, a smile on her lips giving away her apparent satisfaction of Jim's reaction to her ideas.

"Now, angel, let's not get cocky over some of that thinking of yours. You'll tax yourself and get weaker. Wait until you're feeling better."

Jim could hear some chuckles behind him and knew the other officers in the room were amused by Debra's take-charge attitude. He would normally have been annoyed by it, but as he saw the gleam in Debra's eyes, he could only play along and hope she was made to feel better by their amusement.

"Jim, I've always said it takes a woman to see what should be done. And as for me being cocky, let me tell you, it wasn't fun to look into the eyes of Officer Benson as he plunged his knife into me. I only hope he realizes that his identity is now known. He's also Frank Spencer, isn't he Jim?"

"You never cease to amaze me, Debra. Right again. Next you'll be telling me that Walter Grieder is also Frank Spencer."

Debra looked quizzically at Jim.

"Who?"

"Grieder, Walter Grieder. The name you pointed at in the file just before you passed out this morning."

Debra hesitated, and then realizing what Jim was referring to, smiled and shook her head.

"I was trying to indicate that my attacker was Benson. I started to scroll a large "B" on the paper. Guess I never quite finished it"

Suddenly the lights came back on, as well as sounds of shouting from outside the room. Jim swung around to face the door, reaching for his gun in anticipation of imminent danger. But it was only Harry, and he seemed rather uptight about something.

"Jim, I'm sorry. Truly I am. I tried to see if our "friend" would listen to reason. I made a mistake by calling him Spencer instead of Benson. It triggered him to jumping and getting to the main power switch. Somehow he had also disabled the transfer switch for the emergency power. Got an electrician and made a temporary connection. However, now that he knows we all know who he is, he'll try disappearing, this time permanently."

Jim frowned.

"I doubt that. He's cunning and quite capable. He is hell bent on getting to Debra, or he wouldn't have risked coming here to begin with. I think we had all better stay on high alert."

"You're damned right about that."

It was Mike speaking as he entered the room.

"Our Frank Spencer is up to something. I happened to go back down the stairway to have a look. Saw movement coming up to street level and just shot wildly at the moving figure. Thought I hit something, but all I found at the bottom was a broken latch to a door leading into the boiler room. Went in, but there wasn't anyone there. However, there were drops of blood on the steps. I think I might have hit him, though I haven't any idea as to where he might have gone. This guy is almost inhuman. In his condition he'll probably be as dangerous as a wild animal."

Jim turned back to face Debra. He saw tears in her eyes as she took a deep breath. She had apparently put on a show for Jim, hoping not to give away the fact that she was terrified of still being the target. He sat down on the bed alongside of her, placed his arms around her, and held her tightly. She gasped, and Jim realized she was feeling the pressure of his hug on her wound. He immediately relaxed his grip.

"Sorry Debra. I forgot for the moment about your chest."

Smiling, Debra reached over and kissed Jim. Whispering in his ear so that only Jim could hear, she consoled him.

"Well that's a first. You forgot about my chest, did you?"

Jim could sense the energy and feistiness that was Debra. He smiled and allowed himself the pleasure of feeling her lips near his cheek. Moving back after a few moments, he grinned and gave her a wink.

"Not really; just momentary disassociation."

The two smiled at each other. Jim could see Debra showing signs of weakness, though she was fighting not to give her frailty away. He took a deep breath, as he was also feeling tired. Jim felt as if this day was by far the longest day in his life. And it wasn't over yet.

Spencer was still somewhere in the hospital, hiding and waiting to seize upon the moment when someone let down their guard, or made the wrong move. Anything! A last chance to take the life of the one he loved so very much. Jim was determined not to let that happen.

He kissed Debra, told her to rest and not to be concerned; he was there and not even the devil himself could get into the room. She smiled, closed her eyes and drifted into a light sleep.

Jim motioned to Harry and Mike, and the three stepped out of the room, leaving the officer at the bedside. Jim saw the confidence Debra had in his commitment of protection. Now, if he could be as confident himself. That would help take the edge off the imminent danger that was at hand.

Chapter 14

Three hours had past since the last sighting of Spencer. More police had been brought in and the visitors were directed to leave, giving a less congested area for observation. The patients that were not immobile were sent to the main lobby to wait out the vigil until the building was safe from potential danger. Everyone thought the main lobby would be the least likely place for Spencer to show up.

The nurses and aids were directed to stay in the rooms with the patients restricted to beds and not to leave any patient unattended. This would discourage Spencer from using a patient as a bargaining chip, and provide some comfort for the patient's peace of mind with all that was taking place.

Jim, Harry and Mike set up a makeshift command post at the nurse's station on the third floor. All calls and directions would be received and transmitted from that point. It took several trips outside to dissuade the news media from endeavoring to access the hospital and turn the situation into a circus. Jim had always cooperated with the media, but this time he was adamant about not having them around. It would be so easy for Spencer to impersonate a news team member and work himself right to the room before he was noticed. Much too risky. It also made surveillance extremely difficult, having cameras, lights, wires and other equipment moving about the floor.

Mike and Harry let Jim take complete charge of the operation. They were sure that if anyone would leave no stone unturned, it was Jim since he had the biggest stake in the events. And they were also sure he wouldn't have allowed it to be any other way. The third floor especially, was clear of all moving objects such as carts, wheelchairs, maintenance materials, and housekeeping supplies.

Two policemen were stationed at each end of both corridors on the north and south sides. One policeman was stationed at every door to a stairwell. Two officers who had their guns in hand just in case the elevator doors opened to reveal an armed man watchfully kept the elevators, which opened onto the floor at the nurse's station, in sight.

Every contingency imaginable had been thought of and covered. It seemed impossible for anyone to even scratch their nose and not be seen by some law official.

Once everything was in place, it became a cat and mouse game of how, where, and when Spencer would make his move. Mike kept himself occupied by watching the spare television set that one of the nurses had set up for them. The events at the hospital had taken on crisis proportions locally and even nationally. Local programs had been replaced with news footage of what was going on, and who was to answer for the operation that was disrupting the lives and safety of so many Western New Yorkers.

Harry glanced at the television occasionally, but primarily he was preoccupied with a crossword puzzle in the newspaper that he had acquired in one of his rounds of the rooms on the third floor that he personally made every fifteen minutes.

Jim spent most of his time looking in on Debra, who had stayed asleep during the entire transformation. He even stood watch at her side during one of the shifts. Jim had established a rotation of the officers in and outside her room so that fatigue or boredom didn't dull the alertness of the team that protected Debra. He became familiar with each officer on a personal basis. He also made sure they all knew each other very well. It would be impossible for Spencer to replace any one of them, or claim he was a substitute. Every move the officers made was under observation by the others. If nothing else held, that one room was impenetrable.

More time passed. By eight o'clock everyone agreed they needed something to eat in order to function at their peak. Every floor was directed to order something from the hospital kitchen, which still had a full staff due to the situation. The kitchen said they would try to comply in a timely fashion and, by eight thirty the food began to arrive. Jim even ordered a cheeseburger, though he was so tense that he wasn't sure he could eat it, let alone digest it. He asked Mike and Harry several times if they thought he had overlooked anything. They couldn't come up with another suggestion. They had even done a door-by-door search from the roof to the basement hoping to run into their man. Nothing was found.

"Where is that bastard. Harry, where would you hide in a place like this?"

"Well, Jim, the man's built somewhat like me. I could never manage a network of air ducts, so that's out. Stairs get you nowhere if you can't open a door without confronting an armed foe. You can't look like hospital staff because all the staff here has been here throughout the time without replacement. Which brings up a good question; do we allow the change of shifts?"

"No. That would give him a great opportunity to slip by us. Maybe that's what he's waiting for. If it is, he's in for a big disappointment; no easy way to get out, or a way in. Whatever he's planning, it cannot be afforded to him."

"I can't think of any other means, my friend. Pity."

"How about you, Mike? Can you think of anything I've overlooked? Mike!"

A startled Mike looked away from the television and at Jim.

"What's that, Jim? I wasn't listening."

"What the hell is so important on television that you can ignore our situation here?"

"It's those damned news anchors. See there? They're interviewing some nerd that believes we are all crazy and are here just to pressure the nursing industry into learning methods of self-protection in the case of a terrorist overtaking. What crap. Where do they find these jerks anyway?"

Jim could see that Mike was totally obsessed by the television and would be of little use as far as contributing ideas. He was about to turn away from the set when something caught his eye. Quickly Jim's eyes scanned the scene that the camera was focused on. The camera was aimed at the employee entrance to the hospital where the reporter was interviewing someone, but that wasn't what Jim was looking at.

In the distance behind the focus of the camera was a figure of someone wearing a police uniform. It was slowly making its way from the employee entrance towards where the main lobby entrance was. The picture of the figure was fuzzy, but it was the color that Jim was noticing. The color of the uniform was of an officer in training. Jim yelled to Harry as he headed for the nearest stairwell.

"I think Spencer is outside the building headed towards the main entrance to the lobby. Tell our people down there to block off the entrance. Hurry!"

"How the hell do you know that?"

"Don't ask, just do!"

Jim was having an adrenalin rush as he entered the nearest stairwell and sped down the steps two at a time. There were a lot of innocent people down there, and they were there at his direction. If something happened to any of them, he would never be able to live with it. He had to stop Spencer.

Once he reached the street level, he opened the door and burst into the lobby. The first thing he noticed was the absence of a police officer at the door to the stairs. Where the hell were his men! People were all over the place, some wandering around looking lost while others were engaged in deep conversations, presumably about what was happening to them, but no police officers. Damn!

Suddenly a hand grabbed at his shoulder. He swung around and was about to smash his fist into the person, but luckily was stopped by another hand from behind grabbing at his arm.

"Hold it Lieutenant! It's us, not the enemy."

A sweat had begun to cover Jim's forehead and under the collar of his shirt. He saw a blurred feature of a face for only a second. Then he recognized the face as being one of his deputies.

"Lieutenant, you've got to slow down. You might hurt the wrong people the way you're headed."

Jim heard what the sergeant was saying. Taking a deep breadth, he looked around at the people. They were all staring at him as if to say 'what's wrong with him?' Jim was not presenting the good picture of confidence that he should be exhibiting. Jim collected himself, smiled at the officer, and apologized.

"Sorry Sal, I guess I lost it. My concern was for these people. When I didn't see any officers around, I got panicky."

"We're all at the entrance, on your orders, to stop this Spencer fellow who you say is outside and headed this way."

Of course. Jim felt a moment of foolishness creep into his body. How stupid of him. With an attitude of confidence and control he proceeded towards the entrance. As he and the sergeant approached, the figure of a police officer appeared outside the entrance of the lobby. Instantly he was surrounded and taken off to the side, hands behind his head. Jim hastily walked over and looked at the man. His build was that of Spencer, but the face was hard and rugged. And the shield on his uniform was that of a special officer provided for internal security. It wasn't Spencer. He wasn't even a policeman.

"Hey, what gives? Can't a guy have a cigarette without being mauled by the police?"

Jim asked a few questions, apologized for the mistake, and advised the man not to leave his post until the person they were after was caught. Then he walked back into the lobby, headed towards the elevators, and thanked the men for being quick in their response. Asking the sergeant to radio his arrival on three by elevator, Jim returned to the third floor, and the criticism of Mike.

"You sure made an ass of yourself this time. What the hell got into you, Jim? If Spencer were outside where you thought you saw him, he would be long gone. He wouldn't return to the most populated area."

Jim realized Mike was partially right. Spencer was after his satisfaction. He was determined not to be deprived his success at killing Debra. Why would he ever be outside where he would be spotted? Jim didn't say anything for the next thirty minutes. He looked in on Debra, saw she was still sleeping, and remained at the nurse's station.

Around nine the elevator door opened and a man with a cart full of food emerged. Jim looked away from the person to avoid being seen with a frown of disinterest on his face. Food, at this moment, repulsed him. He heard the officer at the elevator direct the man as to where the food should be placed. Jim paid little attention to anything that was going on between the two.

Harry had just returned from his rounds and was deeply into his crossword puzzle. Mike was again glued to the television. Everything seemed in order and relatively quiet. Jim mused over his reaction to what he had seen with regard to the figure in the television earlier.

As Jim thought more about it, it became obvious that if Spencer were to succeed at his goal, he would be changing his appearance rather than continuing to look as he had at first. Somehow, Spencer would have to shed that uniform and don another to disguise his appearance. But what, thought Jim. What would be a perfect disguise for Spencer? A doctor or nurse was out, since every doctor and nurse was known on the floor and would remain without replacement until the very end.

As Jim's thoughts reflected on possibilities, his eye caught the figure of the man from the kitchen wheeling the cart with some remaining food in the direction of Debra's room. From the rear, the figure looked impressive, with a broad span at the shoulders and so tall that he had to stoop to hold the cart's handle.

Moments passed without any further emotion. Then suddenly, Jim looked long and hard at the back of the man as he approached Debra's room. For some unknown reason, Jim felt a sudden urge to talk to the man. He stood up and, remaining at the station, called out to the person.

"Excuse me! I don't recall any rooms in that direction placing an order.

Hold on for just one second."

In an instant, the man shoved the cart off to the side, produced a gun and fired at the trooper standing in front of Debra's room. The shot brought Harry and Mike to immediate attention. Jim reached for his gun only to see the trooper slump to the floor and the assailant dart into a room directly across from Debra's room. Jim yelled out to alert the officer in the room that Spencer was directly across the way, but his shout came a moment too late. The door to Debra's room had opened and another shot fired. The policeman that was with Debra didn't have a chance. The officer had his gun out and fired it as the impact of the bullet he received hit him. His shot went into the ceiling as he fell backwards into the room.

Again Jim shouted out.

"Stay where you are, Debra! Don't move or make a sound. He can't get to you without getting his head blown off. Trust me on that one."

The last sentence was for Spencer's benefit rather than Debra's. He heard footsteps behind him and knew there were at least two more guns other than his own aimed at the space that separated the two rooms. Any move into the corridor would be an act of suicide.

As Jim reached within feet of the two opposing rooms, he stopped and placed his back against the wall of the corridor, his eyes looking at Debra's open door. He could see the soles of the officer's shoes and had to assume the shot he had received was rendering the officer unconscious or, worse yet, he was dead.

The trooper just in front of him was face up, blood coming from his left temple, his eyes open and lifeless. Jim felt outrage. He wanted, more than anything to turn and rush the door at his left, shooting furiously as he did so. But training and common sense told him that would be futile and dangerous.

Mike and Harry had come up beside Jim and also had their backs to the wall. From the nurse's station and well into the corridor he saw a number of deputies, some standing and some kneeling on one knee, all with their weapons pointed in the direction of the two rooms. To his left was a similar arrangement. The corridor was totally blocked. Spencer had nowhere to go. They had him.

Jim motioned for everyone to get against the wall. It was too risky, with two separate groups facing one another; they could easily shoot one of their own. Then Jim spoke loudly and deliberately.

"Spencer, you have nowhere to go. You are covered and we are all armed and ready to blast your head off if you make any move to leave that room. Hear me?"

Silence. Total silence. Jim couldn't imagine anyone not realizing their situation and surrendering immediately. Yet there was no response.

"Spencer, throw out your weapon and acknowledge that you heard me. Now!"

There still was no sound from within the room. Then Jim heard the faint sound of weeping coming from Debra's room. Without a moment's hesitation, and without care for his own endangerment, Jim rushed at Debra's room and leaped over the body of the officer on the floor, landed on his back and rolled over towards Debra's bed, gun ready to shoot.

For what seemed like forever he remained on the floor. He could still hear Debra, and he could see that he was the only other person in the room. He quickly got to his feet and stood beside the bed. Debra was awake, her eyes wide open; tears were streaming down her cheeks. She looked at Jim and tried to speak, but somehow nothing came out from her mouth. Jim could see she was petrified. Giving her a big kiss, he whispered into her ear.

"We've got him cornered across the hall. There's no way he can elude us. Relax, angel, I'll see that you remain safe. I love you."

His words had a comforting effect on Debra. She smiled, wiped her eyes and mouthed the words I love you too. Jim's anger, which had momentarily subsided, now welled up in him even stronger than before. What the hell was that bastard doing? He must realize the futility of his situation. And Jim was also somewhat surprised that no attempt from Spencer to shot him as he entered Debra's room had occurred.

Something didn't seem right. Carefully he walked to within a few feet of the doorway. A quick glance at the officer on the floor told him that Spencer had downed two officers permanently. Then he cautiously peered around the frame of the doorway at the door across from him. It was closed. There seemed to be no other choice but to go across the corridor and open the door.

Jim quickly exited Debra's room and placed his back against the frame of the closed door. From his right came a sudden sound of breathing and a voice he knew so well whispered in his ear.

"Pity, good fellow. No other choice, I agree. But let me do the honors; you back me up in case, eye?"

"No, Harry. He's mine!"

"I'm younger; better reflexes."

"I need to do this, Harry; for Debra."

"If it's for Debra you say, then what the prize if victory means death?"

For a brief second Jim had to look at Harry with a smile.

"Aren't you sick of poetry on this case?"

Harry just shrugged.

"And what the victory if there is no satisfaction?"

Harry, resigned to giving Jim his wish, moved away from him just far enough to give Jim room to move while remaining close enough to spring into the doorway that was about to be opened. Jim reached around with his right hand and gently took hold of the door handle. He started to turn the handle ever so slowly. Shit!

"What's wrong, old boy?"

"Damn it, it's locked!"

This presented a bad scenario. Jim would have to stand directly in front of the door and either shoot the handle, hoping to hit the lock and destroy it, or kick the door open. Either way, he would be a prime target. Taking a deep breadth, he turned, stepped directly in front of the door and decided to attempt both at the same moment.

Lifting his gun and aiming at where he hoped the lock was, and raising his left leg at the same time he started to squeeze the trigger. At the precise moment that he fired, he heard a weak voice directly behind him.

"No, Jim."

Jim saw life flash before his eyes. Somehow he fired, kicked and swung around, throwing himself at Debra, who was standing in the doorway of her room. At the same time, there was a loud explosion, and Jim could feel a strong heat across his back.

He landed on Debra as she fell over the body of the dead officer and onto the floor. Then he heard shouting, and the voice of Harry, and someone batting something across his back.

"I take it back, old chap. Your reflexes are still excellent. How you managed all three simultaneously is quite amazing."

Jim, somewhat confused, lifted himself off of Debra. Seeing that she had blood on her gown and was in pain from her movements, Jim helped her back to the bed. Then he removed his jacket, or what was left of it. It was scorched and in two pieces. Jim felt dazed and sat down on the bed. He felt the soft touch of Debra's hand on his shoulder.

"I had a feeling about you. It said you were in danger. I couldn't ignore it."

"Bloody good thing, Debra. Jim here opened a door to hell itself. That Spencer chap must have some plastic explosives on him. He had the door rigged to explode the second it was opened. Jim would have been dead if it weren't for you. Let me get a nurse to tend to those stitches. They've likely opened."

Jim took several minutes to orient himself and to capture the fact that he had almost been killed. He felt cold and sweaty. It was as if he had died and then returned back to the living.

By now, the explosion had sent a frenzy through the hospital and the media outside was demanding to know what had happened. Mike came into the room to check on Jim.

"You should see what they're doing out there. You are dead, but OK. You risked lives, but you're a hero. The media doesn't know or care about what really happened. Only news worth talking about is that Spencer got out of the room through the sleeve under the window that was originally designed for the heater, and his whereabouts are still unknown. Wouldn't have the nerve myself, but he actually used a notch of probably no more than an inch between each exterior block to move along the outside until he could reach the roof of the cafeteria."

Jim shook his head in disbelief. All that for nothing. Back to square one. The nurse came in and changed the dressing on Debra's surgery, lectured Jim about trying to keep from pouncing on the patient, then treated Jim with some cream for the burns he had received on his neck and scalp from the explosion. Thank God that Debra's stitches still held, or Jim would never have forgiven himself.

His near brush with death had taken a lot out of Jim and exhaustion was creeping up on him. Debra had been given a mild sedative and was close to being asleep by the time Jim found the energy to get up and walk back to the nurse's station. There were now two officers in the room with Debra and two outside the door.

Harry was munching on a croissant and Mike was wiping the remnants of some mustard from a hot dog from his lips. Jim felt the need for some energy and, finding his cheeseburger untouched, threw it into the microwave for a minute and downed it with an apple juice chaser. No one spoke a word during those few minutes. Mike, eyes glued to the television, was mumbling about the stupidity of the media and the public in general. Harry looked like he could use a nap, but remained attentive to his surroundings, as if expecting all hell to break loose at any moment. Finally it was Jim that broke the silence.

"OK guys, give me a hint. What comes next? What can Spencer possibly come up with now?"

Harry responded with a very logical opinion.

"I think Spencer will do nothing until he realizes that there will not be a change of shift. He's bloody well prepared with something there. What he'll do after that, only The Lord knows."

For a change, Mike was attentive to the conversation.

"I think we should be thinking a new strategy. With the introduction of explosives, it is now evident that Spencer has every intention of killing Debra by killing himself as well. That episode a short while ago was a test to see where we have people and what our capabilities are. I don't think he really expected to succeed the first time around. He carried the explosive just in case, and unexpectedly used it to his advantage. But now that he sees how we are thinking he will concentrate on making his second attempt a success. All he needs is to gain access to Debra's room and it's all over. He wins; we lose."

For the first time that evening, Jim agreed with Mike's analysis of the situation.

"So? What can we do to change things and turn the advantage around to our side? He has the advantage of the element of surprise. He has the entire floor analyzed; every position of resistance located. This guy is trained to see and record in his mind the most minuscule detail. He has us exactly where he wants us and can predict our moves and reactions. What can we do to change things? And don't lose sight of the fact that his marksmanship is deadly accurate."

Harry spoke bluntly.

"Reconfigure your ideas about those men at Debra's room. They are no match for Spencer's skills and marksmanship. They are sitting ducks waiting to be slaughtered."

Jim saw merit in the idea of a restructure of Debra's protection, but what? Numbers weren't the answer. It had to be something that wasn't noticeable to the eye. Spencer would be looking for the men at the door to her room.

The men inside could be removed from harms way, but that would be leaving Debra alone. Spencer's cunning might have concocted an access that no one conceived possible. Without a deterrent in the room, the result would be swift and deadly. It could be assumed that Spencer would not be aware that Debra was alone, but that left Jim too uncomfortable to even consider such a gamble.

Mike had turned back to view the television once again. Jim became annoyed.

"Mike, I wish the media were here instead of in that television. At least then I would have some of your attention focused on our situation."

"That's it! The very thing! Pity."

"Harry, what the hell are you babbling about?"

"That's your answer, Jim. The change that could throw a monkey wrench into Spencer's plans. Invite a restricted representation of the news media to spend time in Debra's presence. You know, like an exclusive interview, or something. Time it around the usual schedule for shift change. Don't mention it until the very last moment, so Spencer doesn't get wind of it before he plans to make his move. The media will jump at the chance, with or without preparation."

Jim rubbed his chin absentmindedly and thought about the possibilities. Mike had his attention back on Jim's search for an answer.

"Harry has something. It sure would catch him off guard to come here ready to create hell only to be confronted by a set of lights and a television camera. He won't be expecting that."

"And we could have the crew of technicians both inside and outside the room, making entry impossible without being detected."

Jim liked the idea. He knew Mike would work with it, since he might get the chance to needle the news anchor about their presentations thus far. Harry would stand in the background, observing and hopefully spotting Spencer's entrance on the scene. Only one person Jim would have to convince to go along with the plan. The biggest hurdle of all.

"No way!"

"But Debra, it's a sure fire way of throwing Spencer off and protecting your safety."

"It's a sure fire way of getting me killed, and on public television of all places."

Jim had felt bad about disturbing Debra's sleep, but with the hour of eleven approaching he had no other choice than to prepare her. And true to expectations, he was being met with resistance.

"Debra, Spencer is devious and quite capable of most anything. And he won't give up until he satisfies his ego by killing you, no matter how many others he takes down with him. This unexpected scene gives us the only edge we ever hope to have in deterring his efforts and stopping him once and for all."

"By making me an even bigger target than I already am?"

"That's exactly what he'll least expect. Don't you see he knows we will do anything to protect you, hide you or surround you? Never in a million years will he expect you to be up and giving an interview on television. It's perfect."

Debra felt weak, but she was sure she could cope with that. It might even be a good thing, taking her mind off of Spencer.

"I need time to prepare. Some makeup and help getting into something more than this ratty hospital gown."

Jim leaned over and kissed her. He was glad to see the energy return to his love in life. He was careful not to look apprehensive or to speak of any fears he had.

"Now I'm sure you are my true love in life."

"Your crazy true love, I'm afraid. I have to be crazy to agree to this insanity."

Jim tried not to press the issue. He just smiled softly at Debra and touched her affectionately on her right cheek.

"The not so crazy, the most beautiful woman in the world."

"Don't press your luck James Hargrove."

Jim got up from the side of the bed and turned towards the doorway. As he headed through it he heard Debra giving her final word for the evening on the subject.

"And if I get killed doing this, I'll haunt you for the rest of your life. You'll never rest again, do you hear me?"

Jim smiled to himself and walked back to the nurse's station. He knew that was Debra's way of saying I love you, no matter what happens. Jim was determined to make sure nothing bad did happen.

At ten minutes past the hour of eleven, Jim went down to the main lobby and out the front doors. He approached one of the cameramen and told him of his interest in having a camera and crew available immediately to interview the victim and target of all this attention. They would be allowed only one crew and anchor, to be selected amongst themselves as representative of all the networks at the scene. It would be a taped interview only, not live. Jim emphasized that part. The message sent waves of activity through the congestion that made up the networks, their crews and equipment.

Surprisingly, it only took ten minutes before one of the local networks grouped and met Jim at the lobby entrance. Jim recognized the anchor, greeted her with a smile and a word of caution about what she might see during the interview, and escorted her and the crew, armed with cameras and equipment to the third floor and Debra's room.

During the trip to the third floor, the lights and cameras scanned the scene in the main lobby and followed Jim and the anchor into the elevator and, once on the third floor, along the corridor to the room. All the while the anchor kept recording a description of the surroundings, asking for comments occasionally from Jim. Everything seemed on the surface to be calm and controlled.

What Jim deliberately withheld was the picture of men behind every door, on every stairwell, in every empty room all with weapons drawn and watchful eyes as they looked for any sign of anything out of place; anyone unfamiliar that looked suspicious. Little did the media know that they were walking into a virtual war zone. Jim knew he'd catch hell for not saying anything. The price he'd have to pay for protecting Debra.

For the next fifteen minutes there was a beehive of activity as the crews set up the lights and cameras. Jim made it a point not to show himself at the door of Debra's room for two reasons. First, he didn't want to see the look on Debra's face as she tried to cope with being a national figure on television. Second, Jim was nervous and didn't want that conveyed to his love.

He kept glancing at his watch and at the clock on the wall of the nurse's station, waiting for something to happen. He knew it was inevitable and would come; he just didn't like not knowing when and from where. As predicted, Mike was bending the anchor's ear as the crew readied for the taping. He felt sorry for her, knowing Mike was letting all his disgust at the coverage rest on her shoulders.

Harry had settled himself at the corner of the corridor to Debra's room, his gaze covering the elevators and the corridor in both directions. He had decided to keep his gun in his hand, knowing the speed and accuracy of their foe. This made the head nurse very unnerved. Jim advised her to be ready to fall to the floor at the least sound of imminent danger. All was ready and going as planned. Now came the worst of it. The wait. Time seemed to slow down as Jim kept watching the clock. Eleven thirty. Eleven forty. Eleven forty-two.

It was the voice of the head nurse that broke Jim's trance.

"That's strange. There are no operations scheduled at this time of night."

"Why do you say that?"

Jim saw the look of confusion on the nurse's face.

"There's a fellow standing just back of the door where the television crew is that's wearing a surgical gown. He still has his mask on and his gloves. Very unusual."

Jim reached for his gun and gestured for the nurse to duck down behind

183

the desk. Harry, seeing Jim's movements, gripped tightly on his weapon and shrugged, silently questioning the move. Jim nodded his head at the direction of the man in the gown and mask. Harry picked up on it immediately. Jim moved back and out of sight of the figure. Harry moved back and joined Jim.

"You think it's him, Jim?"

"I'd say so. He's wearing what is usually left at the OR. I'm going to go down the nearest stair and come up the stairs directly behind him. Radio my moves and the situation to everyone. We have to play this right or a lot of people are going to be hurt or killed."

"And what, if I might ask, are you going to do? Just ask him to raise his hands and give up?"

Jim knew Harry was needling him. But the truth was, Jim didn't know yet what he was going to do.

"Beats me."

"Jolly bad scenario. Better do better."

Then Jim had an idea. He ducked down and gestured to the head nurse to move closer to him.

"Is there anything here at the station that I can use to render someone unconscious? It has to be fast, and it has to be here."

For a moment the nurse seemed stumped. Then she raised a finger, went to a small refrigerator, and took a small bottle out of it, handing it to Jim.

"It's left here only for emergencies. Not used much anymore."

Jim read the label. Ether. She handed Jim a large gauze pad.

"When you're ready, just pour onto the gauze and hold over the face. He'll be out in a minute."

"A minute? I hope it takes less time than that; I'm not much of a match in strength for a Navy Seal."

All the nurse could do was give Jim a smile. Jim went back to Harry and directed him to watch for when he places the gauze over Spencer's face, then come running like hell to help keep him restrained until the ether took affect.

"And Harry."

"Yes?"

"Don't spare the gas on your way over."

Harry smiled at Jim.

"Pity."

Jim hoped that meant yes, and not what it sounded like.

Exiting the floor, Jim went down to the second floor, opened it and was greeted by a trooper.

"Good luck, sir. Everyone is confident in you."

"Well, I'm glad someone is; I'm not."

Jim approached the stair that would lead him up to approximately where Spencer was standing. Another officer gave him a word of confidence. He thanked her and, upon entering the stairwell, started to climb. He was beginning to feel his heart pounding inside his chest. His breathing became rapid, and sweat was prominent from head to toe. It had been a long time since he had ever felt like this.

He was scared. Scared that Spencer might kill others. Scared that he would not be able to hold Spencer long enough for the ether to take affect, and seeing his love get killed. And ultimately, Jim was scared that today might be his last day alive.

He reflected on whether or not he should take back up with him. That was risky; if Spencer caught a glimpse of more than one person moving towards him, it might prompt him to discharging the explosive immediately. There were too many lives to risk.

Jim kept going over and over in his mind exactly what he would do. As he reached the third floor, he realized that he had forgotten about the officer assigned to that door. At the top of the flight of steps lay the body of an Amherst police officer, his throat cut from ear to ear. The landing was a sea of blood. Jim's mind went from fear to anger. The bastard has no heart. He is vicious and vindictive.

Blood began to swell inside Jim as he started to prepare to enter the corridor. He decided it best to have the gauze already saturated before going out. Less chance of his movement being spotted and less time to get ready to strike. Jim had to remember to keep his breathing off to the side to avoid inhaling the fumes himself. Ready, he slowly opened the door to the corridor.

The corridor hummed with the sound of voices coming from within Debra's room. The bright lights both inside the room and outside in the corridor afforded a small amount of distraction. A few onlookers were at the entrance to the room, in spite of the direction that no one but the media be there. In a way it gave entrance to the room greater difficulty, which was probably why Spencer hadn't made any move as yet.

Jim looked at the back of the figure in the surgical gown and mask. Jim was surprised that Spencer thought he would be less conspicuous in them. In actuality, Spencer stood out like a sore thumb. Then, in retrospect, Jim's thoughts turned to the well trained Spencer and how he had handled his appearances and disappearances. Flawlessly. Suddenly Jim felt panic wrench at his stomach. Spencer's target had changed; it was no longer Debra.

With deliberation, Jim's target slowly turned until it was facing him. Raising his left hand, the facemask was loosened until it fell away to reveal the menacing grin of Spencer. His eyes stood fixed as he glared coldly at Jim. If there was a heart behind the life of the individual in front of Jim, it was well hidden by hatred. The new target for Spencer was himself.

As the shock of this revelation whelmed over him, Jim's mind began to race. He had no idea where Spencer had placed the explosive on his person, but he assumed it was strapped to him so as to keep his hands free. Jim had to avoid contact with the explosive or it would be over in an instant. Spencer's eyes were fixed on Jim's throat. In Spencer's right hand was the weapon that had reeked so much destruction since this morning. The blade had to be at least eight inches long.

Jim felt the cold, slippery feeling of the ether-drenched gauze in his hand. What was he supposed to do with it now? Spencer was facing him, not with his back to Jim. The gauze was useless so he dropped it to the floor. Jim could see the end of life in front of him.

At any moment he expected Spencer to lunge at him, igniting the explosive and ending the hopes and dreams he held deep in his heart for a life of happiness with Debra. Jim also felt remorse at having to disappoint Debra, depriving her of what he had promised would be a beautiful life together. He had no control of what was about to happen. Jim felt frustration; any move would be futile.

In an instant, Spencer suddenly moved towards Jim. A moment later, Jim was holding Spencer's right arm and desperately trying to overcome the brute strength of the former Navy Seal. It was a losing battle.

Spencer's left hand grabbed at Jim's throat and the vise-like grip around his neck became unmerciful as the power of both arms brought Jim to his knees.

Jim could hear shouting all around him. He could not make out what they were saying. A woman screamed, her cry ringing endlessly in his ears. Then his head hit the floor, his face being forced onto the ether-drenched gauze he had dropped to the floor moments earlier. Jim could not help but to inhale the toxic fumes it was releasing.

Whatever strength Jim had suddenly left him. His arms felt limp and the room around him began to spin. He now had both hands on the arm with the knife. He could feel the arm pushing slowly upwards, heading for the throat that was now parched with a sweet taste from the chemical he was inhaling.

Jim tried as hard as he could to control that arm. Then there was nothing but darkness and silence.

Jim awoke to the sounds of voices. They sounded far off in the distance at first, and then slowly they zeroed in on his hearing until they became almost deafening. Jim tried to open his eyes, but the eyelids felt like they were lead weights and glued in place. When he did manage to open them, he saw the ceiling of a room, and it was spinning around, making him so dizzy he felt nauseous. He closed them again to escape the nausea. Then he heard a voice that was unmistakably Debra's.

"Jim honey, are you awake? I thought you'd never wake up. Please, Jim, try to open your eyes."

Jim tried to speak, but the saliva in his mouth felt so thick he almost gagged. Then after another couple of minutes, Jim managed to open his eyes. The room had settled down, and he was able to manage a look around him.

Debra was sitting at the edge of the bed he was lying on, a worried look on her face. The room was bright, making seeing difficult. He finally realized it was the lights of the television crew, aimed directly at him. He tried to speak, found he was still unable to, so he waved at the light to indicate he wanted it to go away.

"Enough for awhile, please. Give the man a chance to regain his composure."

The lights went away, but the nausea remained. Finally, unable to control it, he leaned over the side of the bed and vomited. Luckily, a nurse was there, pan in hand to prevent a mess. Jim lay back and closed his eyes again, drifting as if on a cloud.

After what seemed like hours, Jim opened his eyes, sat up in the bed and looked around. His entire body was covered in sweat. He shivered. The nurse gave him a small blanket to cover his shoulders and told him it would take a little while longer for the ether to wear off. Jim asked for something to wash the taste out of his mouth and was given some apple juice.

Debra looked very tired, but the robe she had on to tape her interview made her look fresh and beautiful. And alive! Jim realized that Debra was still alive, and so was he. He reached up and touched his throat, found no bandages, which told him he had escaped the blade held by Spencer. He looked at Debra. She had a huge smile that helped to warm his shivering body.

"He didn't succeed. Spencer was so engrossed in his desire to kill you he made a fatal mistake of not watching his back. Harry arrived to give him a taste of that awful stuff you were using. He also got Spencer's right arm and held onto it. Spencer went unconscious almost immediately after you did. Good thing, too, because the knife had reached within an inch of that very beautiful neck of yours."

Jim had never heard Debra, or anyone else for that matter, refer to his neck as beautiful. But considering what it would look like if Spencer had succeeded, he had to accept Debra's description. Slowly, and with deliberation, Jim swung his feet over the side of the bed and sat up.

He looked at his watch and was amazed that only two hours had passed since his confrontation with Spencer. It seemed like a lot longer, and he was angry with himself for letting the ether get to him. Jim took hold of Debra's hand and stood up. Unsteady on his feet, he immediately sat down again. The nurse, reentering the room, just shook her head in disbelief.

"Lieutenant, you truly are amazing. Most people who get knocked out by ether take a few hours just to recover from the drug's effects. You want to walk already. That's not very wise at this point in time."

Mike had entered the room during the nurse's lecture with Harry right behind him. The two stared at Jim, their faces solemn and void of any real emotion. Jim wasn't sure if what they had to say would be comforting or disappointing. Feeling his strength beginning to return and his ability to speak and focus on his surroundings, Jim began asking a lot of questions. Mike just raised his hands and interrupted Jim.

"Hold it, Jim. Stop all the questions. Harry will fill in all the pieces as to what, when and how things happened."

"Well. My good fellow, the thought occurred to me as I saw Spencer standing there all decked out, that he was deliberately making himself noticed, rather than hiding. I said to myself, 'Harry? Why would he want to be noticed if he intended to sneak in and do away with his target Debra?' Then it occurred to me that it was because the target wasn't whom we thought. "Then who,' says Harry? Only fellow that came to mind that he had a real hatred for was, excuse me but truth is truth, you know; it's Jim. Then you appeared and I knew that you were a dead man unless I did something fast. I asked the nurse for another bottle of ether and some gauze, saturated it and ran like the wind hoping to get to Spencer before he moved on you.

Things went rather hastily at that point, and I'm not quite sure if it was luck or what. At any rate, you managed to keep him off you just long enough."

Mike picked up where Harry's colorful description of the event left off.

"It turns out Spencer didn't have any explosives on him. Maybe he didn't have any more; maybe he didn't think he required the use of it. Regardless, when he hit the floor and didn't set off any explosion, things calmed down. We confiscated his arsenal consisting of that dagger, two magnums and a few clips of ammunition, placed him on the floor against the wall by the nurse's station and put three deputies around him. Having killed a trooper and two policemen, it would have been suicide for him to even consider attempting an escape. Not that it made any difference to Spencer."

Jim stared at Mike.

"What do you mean 'made any difference'? We didn't let him get away again, did we? Not after all this."

Silence fell over the people surrounding Jim. No one spoke a word. Then Jim heard Harry's voice.

"Pity."

"Pity? Harry, what's pity mean this time?"

Debra leaned over and kissed Jim gently on the cheek.

"Harry is just being his usual English born self. Spencer's dead. He won't be bothering anyone ever again."

Mike and Harry gave Jim a smile of agreement with Debra's words.

"He wasn't sane. Something had snapped inside his head. Maybe the fact that he had been defeated in his purpose; he couldn't handle losing."

"So, what happened?"

Mike continued.

"Apparently his training allowed for some compensation when confronted by a chemical that was causing breathing endangerment. He did get some of it in him, but came out of the effects very quickly. We weren't paying close attention to him, thinking it would be hours before he regained consciousness. Let's just say he tried to add another to his collection of victims and ended up the victim instead."

Before Jim could ask for more information, the familiar face of the coroner came into view as he entered the room. He greeted Jim and the others and made his brief examination known to them.

"The two in the other room died instantly from gunshots to the head. They felt no pain, I'm sure. The poor officer in the stairwell died of a complete loss of almost all of his blood. Cut clean with a knife at the jugular. He had a few moments to feel death arrive, unfortunately. As for our assassin, I never saw so many bullet wounds from head to toe in my entire career. What was the weapon, a machine gun?"

Mike and Harry showed no remorse, their expressions completely deadpan.

189

Harry asked what everyone wanted to know.

"Did he feel pain as he died?"

"I'm sure after the first six bullets, he felt nothing. But those first six, well…"

The coroner, who usually had a lot to say about a corpse, just let the statement hang. Jim saw the whole picture. Nothing else needed saying.

Debra held Jim closely to her side and let a tear run down her cheek. She also understood. Even though she had been the target and the victim of injury from Spencer, she couldn't help but feel compassion for the man. No one, in her mind, ever deserved a brutal death regardless of the circumstances. But still, she felt relieved that the threat had been removed from her life permanently. And glad that Jim had come out of this safe and sound.

She recollected Spencer's face the first time she had met him at the scene of the accident at Tonawanda Creek. That young boyish face of a rookie cop that had appeared so green, and her compassion for him when Jim had made an example of him in front of her. How odd that she should remember only that face, and not the hell that he had produced later on.

Debra felt Jim's hand reach up to wipe the tear from her cheek. He was looking at her, a smile on his face. He saw what she saw; Debra was sure of that. One could only wonder what would have happened if Jim hadn't taken the initiative of covering the accident that started the whole series of events that followed. That vacation would have been wonderful, and someone else would have walked the path that they had followed instead. Who knows? And, as the two looked at each other with only love in their eyes and in their hearts, no one needed to know.

Epilogue

It was a month ago since the case involving the murder of the senator, actually his double, had ended in the death of the man that had almost caused the death of Jim and Debra. As Debra, Jim, and Harry sat in Jim's office discussing the results, there was almost an aura of relaxation.

Debra was feeling much better since her wound was healing, and without complications. Jim was feeling especially good since learning that he was being offered a promotion and a medal for his part in the case. And Harry was glad that Mike had left their company for another assignment.

However, there were a few loose ends that needed attending to before the case could be considered closed. Each was finally getting to fill in the missing pieces that only they knew and not the others.

"So, Harry, what ever became of the hunt for the owner of that filing cabinet?"

Harry grinned and allowed a sigh to escape as he paused to reflect on how he was going to present his findings.

"Well, old chap, I seem to have forgotten to mention who the owner happened to be. In searching through the Amherst roster for the names on those files, it became apparent that they didn't belong to the Amherst Police at all. I decided to take a long shot. Since our Officer Benson was working the Tonawanda Police Department, I enquired of those chaps as to a missing filing cabinet. To much surprise, they indeed had a missing cabinet. Reported missing by none other than Benson. It was his, inherited when he joined their ranks. And it wasn't reported missing until the day before we exposed his identity. That's why no one showed concern for its whereabouts."

Debra was fascinated by all the detective work involved. She had an instinct for finding out information, and a hunger to find out the whys that leads to clues.

"Why do you suppose Benson waited until the last moment, and then elected to report it? There was no longer any use for the files, Dorothy was under arrest, and it was apparent he would be disappearing any day from the area and his masquerade. Why say anything at all?"

Harry smiled and proudly gave Debra her answer.

"Because he thought he would leave with a clean slate. Just another instinct left by his training as a Seal. Pride, my dear, just for pride, nothing more."

"And what about the off color Jim noticed about his uniform?"

"After returning to the academy to finish his training, he was required as a rookie to wear it for the first few months of active duty. Like a trial period, you might say."

"And that brings up a fascinating part about Benson. He looked like a youngster. He had to be at least forty. We never would have ever suspected him of being Frank Spencer."

Harry had this answer as well.

"Mike made mention of that before leaving us. He remembered seeing Spencer's picture and marveling at how young he looked. His records indicated he was used under cover many times because of his 'baby face.' Unfortunately, Mike was not around when you and Jim made acquaintance with Benson, so he had no reason to mention it until he found the connection between your Benson and his Spencer."

Jim interjected with a few pieces of information of his own.

"That leads me to the disposition of Dorothy. Since Spencer was killed, the only link between her and Spencer had also died. Or so she thought. However, Debra, your insurance files on Spencer indicated employment started almost immediately after retiring from the Navy and continuing for almost two years. Yet Dorothy's files showed no employment records for Spencer. She thought that the absence of employment records would alleviate any question as to her link to Spencer. She was wrong. That sparked an investigation into Unisearch that ended with those files that you were to read tying Spencer to the disappearance of many people that turned up as murder victims."

Debra looked puzzled.

"How Jim, if his name isn't mentioned anywhere in those files?"

"Because, due to the system used at Unisearch, his file cases had to be reassigned to other investigators. However, computers being what they are, the transfer couldn't be made successfully unless the database indicated a former investigator. His name was used to linked almost every folder you had. The most recent ones were Barksdale's. Marvelous, this age of computers. It was what our intelligence agencies used to keep track of him as well. It also hung Dorothy on tampering with company records."

"But what about her link to the real senator?"

Jim leaned back in his chair and looked at the ceiling. Then he looked at Harry, who had made no sound since the mention of Dorothy's name.

"Harry, remember when we first arrested Dorothy, how she mentioned that the senator was not the real one? She let that slip out. Remember, Harry?"

Harry shifted restlessly in his chair.

"Bloody poor at thinking before speaking, that's Dorothy."

"And remember when we went through those original files that were supposed to be Barksdale's but some of them turned out to be misfiled letters to Dorothy from the real senator? You remember that too, don't you Debra?"

Debra's eyes were open and eager as she recollected those papers.

"Jim, I can still see them in my mind. One in particular was written to Dorothy as if she knew him on a personal basis. Remember, Harry?"

Harry tried not to look uncomfortable, but without much success. Talk about Dorothy was a sore subject with him.

"Vaguely. Oh, I suppose I do! Don't you two feel a bit warm in here?"

"Don't change the subject, Harry. Of course you remember; but none of us put the relationship with Dorothy and the senator into a picture of a threesome. At least not until now."

Debra was all ears. Harry was trying to act disinterested.

"Since Frank Spencer was a Navy Seal, and worked under cover for some of his assignments, doesn't it strike either of you as coincidental that just as the real senator became replaced by his double, that Frank Spencer retired and went to work for Unisearch?"

Harry actually opened his eyes wide. He was becoming intensely drawn into this new light of discovery. Debra was eager for more.

"Why Jim, your investigative prowess is wonderful. But where does the connection between the two originate?"

Jim paused for a moment before continuing.

"Frank Spencer left the employ of the Navy because he had been given the assignment of watchdog for the real senator and refused it. He didn't retire voluntarily, he was asked to resign. It took a lot of coercion by Mike to get the Navy to admit that. Mike could be very resourceful when he wanted."

Jim could see Debra getting even more fascinated by the information.

Harry was beginning to put definitive thoughts together such as dates and places.

"So, old boy, do I smell a plot against our nation?"

"Not against our nation, just the real senator."

"But I still can't associate Spencer with the real senator, or with Dorothy directly either."

Jim got up and walked over to the board still left in his office from the days when it was used to plan strategy.

"Look at the facts. I'll put four names along the top. First the real senator, second Dorothy, third Spencer, and fourth Barksdale. Under the real senator, what do we know? One, he is requested to disappear and become involved in some covert operation only known by the President and certain chosen people. Under Dorothy, we know she has some communications with the real senator that makes her privy to that fact. Then we have Spencer, who is also made privy to that fact when asked to be the senator's bodyguard. Two."

"Hold on, Jim. That right there makes all three with a common knowledge about a secret mission."

"Very good, Harry. You're catching on. Now watch this."

Jim drew a line from the real senator to Spencer.

"Spencer has already refused the assignment. Why?"

There was silence from his colleagues. Jim drew another line between Spencer and Dorothy. Debra was frowning.

"I don't see the connection at this point."

"I did a little further investigating since Dorothy's arrest. It turns out she met the real senator at a convention for the promotion of good will between the Middle East oil tycoons and the United States. She was invited because Unisearch was requested to investigate the whereabouts of one of the sheiks that had mysteriously disappeared. A good will gesture by the United States. How her firm was chosen is still unknown."

"So?"

"So, who else do you think was invited along with a few other specially trained people to provide protection during this event?"

Debra leaped into the conversation.

"Spencer!"

"Right on target. And rumor has it that he spent quite a lot of time the next few days with—"

"Dorothy!"

"Right again."

Harry scratched his chin.

"Old boy, that's nice. But why is that connected to Spencer's refusing the assignment?"

Jim smiled.

"Because Dorothy had coerced Spencer into telling about the double during their tryst. Dorothy convinced Spencer that there was a lot of money to be had if he would bide his time, work at Unisearch doing 'arrangements' with some of her clients, and then nail the big fish when they could kill the senator and threaten to expose his double and thereby extort a fortune for him via the United States Government. At least, that was the plan."

Harry suddenly looked as if he were sulking. Jim surmised it was related to Harry's failure to be Dorothy's latest "flame." Debra smiled at Jim.

"A big ambition, and a formidable target. Wasn't she afraid the government would step in and arrest her?"

"She was anticipating that move. That's where Barksdale comes in."

Jim drew a line between Spencer and Barksdale.

"I found through looking at Barksdale's employment records that he was once in the Navy himself. Remember the photo of Spencer's team with Barksdale in it? He was attached to the Naval Air Base in Guantanamo. He and Spencer were stationed there at the same time."

The line on the board made the answer obvious.

"They had been friends. Spencer was amazed to find his old buddy working for Unisearch. He also felt Barksdale was a threat to the plots being made with Dorothy. But Dorothy, being street wise from her upbringing, suggested they use him as a source of luring their extortion victims into Unisearch, and then later making the whole operation look like it was Barksdale's. The perfect scapegoat."

Jim put down the marker and sat down. Harry still needed a few questions answered.

"How about that motive Debra so advisedly pointed out to us as being absent from our thoughts. Why did they kill the senator's double? He was their big meal ticket to a fortune."

Jim looked passively at the two people seated in front of him. This one would be the coup-de-grace.

"By mistake."

Debra's mouth opened as a look of shock crossed her face. Harry reiterated Jim's statement.

"By mistake? Pray tell, how do you come by that information?"

"Simple deduction my good fellow. Quite elementary."

Debra spoke up like her old self.

"Stop with the Sherlock Holmes bullshit. Give us the facts and just the facts."

Jim smiled. He hadn't heard Debra sound off like that since the case a few years ago involving an investigation that ended up bringing them closer together.

"You know, Debra. A faux pas. A mistake. And stop sounding like Joe Friday."

Debra smiled and gave Jim her complete attention.

"It was the real senator that was supposed to show up in response to the query sent to the White House regarding some wealth that required the presence of Senator William Harrison. Except the message sent to the White House, our infamous letter of late from Dorothy to the senator, never reached the real Harrison. It was assumed to be of a romantic nature and some hot shot at the Capital decided to send the double figuring Dorothy would never be the wiser. So the double got killed as the real McCoy."

Harry seemed unsatisfied.

"But Spencer knew the real senator. Didn't he question the man to determine his legitimacy?"

"Unfortunately, everyone here assumes that Spencer killed the double. He didn't."

Debra and Harry looked at each other and then, in unison, spoke out.

"Barksdale?"

Jim smiled.

"Dorothy."

Debra's voiced amazement.

"How, Jim? How do you know she killed him?"

"She confessed to it. I made a few slips during the last meeting with her and that lawyer Sexton she hired that hinted our Spencer took full credit for all the murders and the planning before dying. In her rage to be given credit as the genius behind it all, she blurted out that Spencer had not shown up on time when Barksdale picked up the senator at the airport, so she hid in the back seat and at the opportune moment choked him to death with her nylon stocking. It wasn't until after, when Spencer as Benson, showed up to dispose of the body, that she saw the face of her victim and realized the mistake she had made."

Harry was staring at Jim in amazement.

"Dorothy? Strangulation? My God, Jim, the strength it takes—"

"Remember Harry, Dorothy grew up on the streets as a mulatto. She built her body up to defend herself against all kinds, both black and white. Too bad you never got the chance to marvel at the exquisite physique she must have. She's a weight lifter, you know."

Harry sighed, reached into his pocket, and handed Jim a twenty. Then he rose from his seat and headed out the door.

"Thanks for reminding me. Pity."

As Harry closed the door, Jim looked towards Debra and smiled.

"A man thing. Sorry."

Debra now knew what the twenty was all about. She smiled and with curiosity asked Jim a question.

"And my worth?"

Jim leaned over and gave her a big kiss on the lips. Then he stroked the side of her face.

"Priceless."

Debra gave up her job with the insurance company. Jim thanked the county for the medal, but rejected his promotion and took an early retirement. Then the two took the vacation that had been so abruptly cancelled. They both are now partners in marriage and as Private Investigators, and have a son who they named after their favorite person. Harry of course.

Harry took the promotion offered originally to Jim and is now wishing he had followed in his superior's footsteps and taken early retirement. And, as expected, he met another feisty beautiful woman and is now toeing the line as the faithful spouse and father of two. We assume.

Dorothy got twenty-five years to life and is now in charge of the files for the warden in her prison facility. She still vows revenge against Jim and Harry. She only mutters profanities about Mike.

No one knows where Mike is, only that he is on a big assignment involving a crisis somewhere in the Middle East. With some senator, we hear.

Until next time, may the wise become more observant, the rich more prudent, and the craftier less diligent so that Harry can spend more time with his family.

The End

Printed in the United States
1003800004B